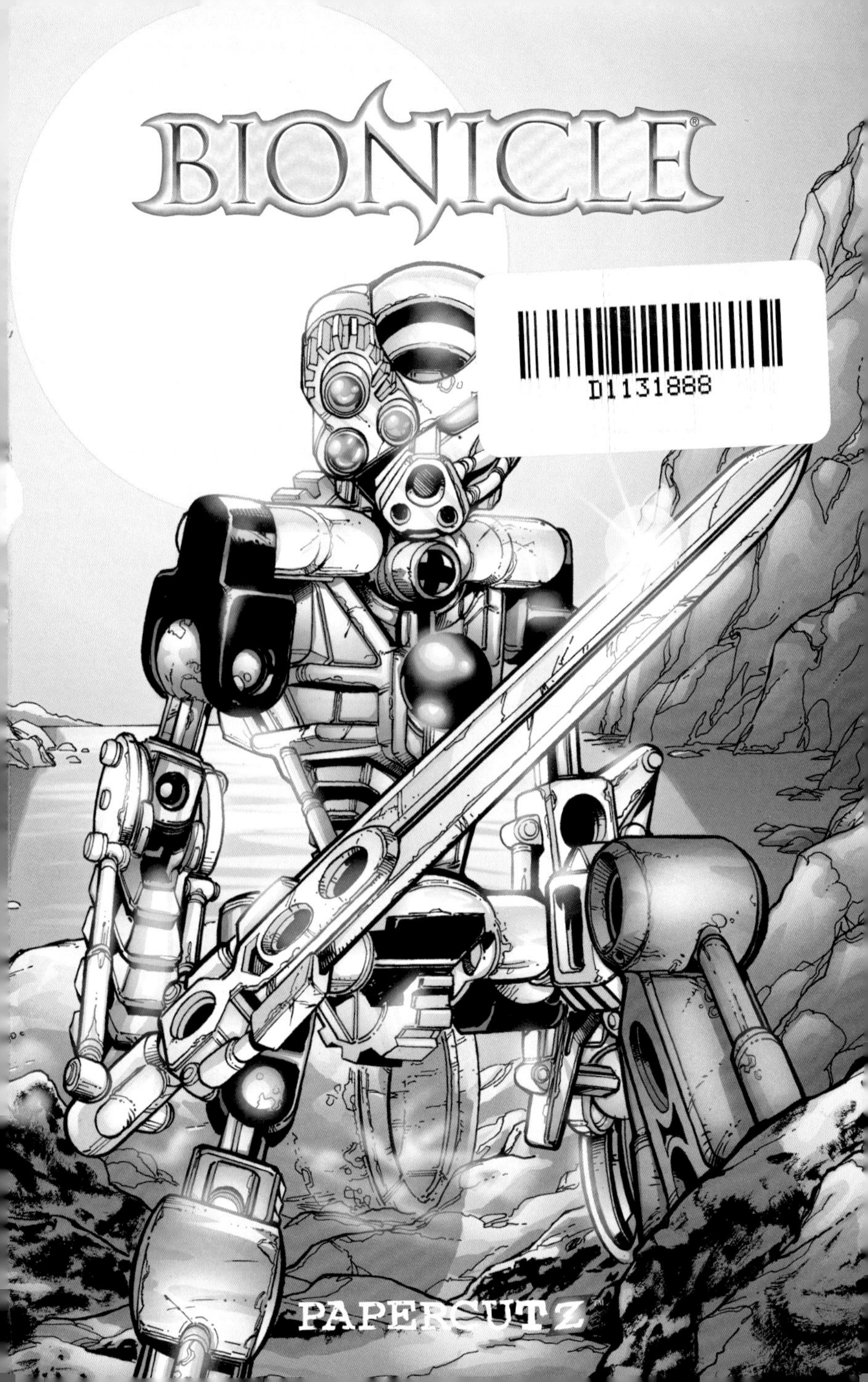
BIONICLE®
PAPERCUTZ™

# BIONICLE® GRAPHIC NOVELS AVAILABLE FROM PAPERCUTZ

Graphic Novel #1
**"The Rise of the Toa Nuva"**

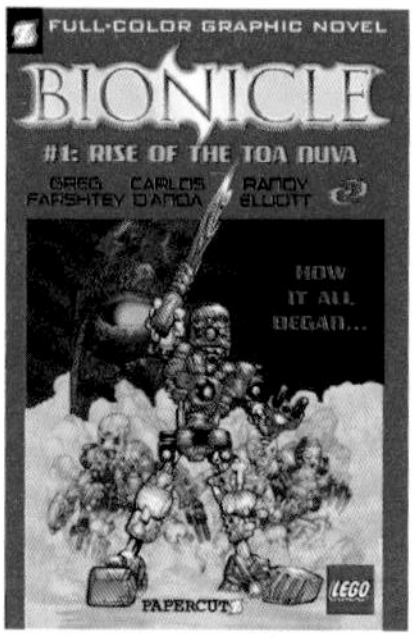
FULL-COLOR GRAPHIC NOVEL
BIONICLE
#1: RISE OF THE TOA NUVA
GREG FARSHTEY
CARLOS D'ANDA
RANDY ELLIOTT
HOW IT ALL BEGAN...
PAPERCUTZ
LEGO

Coming in August: Graphic Novel #2
**"Challenge of the Rahkshi"**

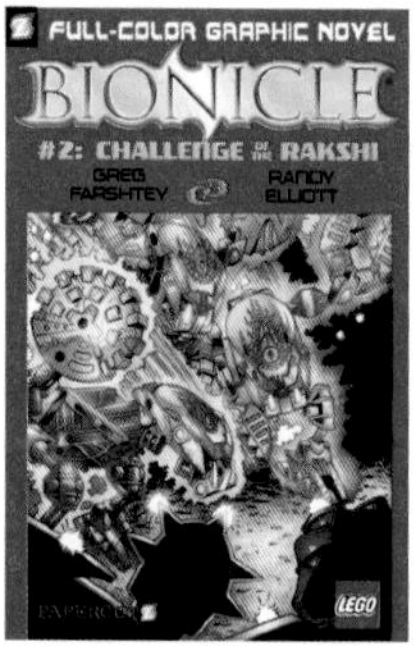
FULL-COLOR GRAPHIC NOVEL
BIONICLE
#2: CHALLENGE OF THE RAKSHI
GREG FARSHTEY
RANDY ELLIOTT
LEGO

Coming in November: Graphic Novel #3
**"City of Legends"**

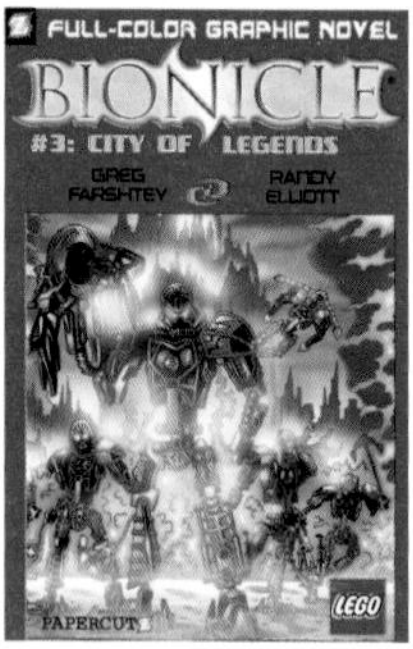
FULL-COLOR GRAPHIC NOVEL
BIONICLE
#3: CITY OF LEGENDS
GREG FARSHTEY
RANDY ELLIOTT
PAPERCUTZ
LEGO

$7.95 each paperback, $12.95 each in hardcover. Please add $4.00 for postage and handling for the first book, add $1.00 for each additional book. Please make check payable to NBM Publishing. Send to: Papercutz, 40 Exchange Place, Suite 1308, New York, NY 10005 • www.papercutz.com

# #1 The Rise of the Toa Nuva

GREG FARSHTEY
Writer
CARLOS D'ANDA
Artist

New York

The Rise of The Toa Nuva

GREG FARSHTEY – Writer
CARLOS D'ANDA, RICHARD BENNETT, RANDY ELLIOTT — Artists
ALEX SINCLAIR, PETER PANTAZIS — Colorists
KEN LOPEZ -- Letterer
JOHN McCARTHY -- Production
JIM SALICRUP
Editor-in-Chief

ISBN 10: 1-59707-109-9 paperback edition
ISBN 13: 978-1-59707-109-3 paperback edition
ISBN 10: 1-59707-110-2 hardcover edition
ISBN 13: 978-1-59707-110-9 hardcover edition


Originally published as comicbooks by DC Comics as BIONICLE #1-8.

Distributed by Macmillan.

10 9 8 7 6 5 4 3 2 1

# CHAPTER ONE

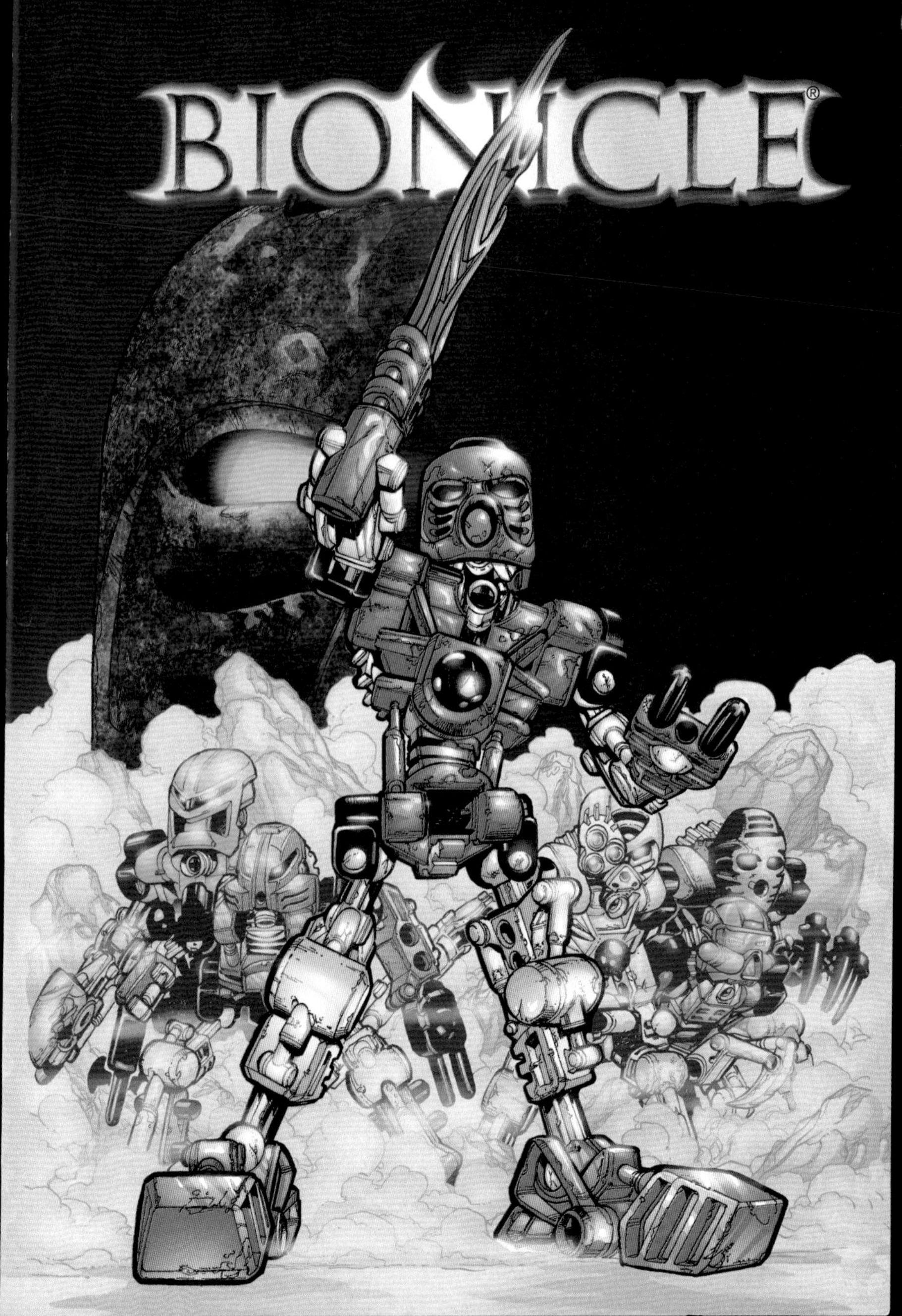
BIONICLE®

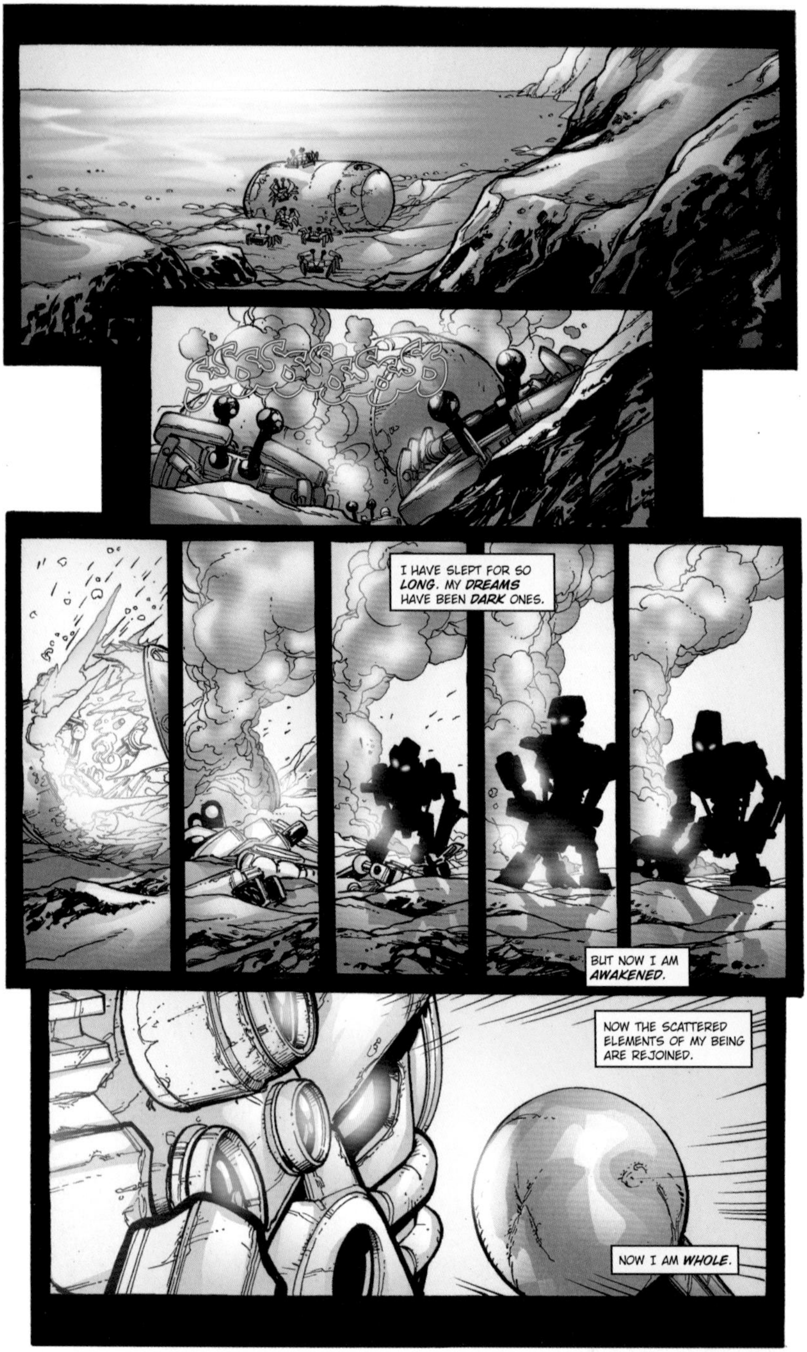
I HAVE SLEPT FOR SO LONG. MY DREAMS HAVE BEEN DARK ONES.
BUT NOW I AM AWAKENED.
NOW THE SCATTERED ELEMENTS OF MY BEING ARE REJOINED.
NOW I AM WHOLE.

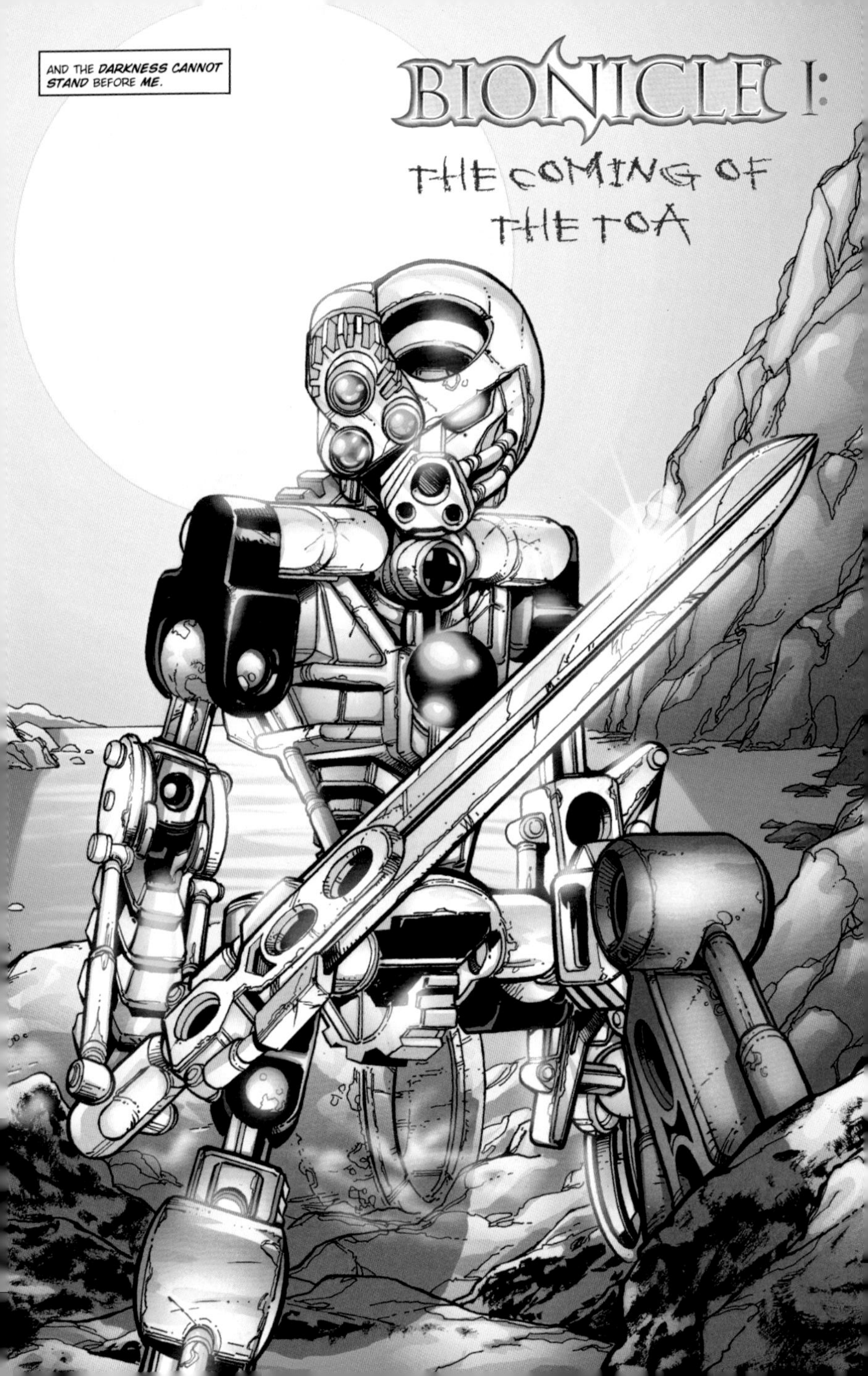
AND THE DARKNESS CANNOT STAND BEFORE ME.
BIONICLE I:
THE COMING OF THE TOA

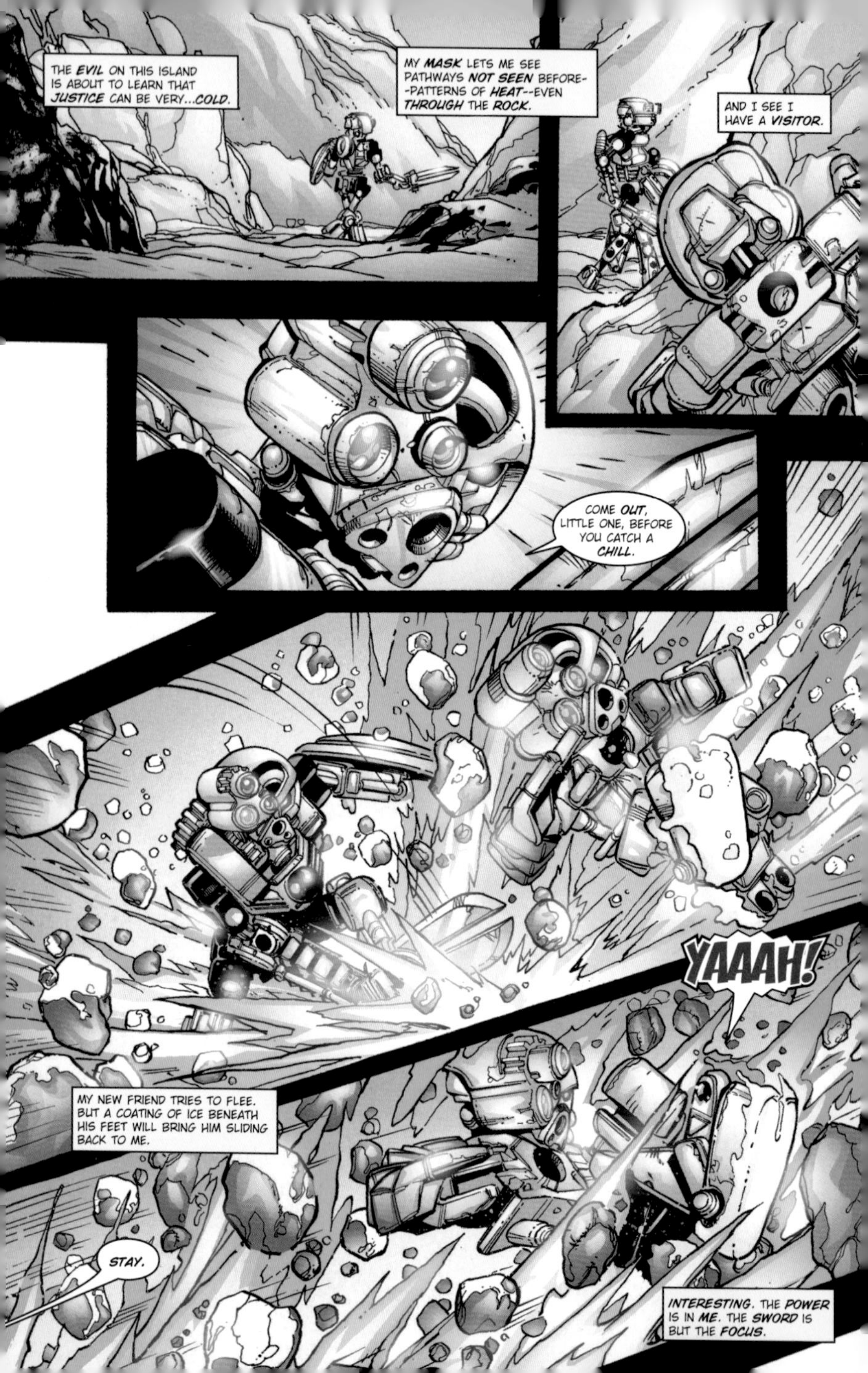
THE EVIL ON THIS ISLAND IS ABOUT TO LEARN THAT JUSTICE CAN BE VERY...COLD.
MY MASK LETS ME SEE PATHWAYS NOT SEEN BEFORE--PATTERNS OF HEAT--EVEN THROUGH THE ROCK.
AND I SEE I HAVE A VISITOR.
COME OUT, LITTLE ONE, BEFORE YOU CATCH A CHILL.
YAAAH!
MY NEW FRIEND TRIES TO FLEE. BUT A COATING OF ICE BENEATH HIS FEET WILL BRING HIM SLIDING BACK TO ME.
STAY.
INTERESTING. THE POWER IS IN ME. THE SWORD IS BUT THE FOCUS.

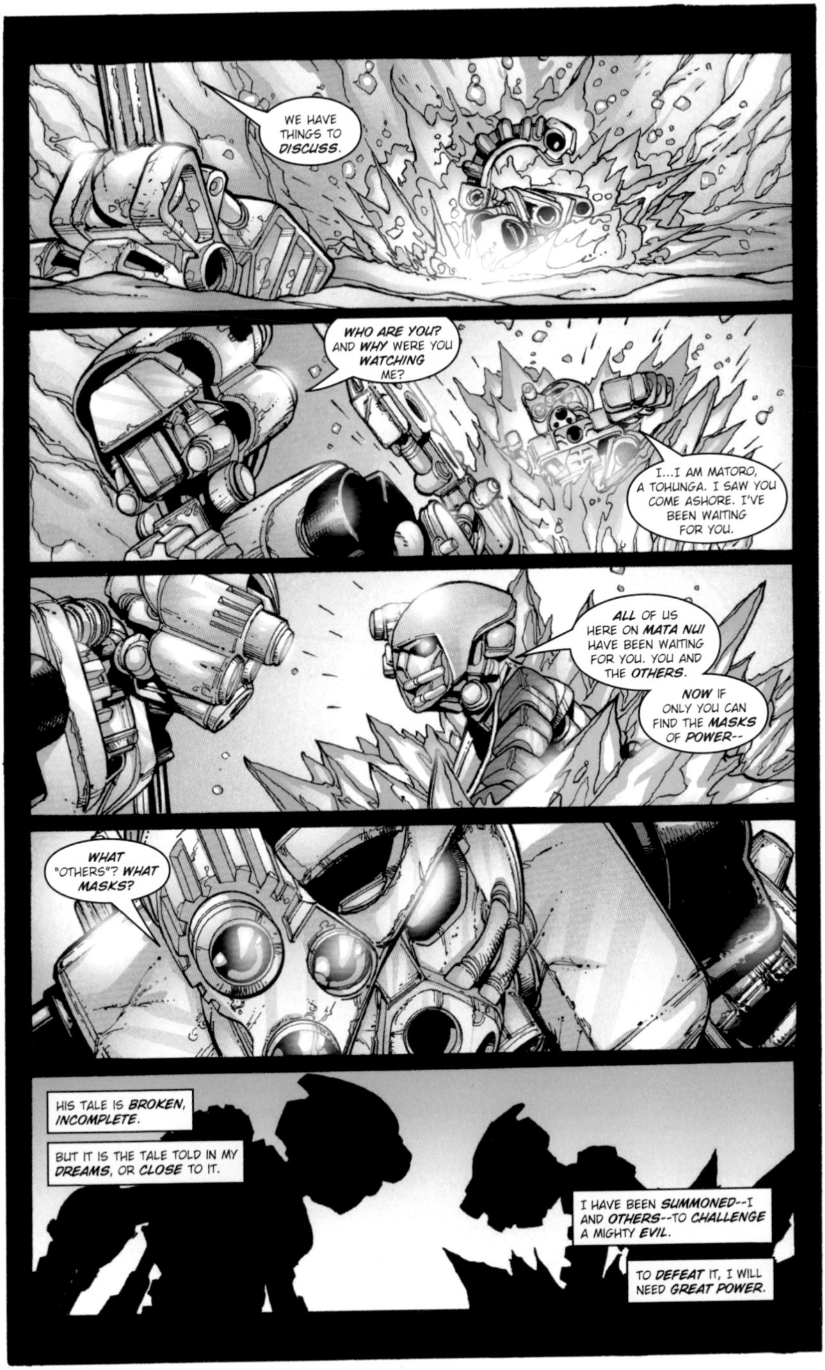
WE HAVE THINGS TO DISCUSS.
WHO ARE YOU? AND WHY WERE YOU WATCHING ME?
I...I AM MATORO, A TOHUNGA. I SAW YOU COME ASHORE. I'VE BEEN WAITING FOR YOU.
ALL OF US HERE ON MATA NUI HAVE BEEN WAITING FOR YOU. YOU AND THE OTHERS.
NOW IF ONLY YOU CAN FIND THE MASKS OF POWER--
WHAT "OTHERS"? WHAT MASKS?
HIS TALE IS BROKEN, INCOMPLETE.
BUT IT IS THE TALE TOLD IN MY DREAMS, OR CLOSE TO IT.
I HAVE BEEN SUMMONED--I AND OTHERS--TO CHALLENGE A MIGHTY EVIL.
TO DEFEAT IT, I WILL NEED GREAT POWER.

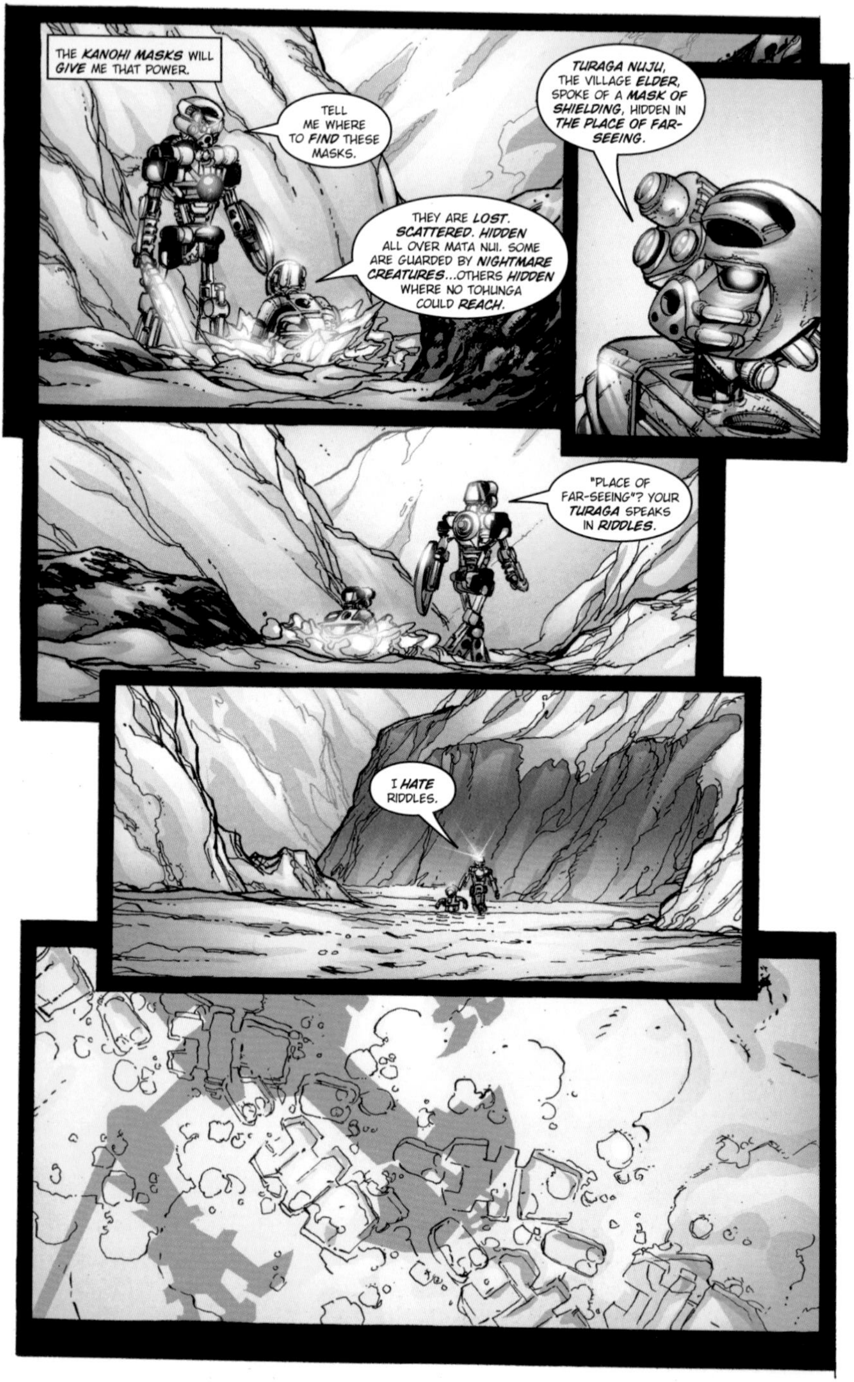
THE KANOHI MASKS WILL GIVE ME THAT POWER.
TELL ME WHERE TO FIND THESE MASKS.
THEY ARE LOST. SCATTERED. HIDDEN ALL OVER MATA NUI. SOME ARE GUARDED BY NIGHTMARE CREATURES...OTHERS HIDDEN WHERE NO TOHUNGA COULD REACH.
TURAGA NUJU, THE VILLAGE ELDER, SPOKE OF A MASK OF SHIELDING, HIDDEN IN THE PLACE OF FAR-SEEING.
"PLACE OF FAR-SEEING"? YOUR TURAGA SPEAKS IN RIDDLES.
I HATE RIDDLES.

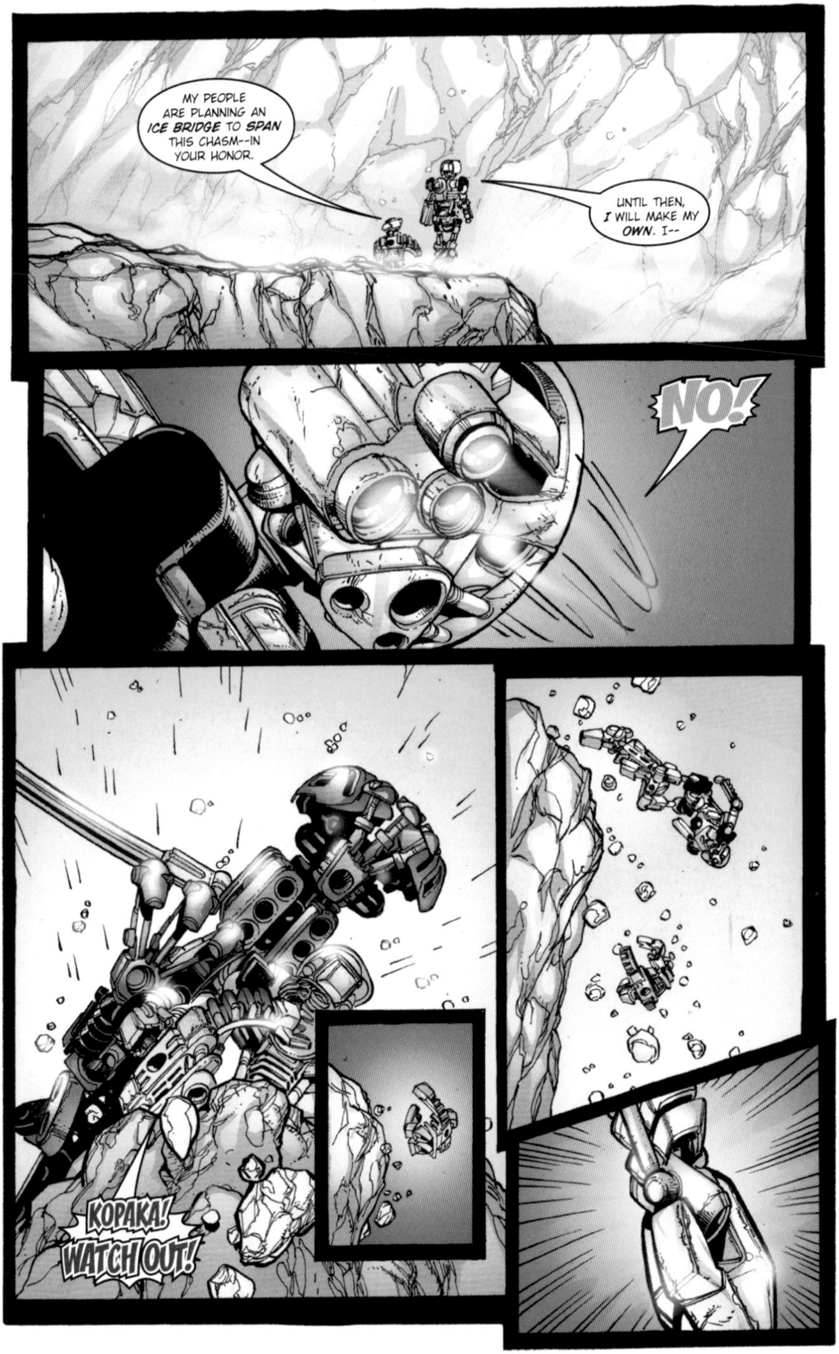
MY PEOPLE ARE PLANNING AN ICE BRIDGE TO SPAN THIS CHASM--IN YOUR HONOR.
UNTIL THEN, I WILL MAKE MY OWN. I--
NO!
KOPAKA! WATCH OUT!

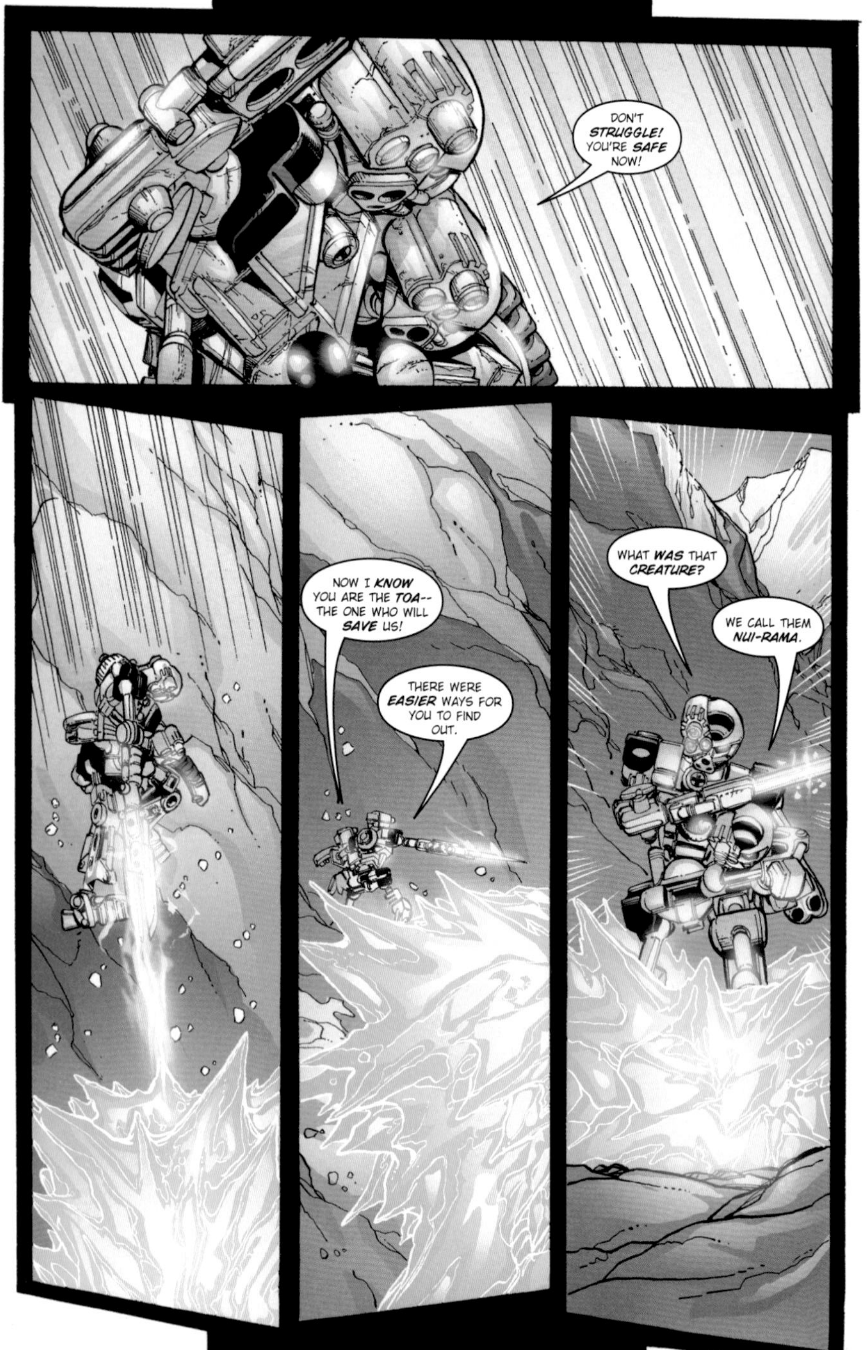
DON'T STRUGGLE! YOU'RE SAFE NOW!
NOW I KNOW YOU ARE THE TOA-- THE ONE WHO WILL SAVE US!
THERE WERE EASIER WAYS FOR YOU TO FIND OUT.
WHAT WAS THAT CREATURE?
WE CALL THEM NUI-RAMA.

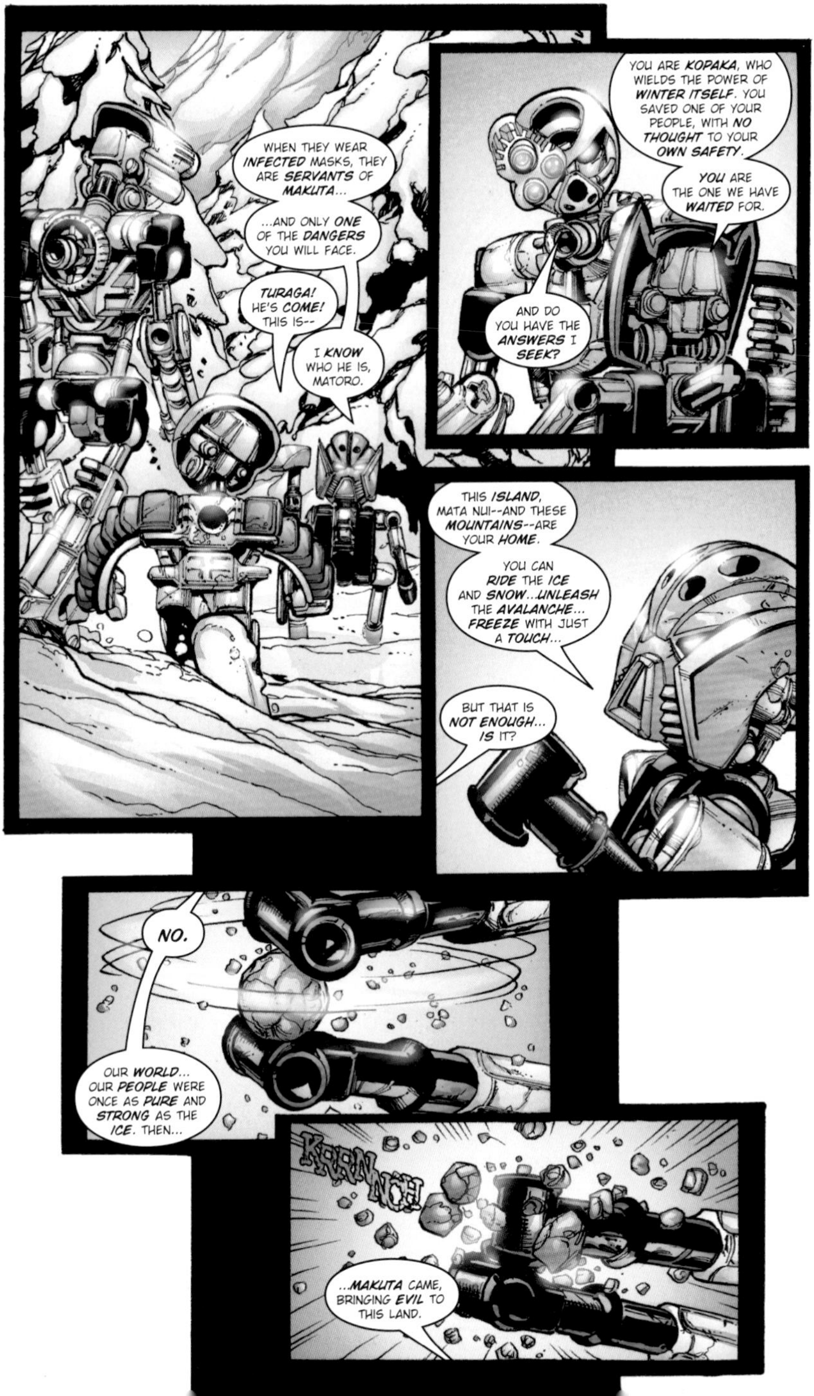
WHEN THEY WEAR INFECTED MASKS, THEY ARE SERVANTS OF MAKUTA...
...AND ONLY ONE OF THE DANGERS YOU WILL FACE.
TURAGA! HE'S COME! THIS IS--
I KNOW WHO HE IS, MATORO.
YOU ARE KOPAKA, WHO WIELDS THE POWER OF WINTER ITSELF. YOU SAVED ONE OF YOUR PEOPLE, WITH NO THOUGHT TO YOUR OWN SAFETY.
YOU ARE THE ONE WE HAVE WAITED FOR.
AND DO YOU HAVE THE ANSWERS I SEEK?
THIS ISLAND, MATA NUI--AND THESE MOUNTAINS--ARE YOUR HOME.
YOU CAN RIDE THE ICE AND SNOW...UNLEASH THE AVALANCHE... FREEZE WITH JUST A TOUCH...
BUT THAT IS NOT ENOUGH... IS IT?
NO.
OUR WORLD... OUR PEOPLE WERE ONCE AS PURE AND STRONG AS THE ICE. THEN...
KRRNNCH!
...MAKUTA CAME, BRINGING EVIL TO THIS LAND.

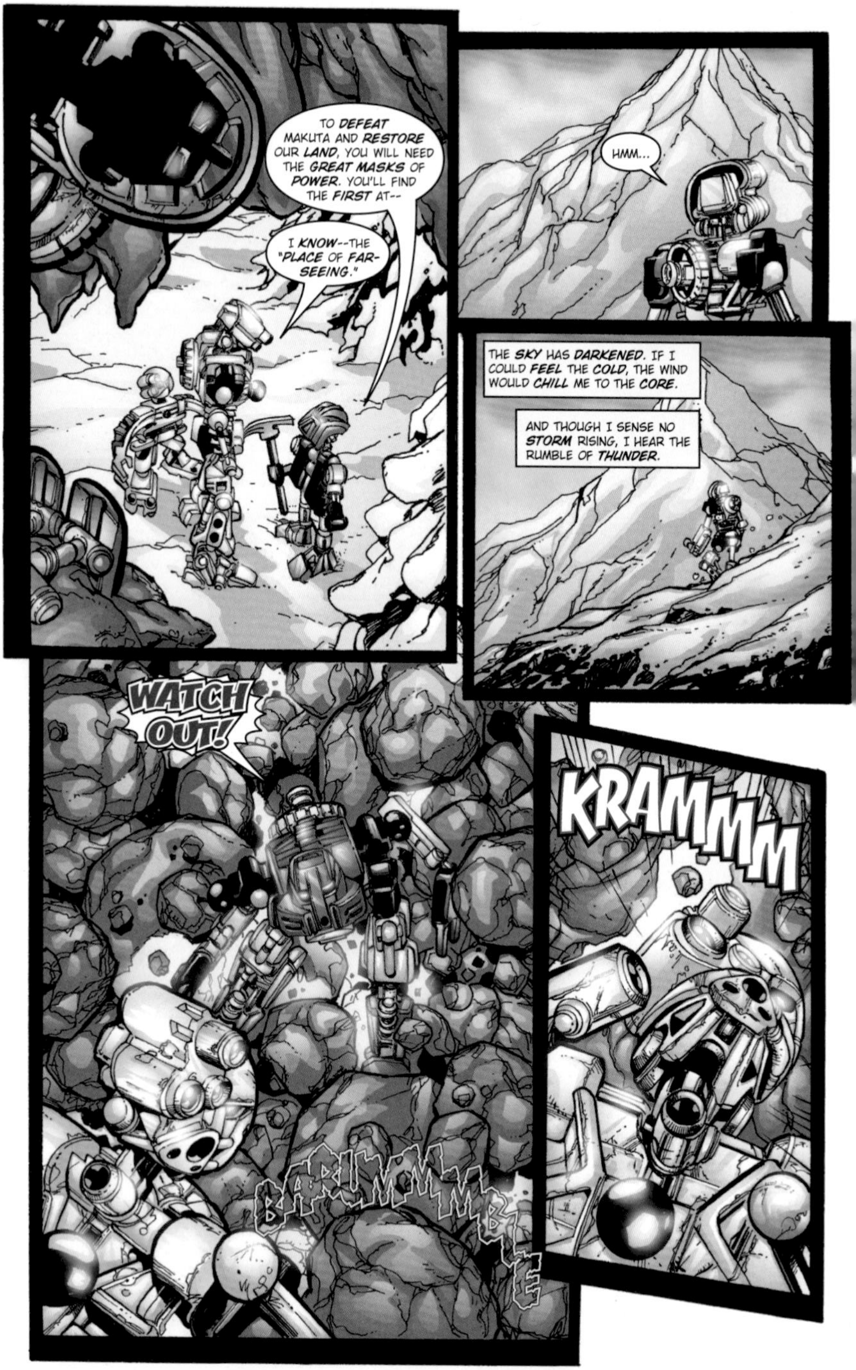
TO DEFEAT MAKUTA AND RESTORE OUR LAND, YOU WILL NEED THE GREAT MASKS OF POWER. YOU'LL FIND THE FIRST AT--
I KNOW--THE "PLACE OF FAR-SEEING."
HMM...
THE SKY HAS DARKENED. IF I COULD FEEL THE COLD, THE WIND WOULD CHILL ME TO THE CORE.
AND THOUGH I SENSE NO STORM RISING, I HEAR THE RUMBLE OF THUNDER.
WATCH OUT!
BARUMMMBLE
KRAMMMM

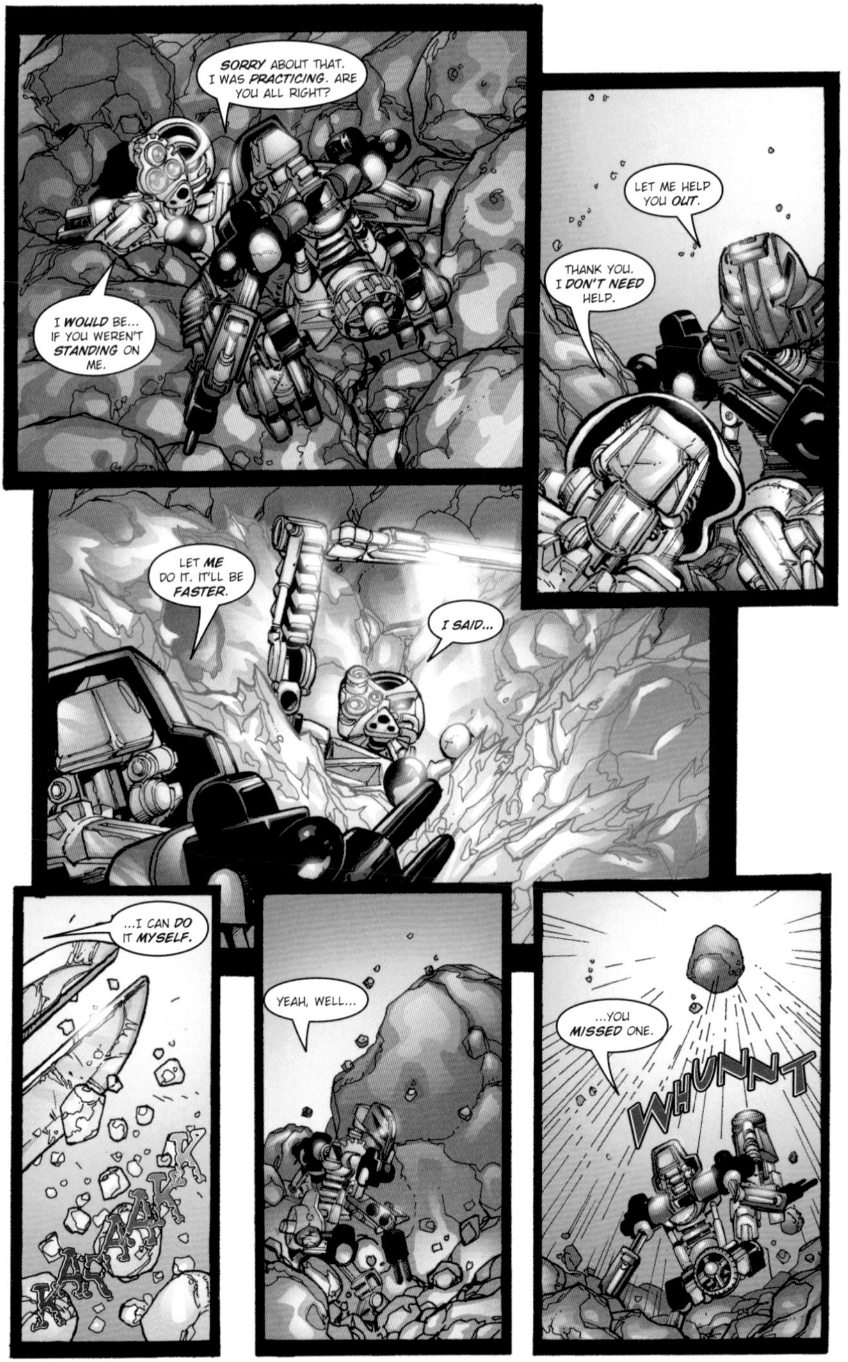
SORRY ABOUT THAT. I WAS PRACTICING. ARE YOU ALL RIGHT?
I WOULD BE... IF YOU WEREN'T STANDING ON ME.
LET ME HELP YOU OUT.
THANK YOU. I DON'T NEED HELP.
LET ME DO IT. IT'LL BE FASTER.
I SAID...
...I CAN DO IT MYSELF.
KAKAAKK
YEAH, WELL...
...YOU MISSED ONE.
WHUNNT

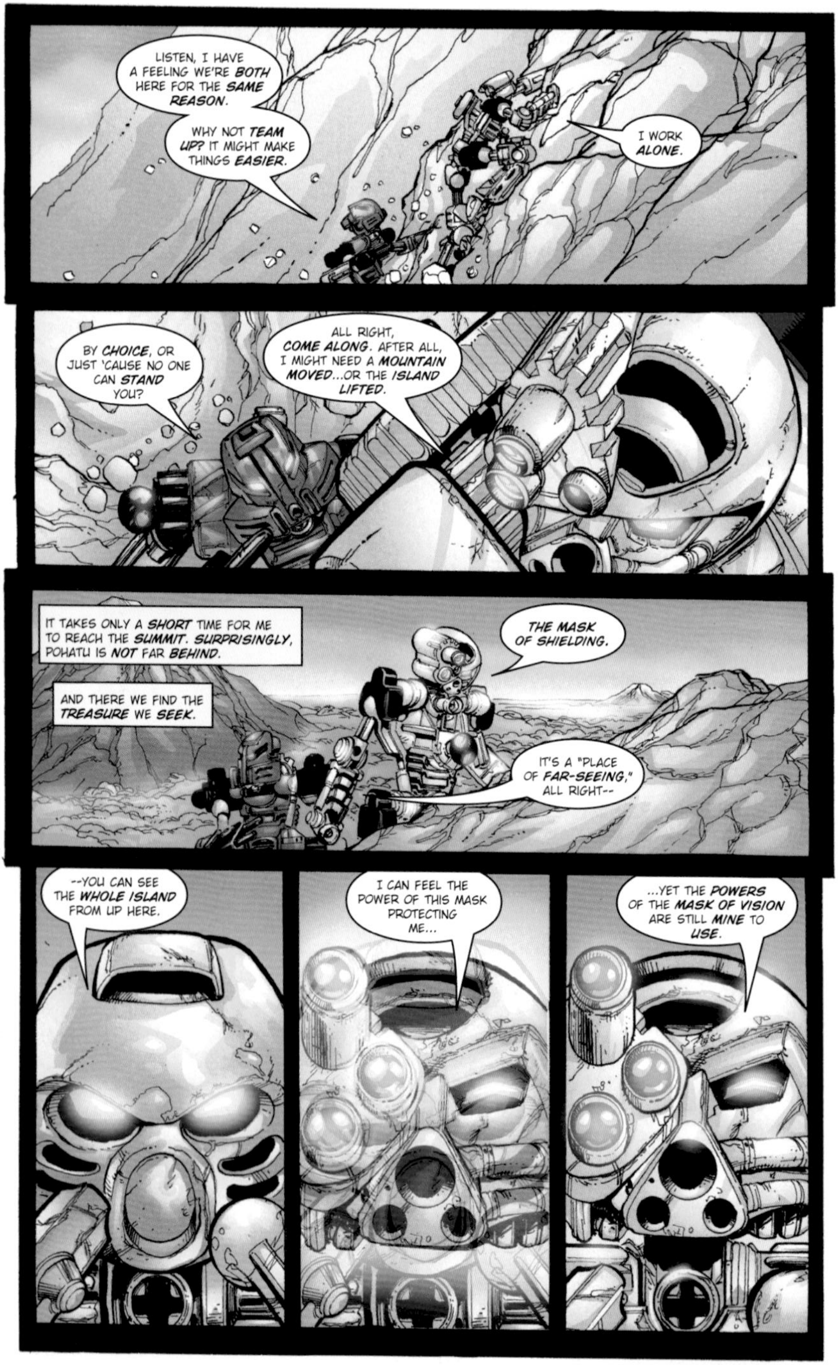
LISTEN, I HAVE A FEELING WE'RE BOTH HERE FOR THE SAME REASON.
WHY NOT TEAM UP? IT MIGHT MAKE THINGS EASIER.
I WORK ALONE.
BY CHOICE, OR JUST 'CAUSE NO ONE CAN STAND YOU?
ALL RIGHT, COME ALONG. AFTER ALL, I MIGHT NEED A MOUNTAIN MOVED...OR THE ISLAND LIFTED.
IT TAKES ONLY A SHORT TIME FOR ME TO REACH THE SUMMIT. SURPRISINGLY, POHATU IS NOT FAR BEHIND.
AND THERE WE FIND THE TREASURE WE SEEK.
THE MASK OF SHIELDING.
IT'S A "PLACE OF FAR-SEEING," ALL RIGHT--
--YOU CAN SEE THE WHOLE ISLAND FROM UP HERE.
I CAN FEEL THE POWER OF THIS MASK PROTECTING ME...
...YET THE POWERS OF THE MASK OF VISION ARE STILL MINE TO USE.

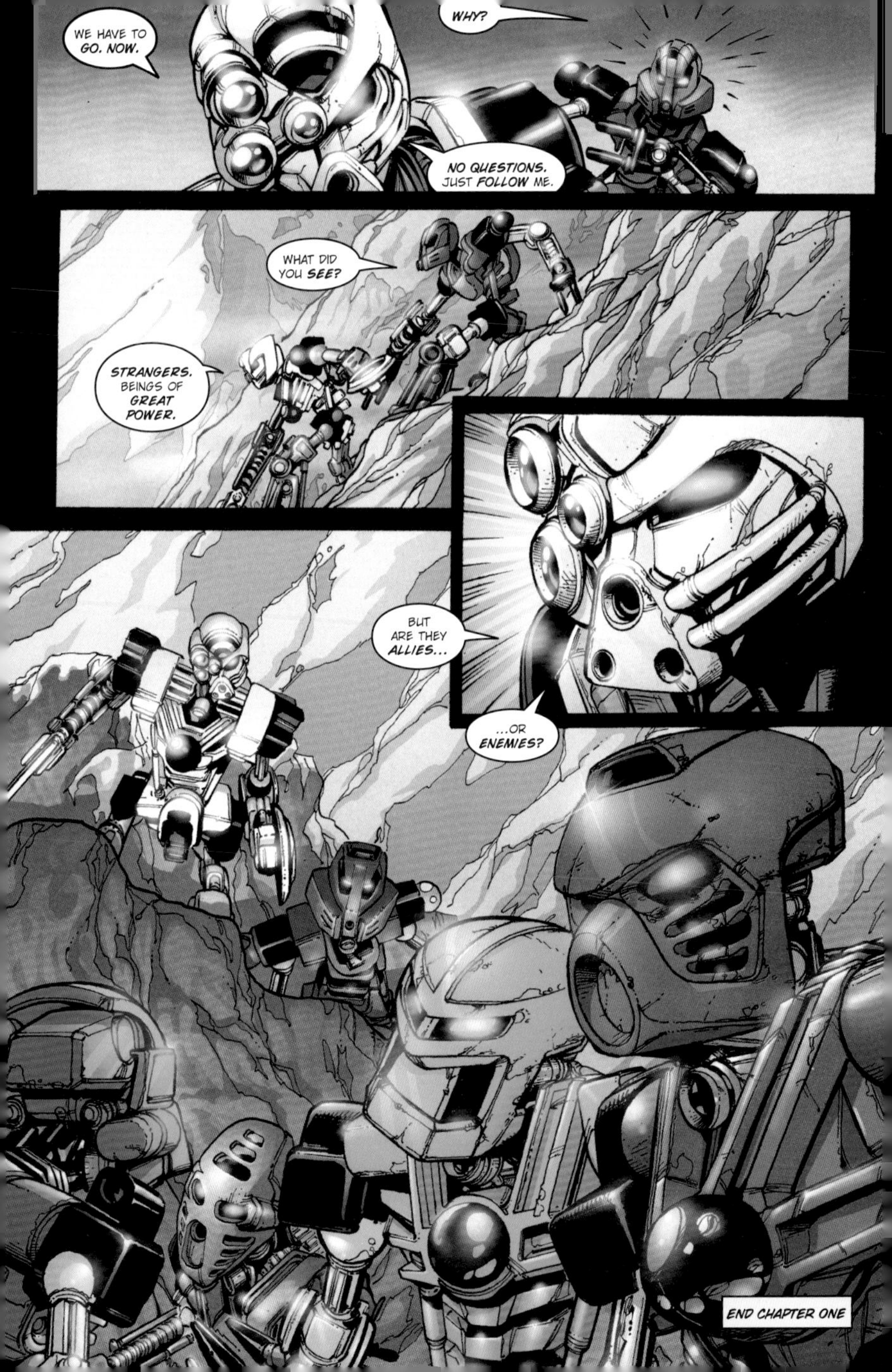
WE HAVE TO GO. NOW.
WHY?
NO QUESTIONS. JUST FOLLOW ME.
WHAT DID YOU SEE?
STRANGERS. BEINGS OF GREAT POWER.
BUT ARE THEY ALLIES...
...OR ENEMIES?
END CHAPTER ONE

# CHAPTER TWO

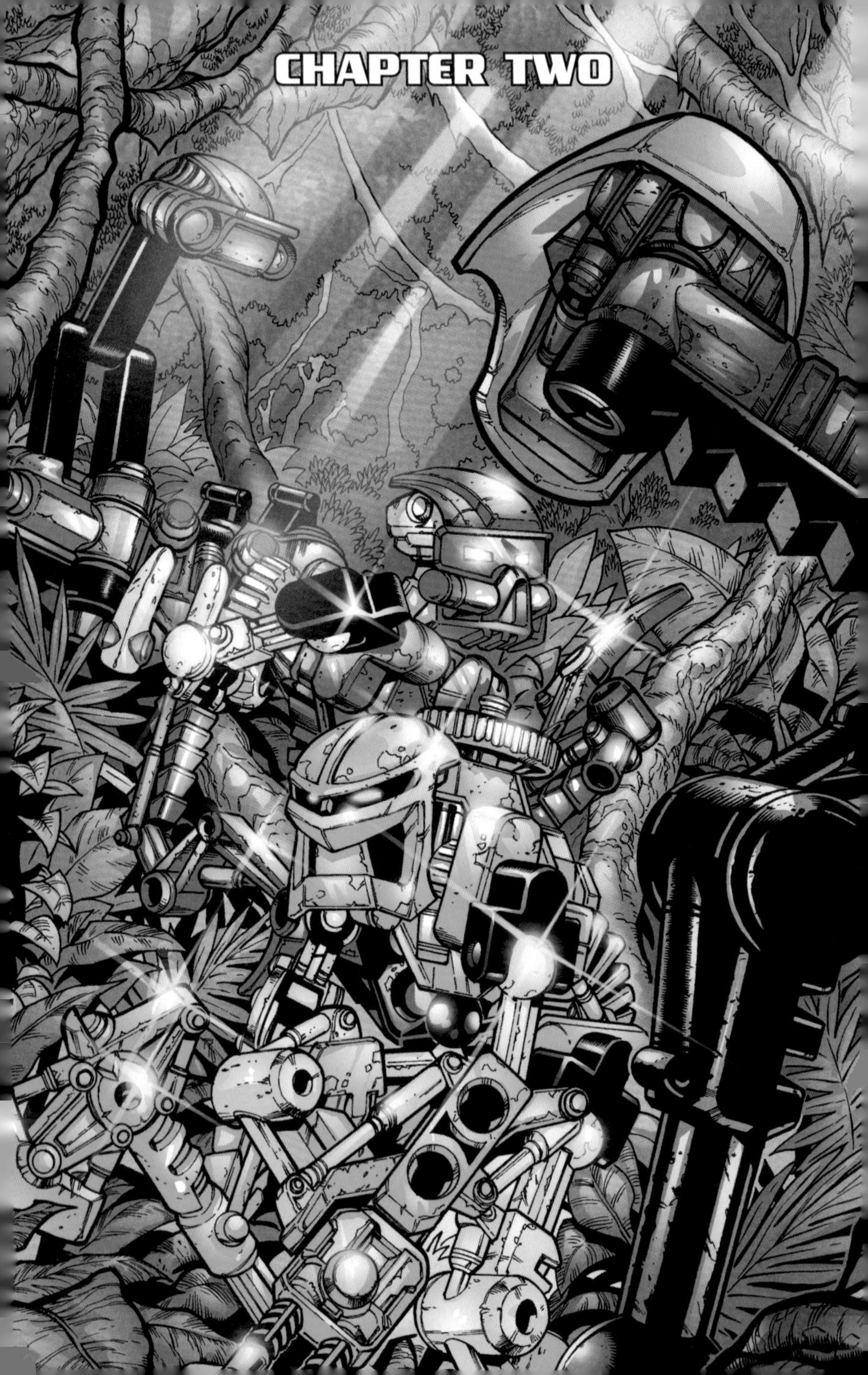

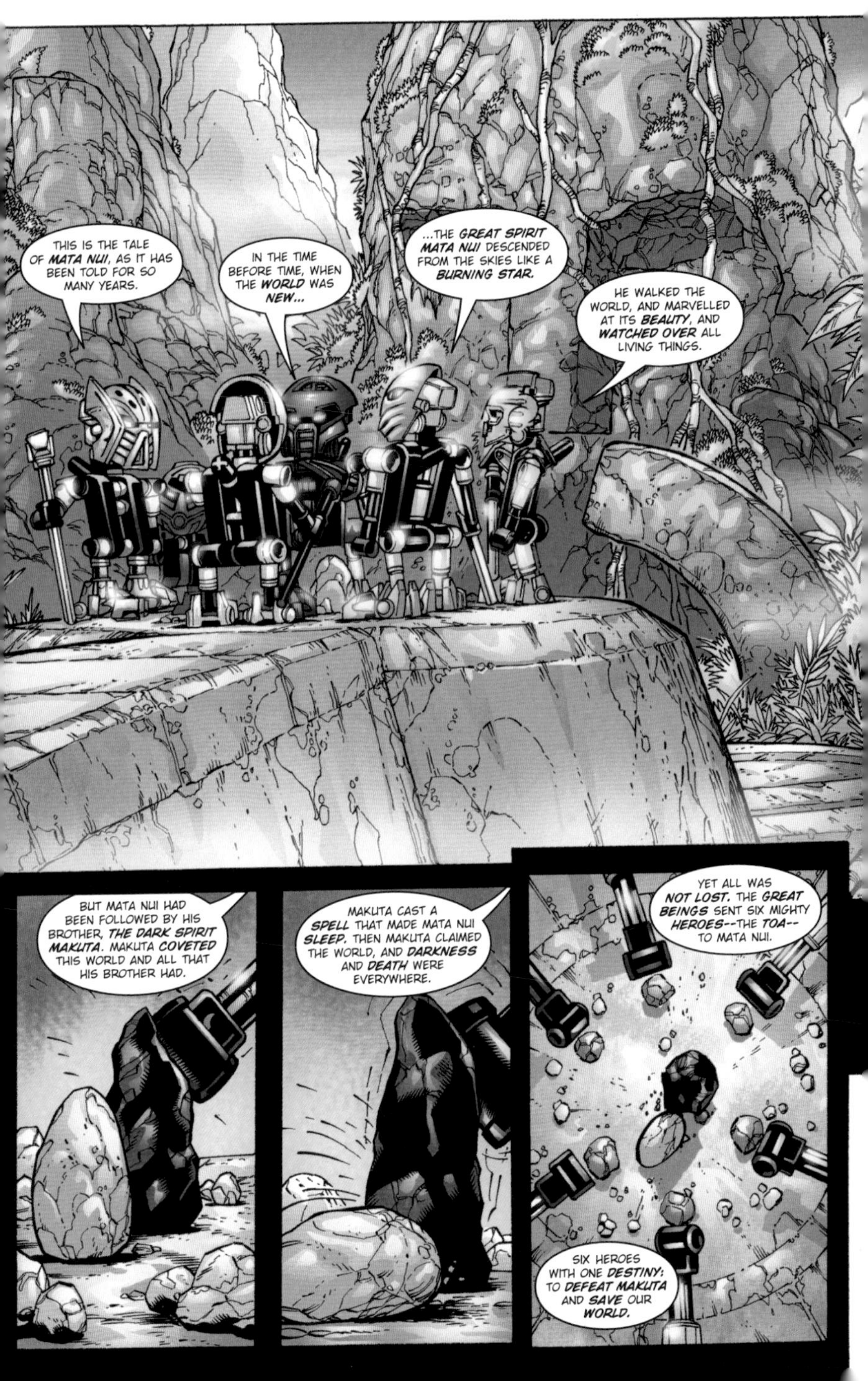
THIS IS THE TALE OF MATA NUI, AS IT HAS BEEN TOLD FOR SO MANY YEARS.
IN THE TIME BEFORE TIME, WHEN THE WORLD WAS NEW...
...THE GREAT SPIRIT MATA NUI DESCENDED FROM THE SKIES LIKE A BURNING STAR.
HE WALKED THE WORLD, AND MARVELLED AT ITS BEAUTY, AND WATCHED OVER ALL LIVING THINGS.
BUT MATA NUI HAD BEEN FOLLOWED BY HIS BROTHER, THE DARK SPIRIT MAKUTA. MAKUTA COVETED THIS WORLD AND ALL THAT HIS BROTHER HAD.
MAKUTA CAST A SPELL THAT MADE MATA NUI SLEEP. THEN MAKUTA CLAIMED THE WORLD, AND DARKNESS AND DEATH WERE EVERYWHERE.
YET ALL WAS NOT LOST. THE GREAT BEINGS SENT SIX MIGHTY HEROES--THE TOA--TO MATA NUI.
SIX HEROES WITH ONE DESTINY: TO DEFEAT MAKUTA AND SAVE OUR WORLD.

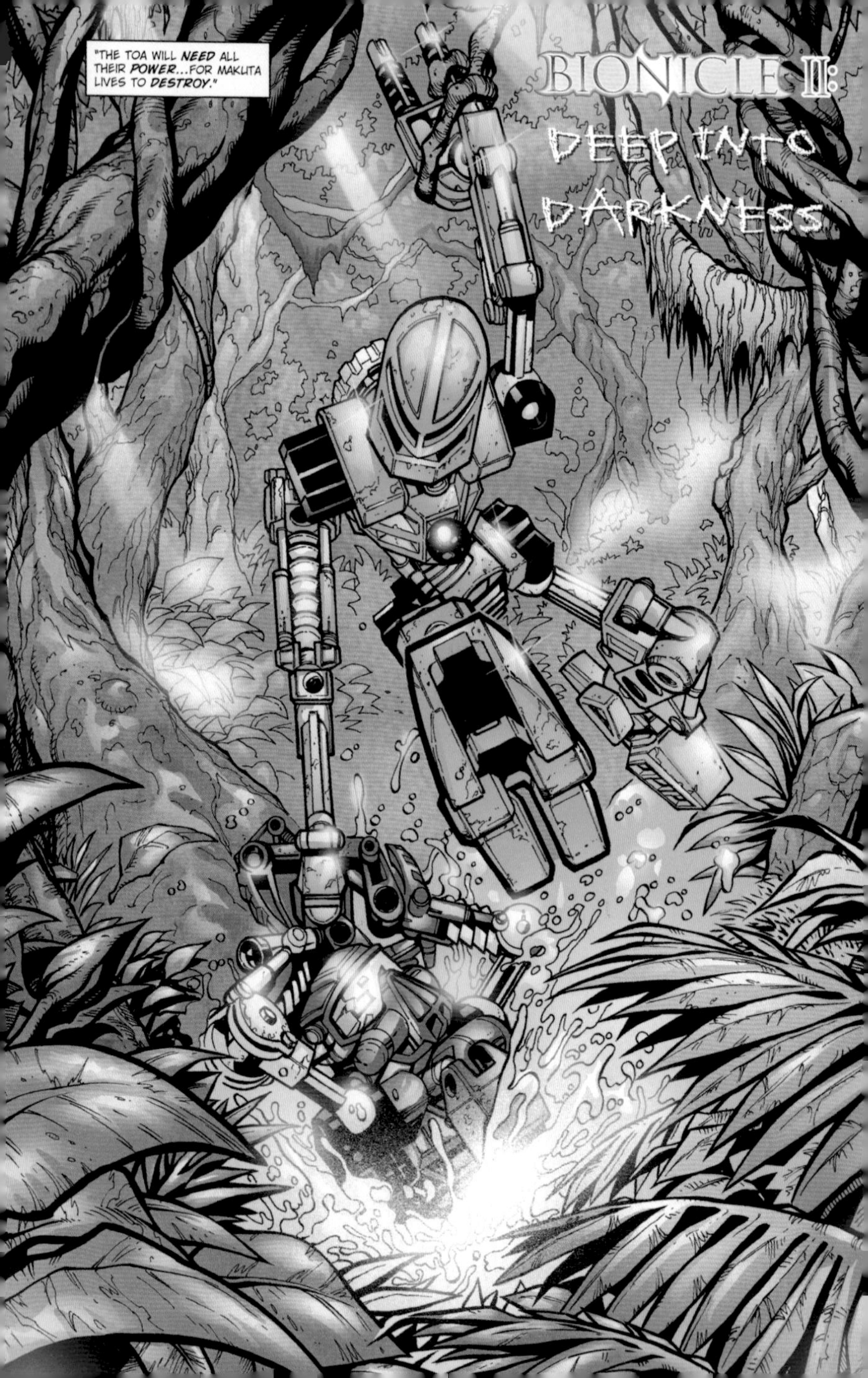
"THE TOA WILL NEED ALL THEIR POWER...FOR MAKUTA LIVES TO DESTROY."
BIONICLE II:
DEEP INTO DARKNESS

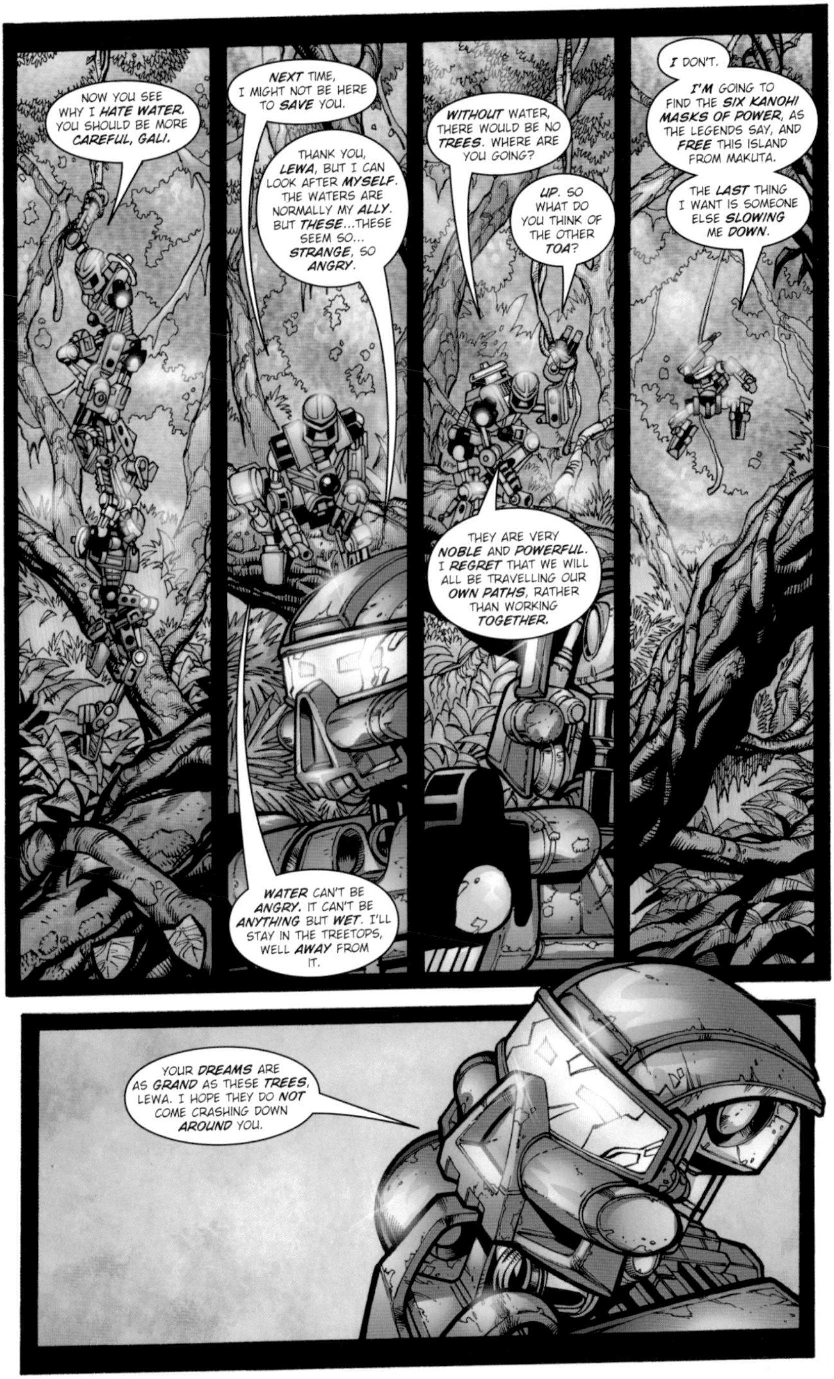
NOW YOU SEE WHY I HATE WATER. YOU SHOULD BE MORE CAREFUL, GALI.
NEXT TIME, I MIGHT NOT BE HERE TO SAVE YOU.
THANK YOU, LEWA, BUT I CAN LOOK AFTER MYSELF. THE WATERS ARE NORMALLY MY ALLY. BUT THESE...THESE SEEM SO... STRANGE, SO ANGRY.
WATER CAN'T BE ANGRY. IT CAN'T BE ANYTHING BUT WET. I'LL STAY IN THE TREETOPS, WELL AWAY FROM IT.
WITHOUT WATER, THERE WOULD BE NO TREES. WHERE ARE YOU GOING?
UP. SO WHAT DO YOU THINK OF THE OTHER TOA?
THEY ARE VERY NOBLE AND POWERFUL. I REGRET THAT WE WILL ALL BE TRAVELLING OUR OWN PATHS, RATHER THAN WORKING TOGETHER.
I DON'T.
I'M GOING TO FIND THE SIX KANOHI MASKS OF POWER, AS THE LEGENDS SAY, AND FREE THIS ISLAND FROM MAKUTA.
THE LAST THING I WANT IS SOMEONE ELSE SLOWING ME DOWN.
YOUR DREAMS ARE AS GRAND AS THESE TREES, LEWA. I HOPE THEY DO NOT COME CRASHING DOWN AROUND YOU.

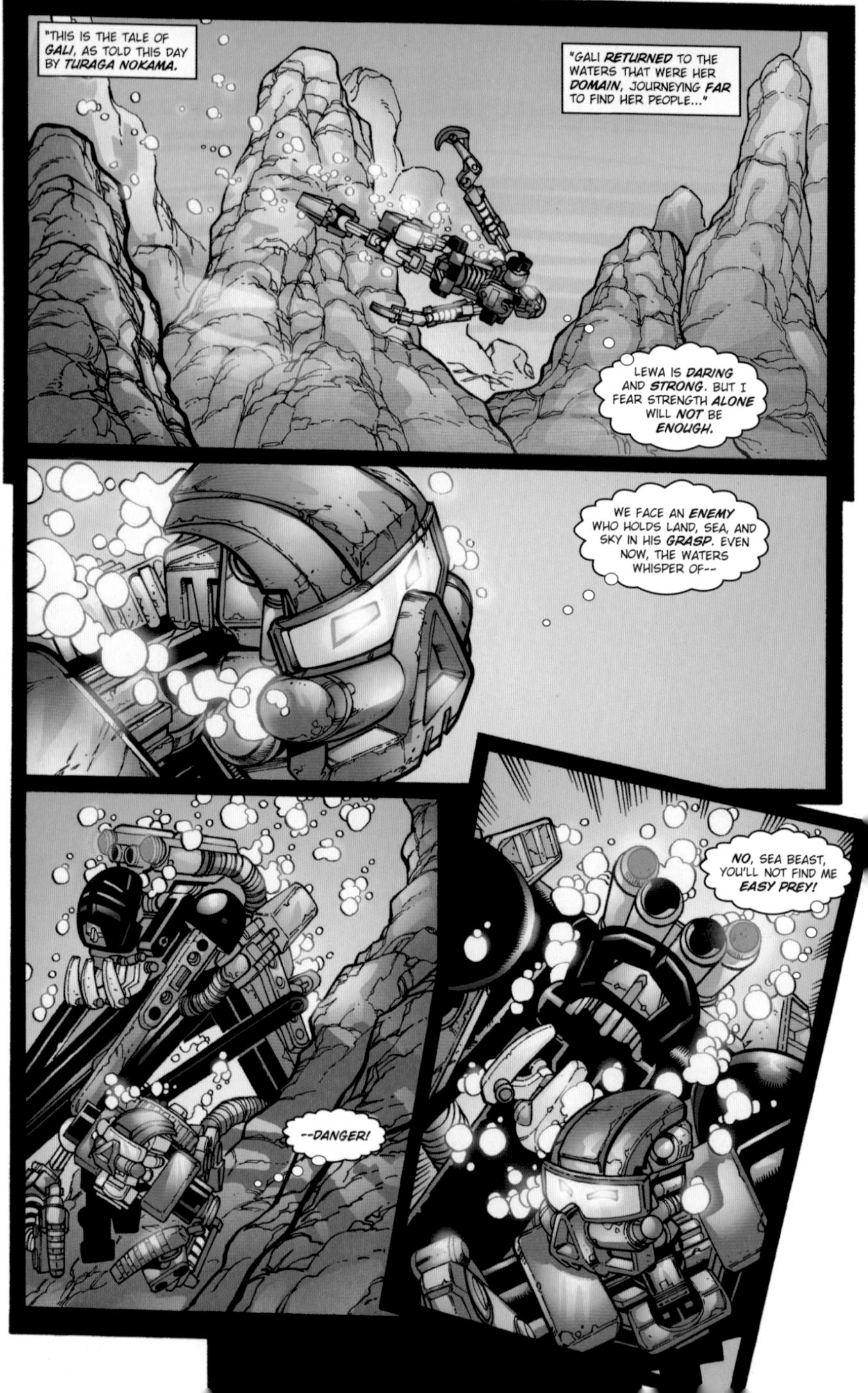
"THIS IS THE TALE OF GALI, AS TOLD THIS DAY BY TURAGA NOKAMA.
"GALI RETURNED TO THE WATERS THAT WERE HER DOMAIN, JOURNEYING FAR TO FIND HER PEOPLE..."
LEWA IS DARING AND STRONG. BUT I FEAR STRENGTH ALONE WILL NOT BE ENOUGH.
WE FACE AN ENEMY WHO HOLDS LAND, SEA, AND SKY IN HIS GRASP. EVEN NOW, THE WATERS WHISPER OF--
--DANGER!
NO, SEA BEAST, YOU'LL NOT FIND ME EASY PREY!

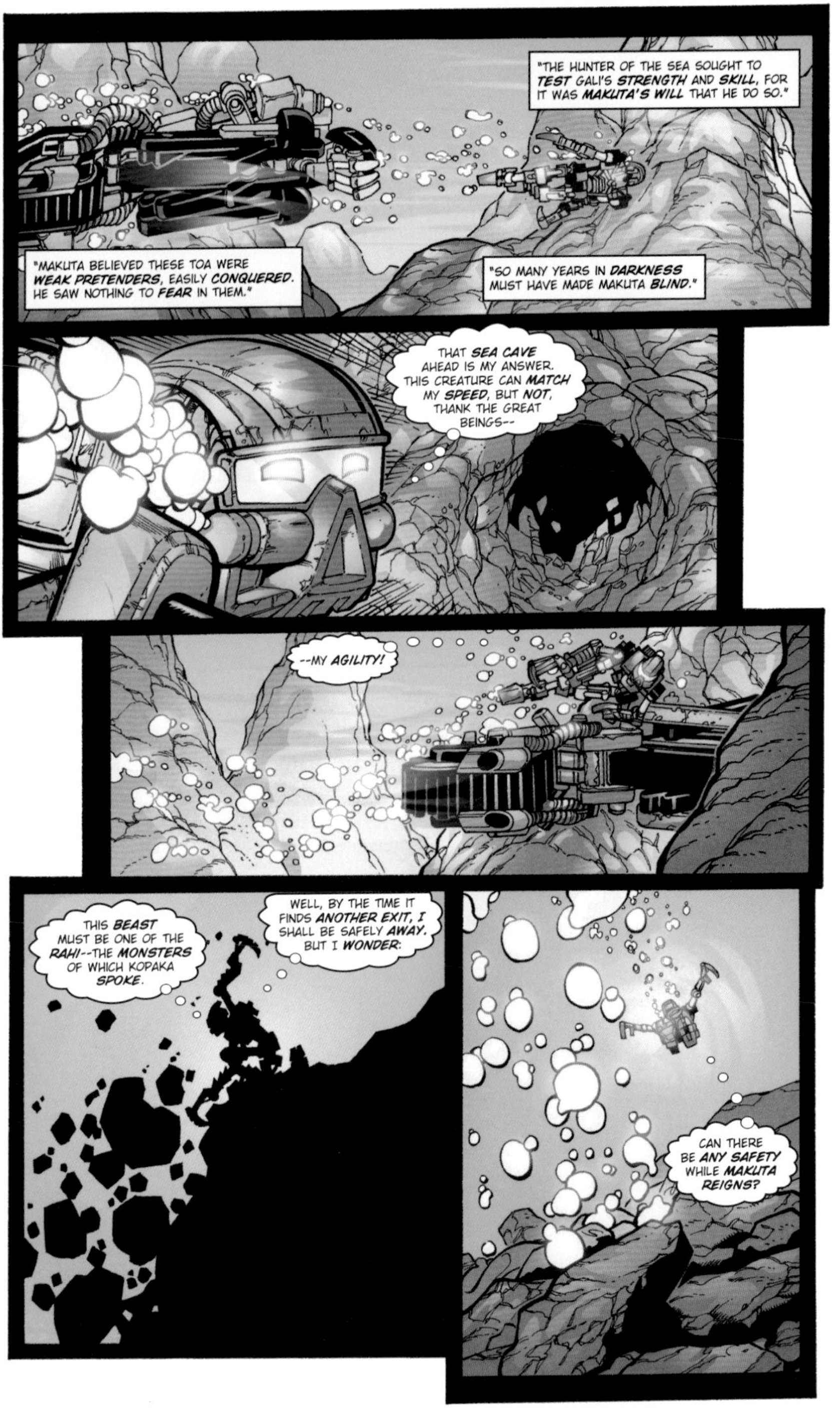
"THE HUNTER OF THE SEA SOUGHT TO TEST GALI'S STRENGTH AND SKILL, FOR IT WAS MAKUTA'S WILL THAT HE DO SO."
"MAKUTA BELIEVED THESE TOA WERE WEAK PRETENDERS, EASILY CONQUERED. HE SAW NOTHING TO FEAR IN THEM."
"SO MANY YEARS IN DARKNESS MUST HAVE MADE MAKUTA BLIND."
THAT SEA CAVE AHEAD IS MY ANSWER. THIS CREATURE CAN MATCH MY SPEED, BUT NOT, THANK THE GREAT BEINGS--
--MY AGILITY!
THIS BEAST MUST BE ONE OF THE RAHI--THE MONSTERS OF WHICH KOPAKA SPOKE.
WELL, BY THE TIME IT FINDS ANOTHER EXIT, I SHALL BE SAFELY AWAY. BUT I WONDER:
CAN THERE BE ANY SAFETY WHILE MAKUTA REIGNS?

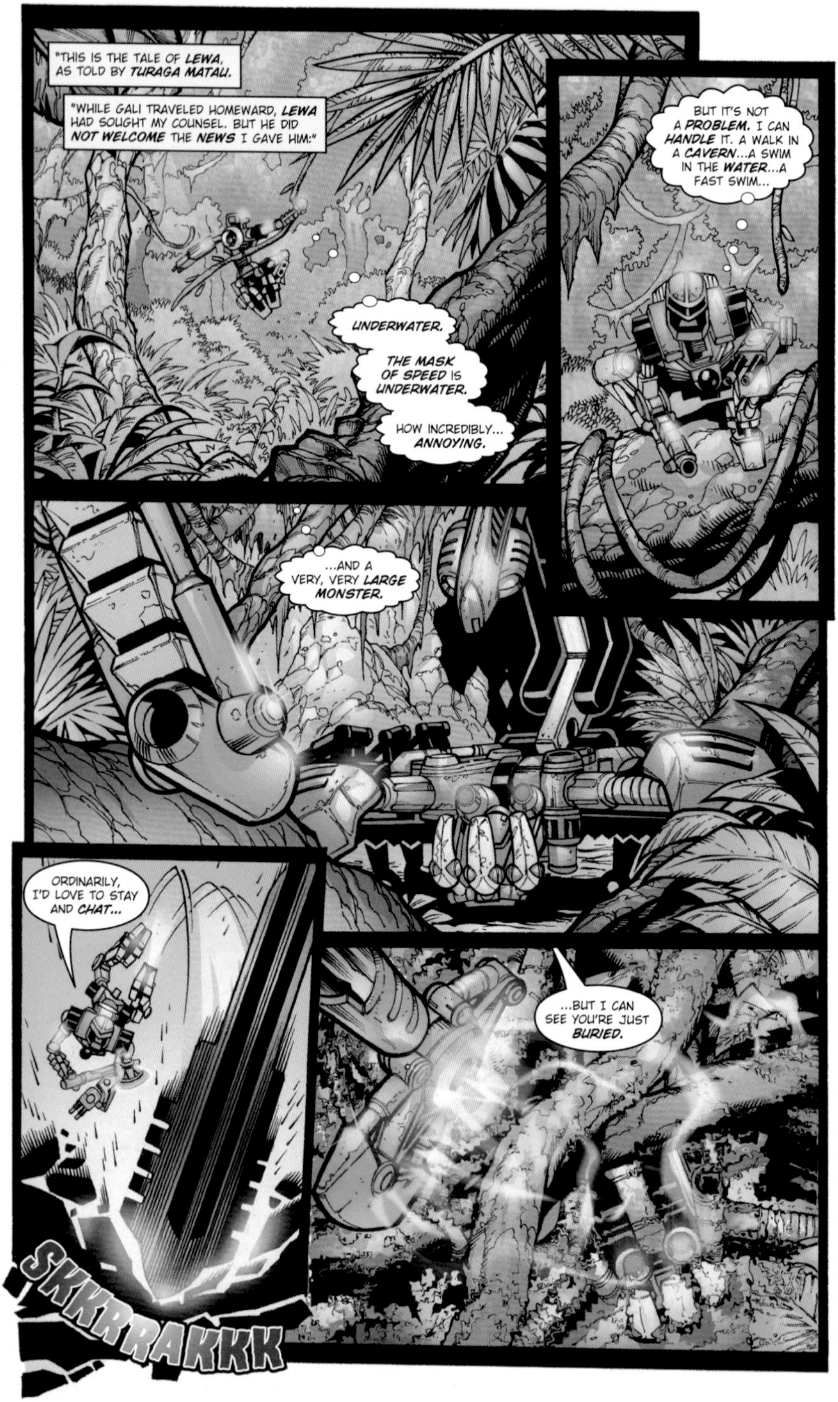
"THIS IS THE TALE OF LEWA, AS TOLD BY TURAGA MATAU.
"WHILE GALI TRAVELED HOMEWARD, LEWA HAD SOUGHT MY COUNSEL. BUT HE DID NOT WELCOME THE NEWS I GAVE HIM:"
UNDERWATER.
THE MASK OF SPEED IS UNDERWATER.
HOW INCREDIBLY... ANNOYING.
BUT IT'S NOT A PROBLEM. I CAN HANDLE IT. A WALK IN A CAVERN...A SWIM IN THE WATER...A FAST SWIM...
...AND A VERY, VERY LARGE MONSTER.
ORDINARILY, I'D LOVE TO STAY AND CHAT...
SKKRRAKKK
...BUT I CAN SEE YOU'RE JUST BURIED.

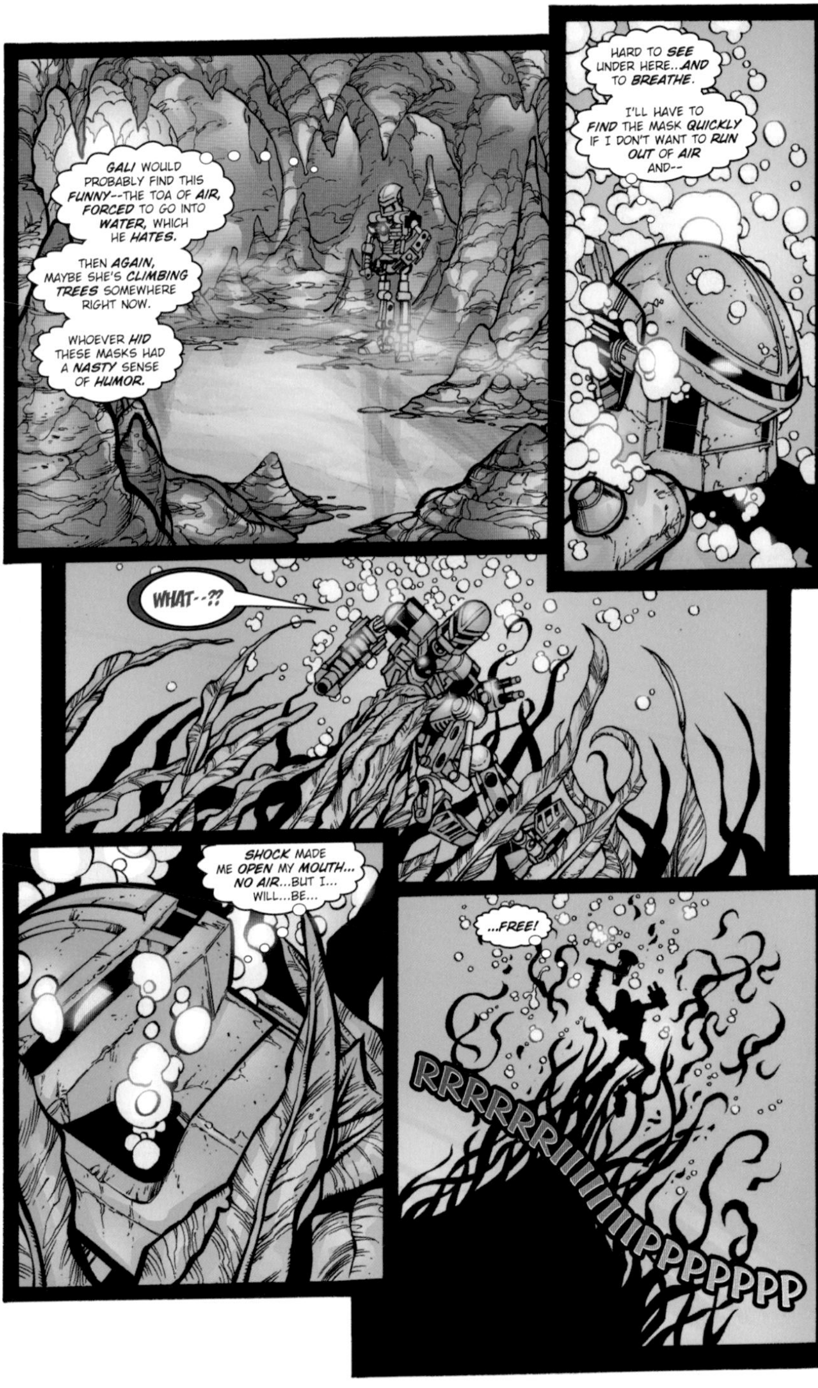
GALI WOULD PROBABLY FIND THIS FUNNY--THE TOA OF AIR, FORCED TO GO INTO WATER, WHICH HE HATES.
THEN AGAIN, MAYBE SHE'S CLIMBING TREES SOMEWHERE RIGHT NOW.
WHOEVER HID THESE MASKS HAD A NASTY SENSE OF HUMOR.
HARD TO SEE UNDER HERE...AND TO BREATHE.
I'LL HAVE TO FIND THE MASK QUICKLY IF I DON'T WANT TO RUN OUT OF AIR AND--
WHAT--??
SHOCK MADE ME OPEN MY MOUTH... NO AIR...BUT I... WILL...BE...
...FREE!
RRRRRRRIIIIIIIIIIIPPPPPPP

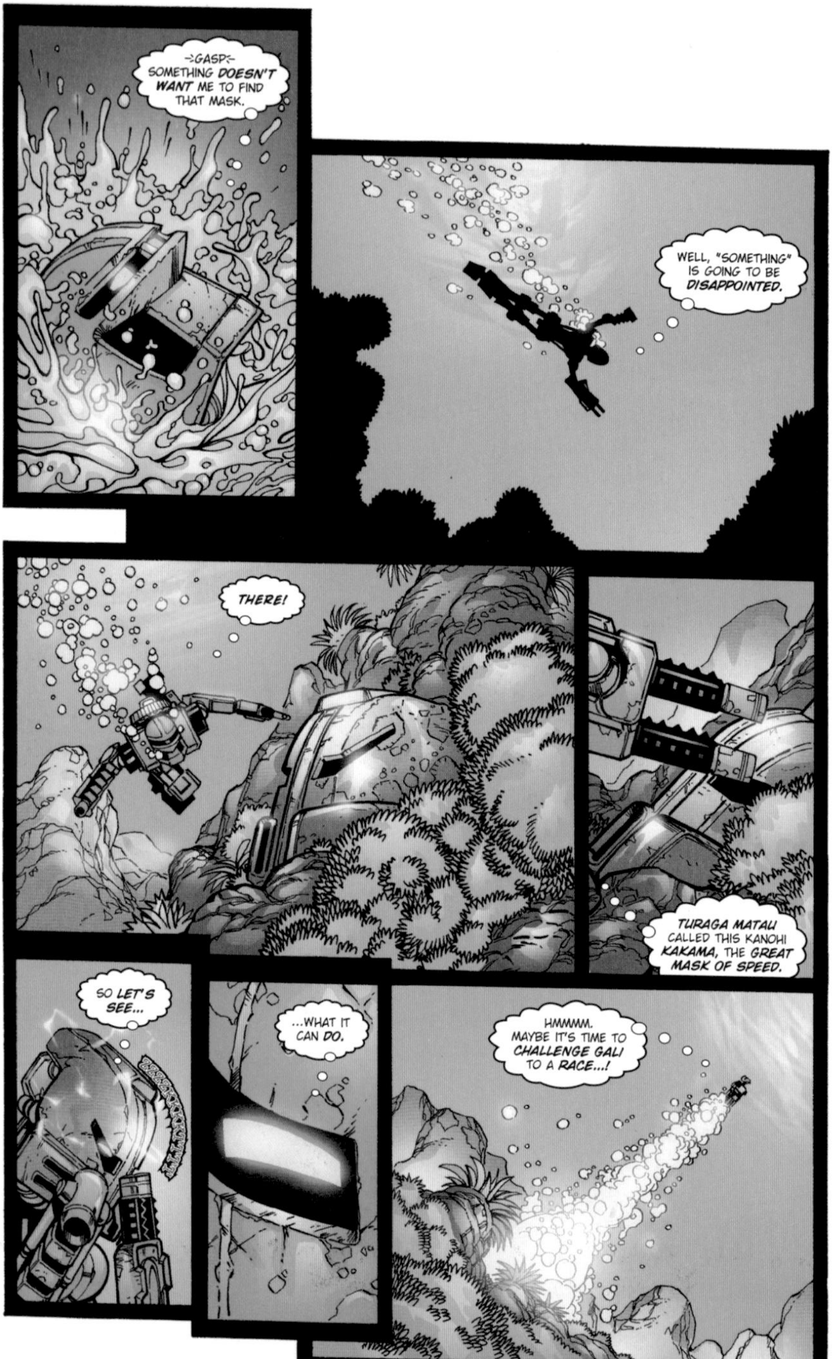

-GASP-
SOMETHING DOESN'T WANT ME TO FIND THAT MASK.
WELL, "SOMETHING" IS GOING TO BE DISAPPOINTED.
THERE!
TURAGA MATAU CALLED THIS KANOHI KAKAMA, THE GREAT MASK OF SPEED.
SO LET'S SEE...
...WHAT IT CAN DO.
HMMMM. MAYBE IT'S TIME TO CHALLENGE GALI TO A RACE...!

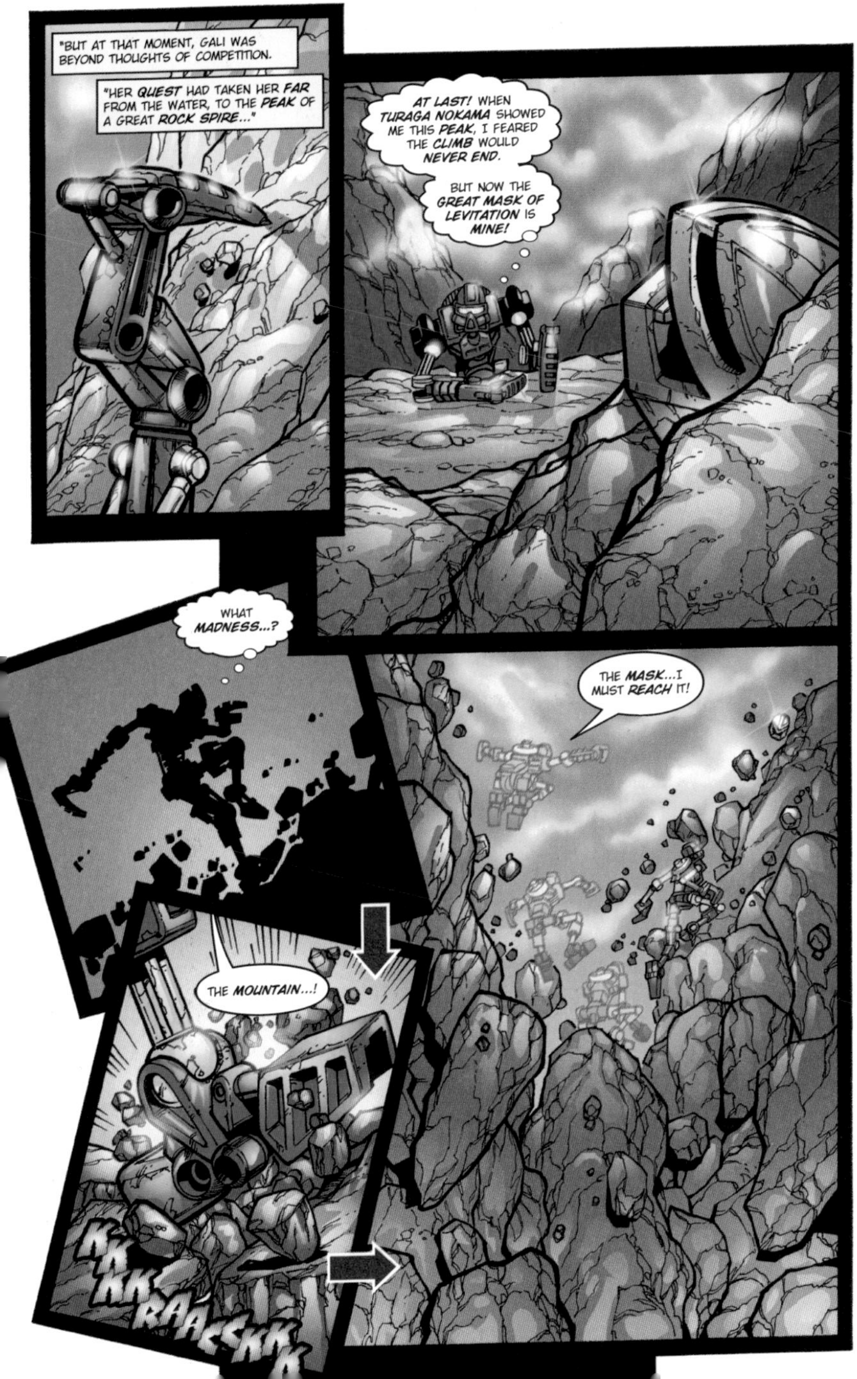
"BUT AT THAT MOMENT, GALI WAS BEYOND THOUGHTS OF COMPETITION.
"HER QUEST HAD TAKEN HER FAR FROM THE WATER, TO THE PEAK OF A GREAT ROCK SPIRE..."
AT LAST! WHEN TURAGA NOKAMA SHOWED ME THIS PEAK, I FEARED THE CLIMB WOULD NEVER END.
BUT NOW THE GREAT MASK OF LEVITATION IS MINE!
WHAT MADNESS...?
THE MASK...I MUST REACH IT!
THE MOUNTAIN...!
KKKKRAACSKKK

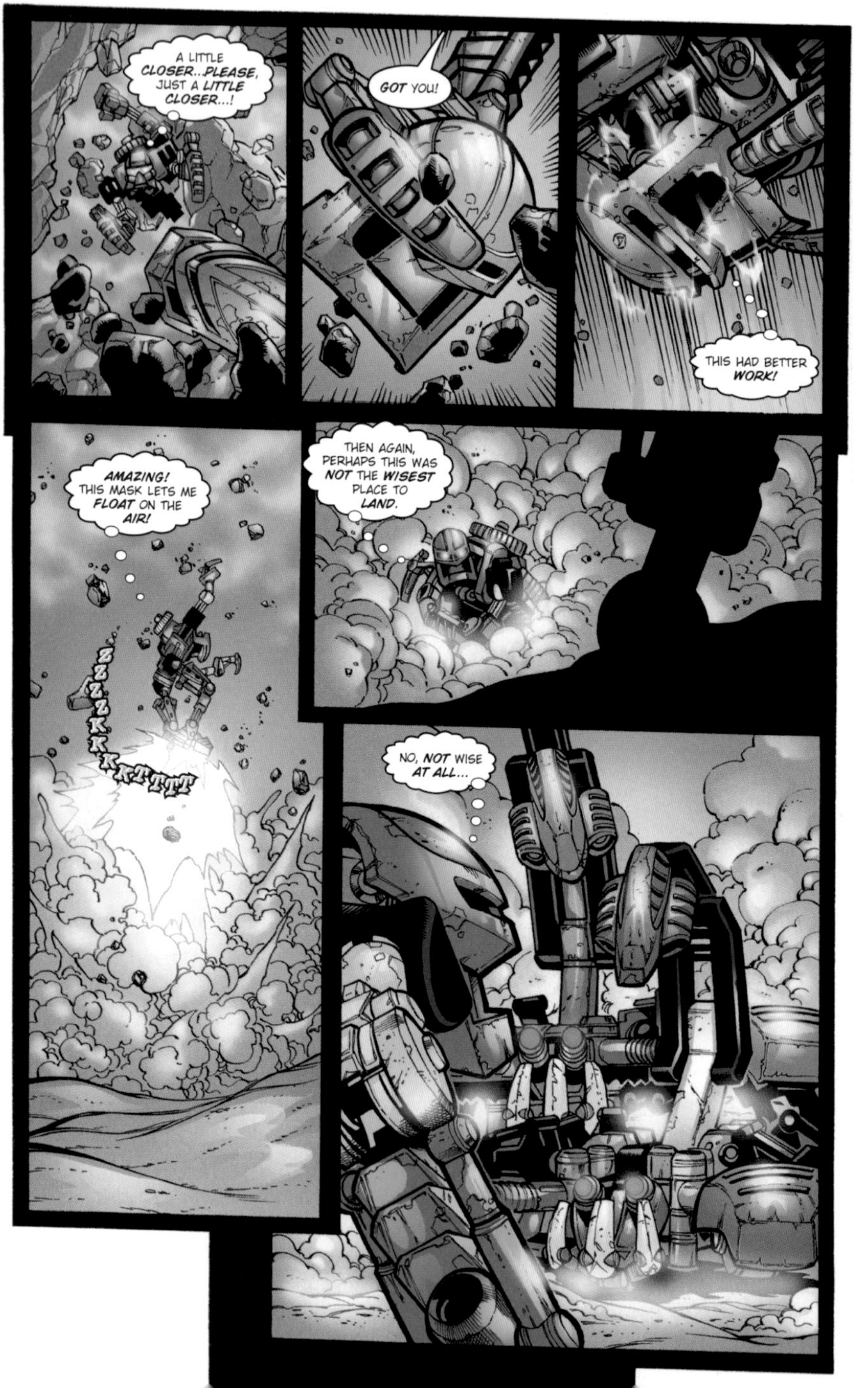
A LITTLE CLOSER...PLEASE, JUST A LITTLE CLOSER...!
GOT YOU!
THIS HAD BETTER WORK!
AMAZING! THIS MASK LETS ME FLOAT ON THE AIR!
ZZZKKKTTTTT
THEN AGAIN, PERHAPS THIS WAS NOT THE WISEST PLACE TO LAND.
NO, NOT WISE AT ALL...

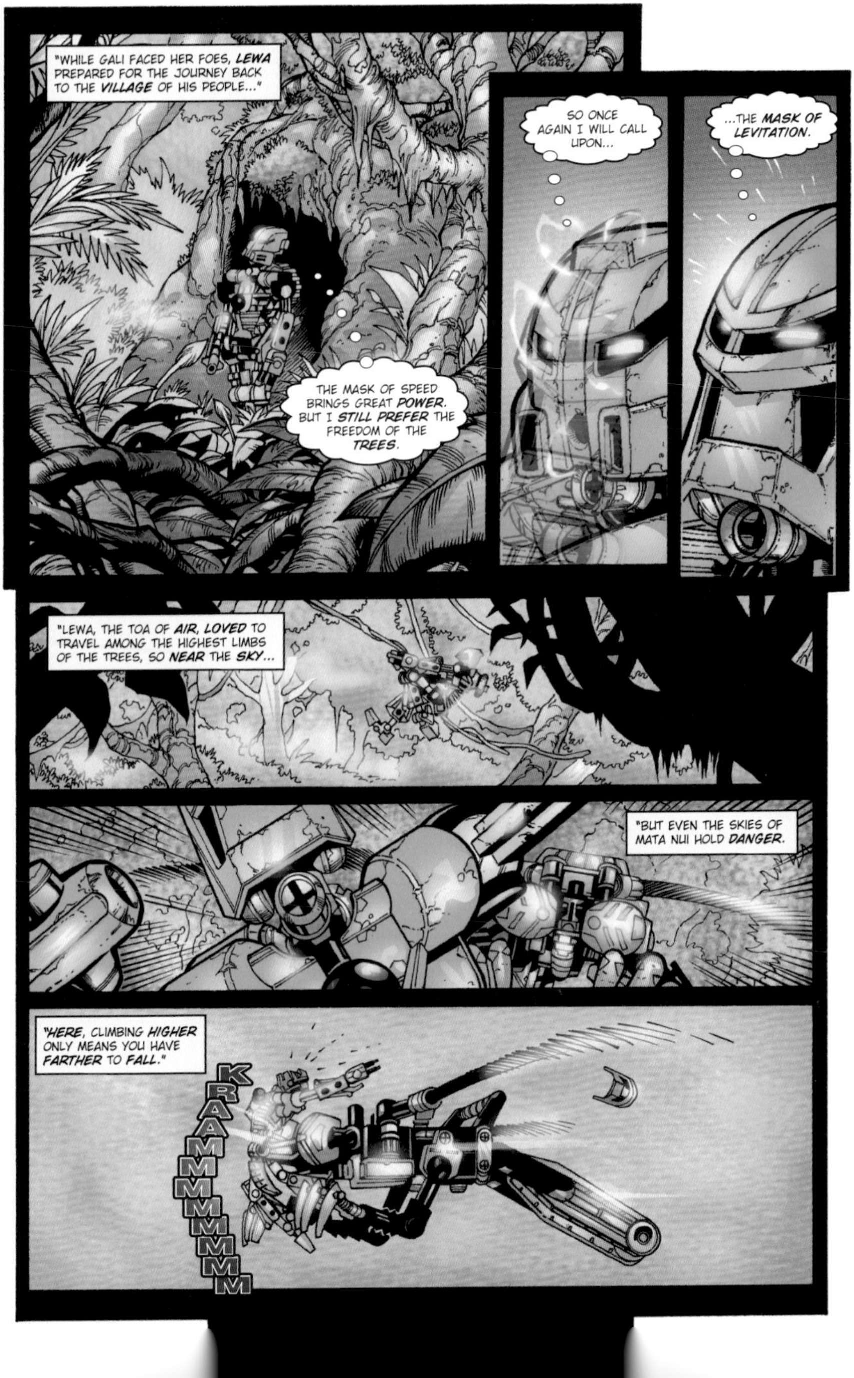
"WHILE GALI FACED HER FOES, LEWA PREPARED FOR THE JOURNEY BACK TO THE VILLAGE OF HIS PEOPLE..."
THE MASK OF SPEED BRINGS GREAT POWER. BUT I STILL PREFER THE FREEDOM OF THE TREES.
SO ONCE AGAIN I WILL CALL UPON...
...THE MASK OF LEVITATION.
"LEWA, THE TOA OF AIR, LOVED TO TRAVEL AMONG THE HIGHEST LIMBS OF THE TREES, SO NEAR THE SKY...
"BUT EVEN THE SKIES OF MATA NUI HOLD DANGER.
"HERE, CLIMBING HIGHER ONLY MEANS YOU HAVE FARTHER TO FALL."
KRAAMMMMMMM

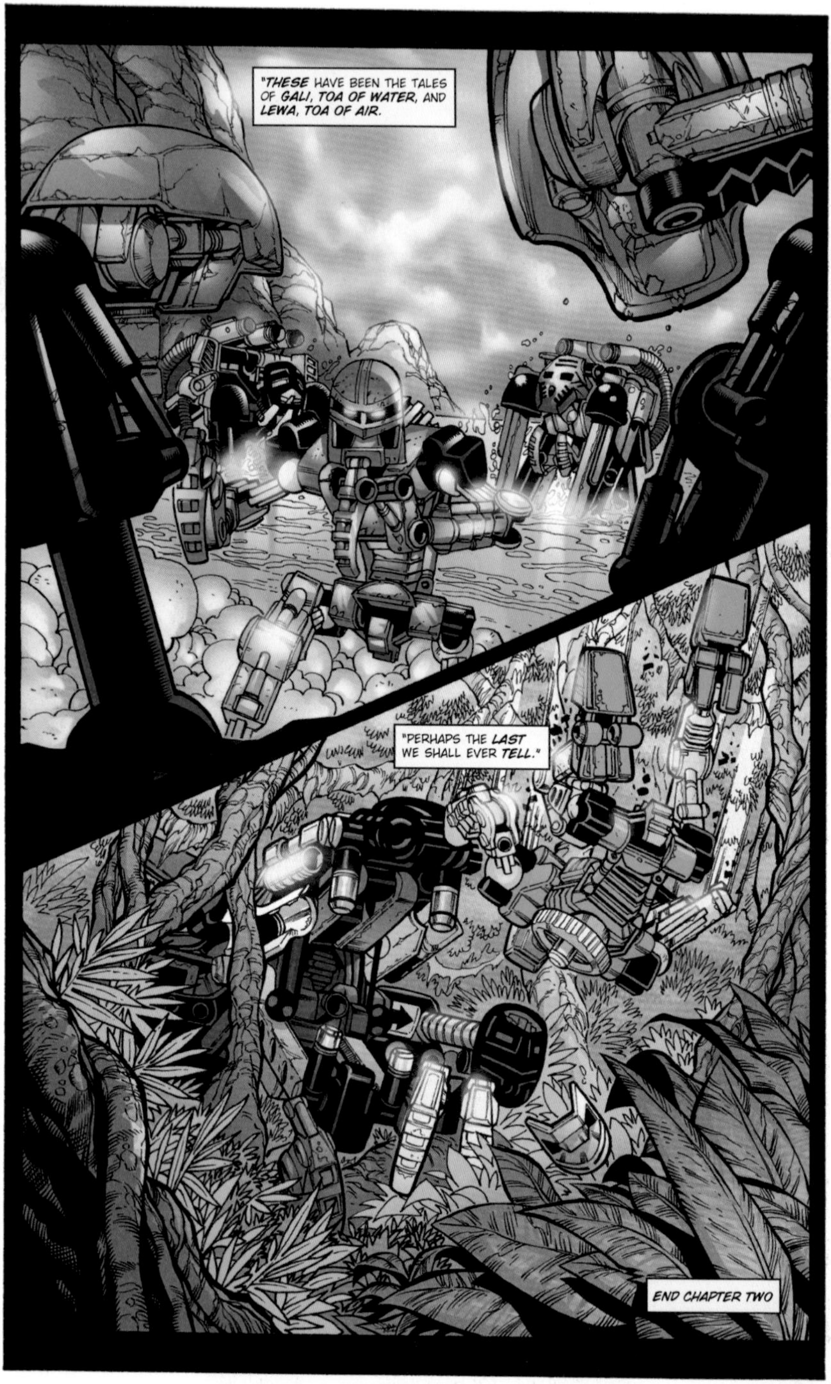
"THESE HAVE BEEN THE TALES OF GALI, TOA OF WATER, AND LEWA, TOA OF AIR.
"PERHAPS THE LAST WE SHALL EVER TELL."
END CHAPTER TWO

# CHAPTER THREE

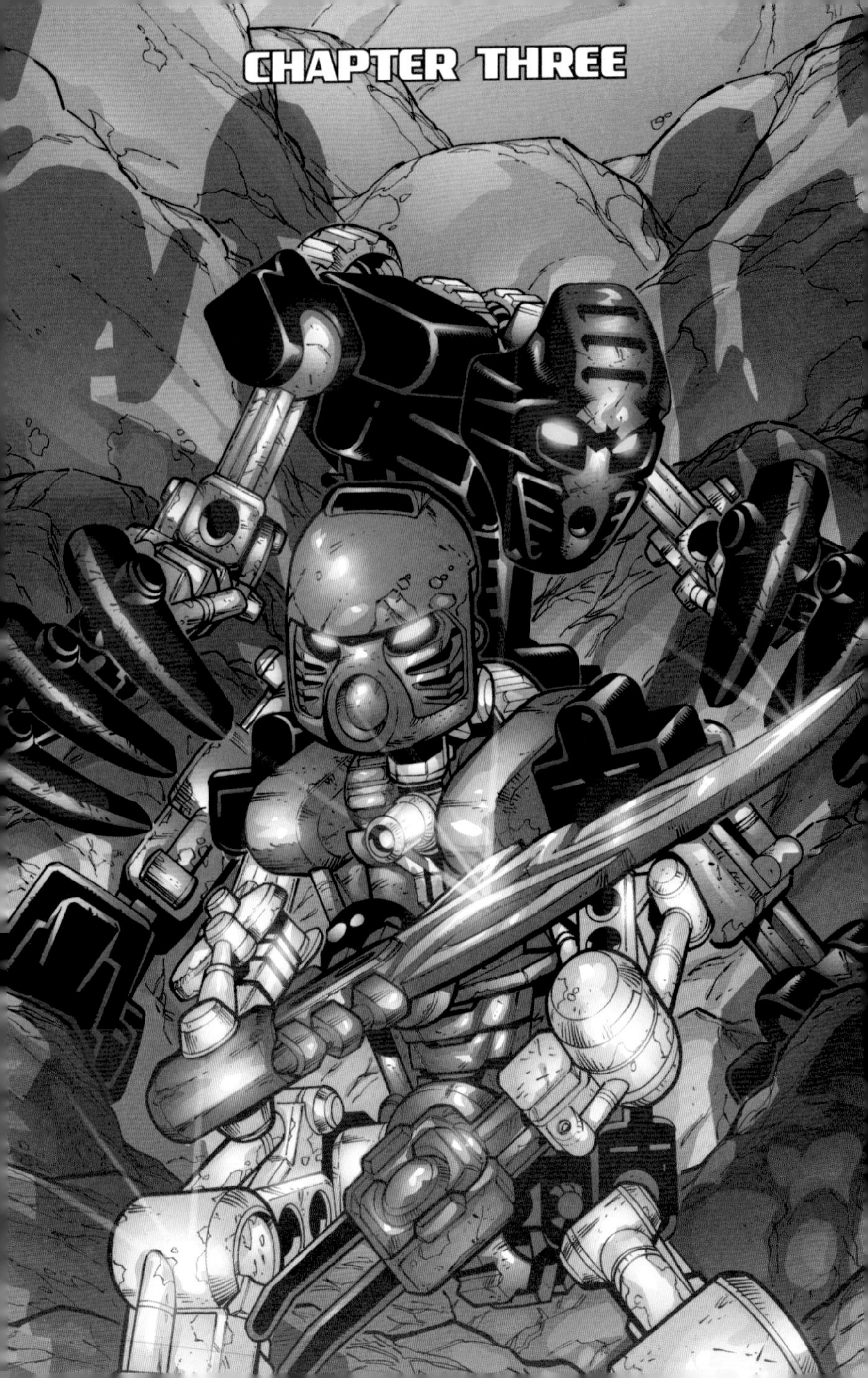

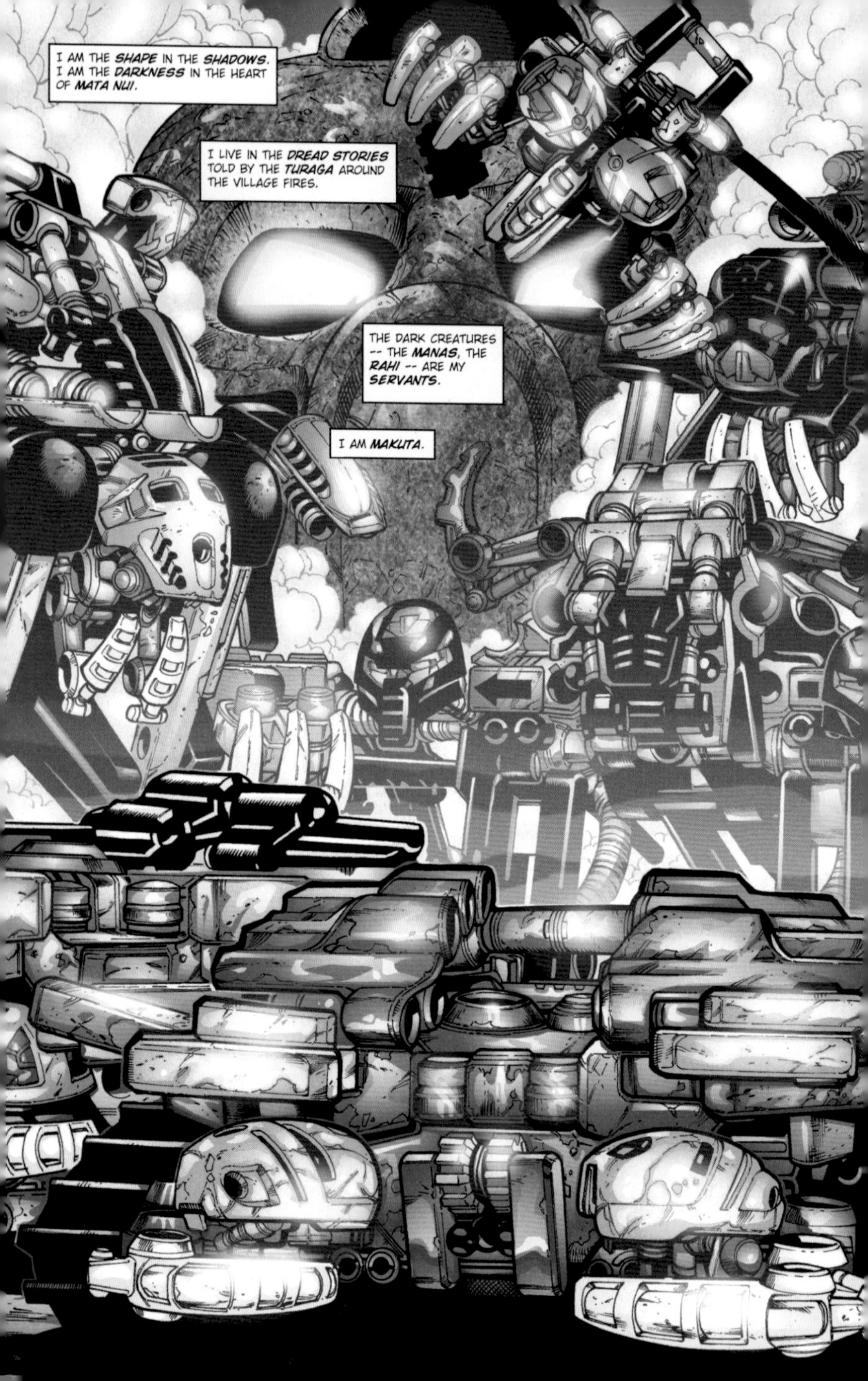
I AM THE SHAPE IN THE SHADOWS. I AM THE DARKNESS IN THE HEART OF MATA NUI.
I LIVE IN THE DREAD STORIES TOLD BY THE TURAGA AROUND THE VILLAGE FIRES.
THE DARK CREATURES -- THE MANAS, THE RAHI -- ARE MY SERVANTS.
I AM MAKUTA.

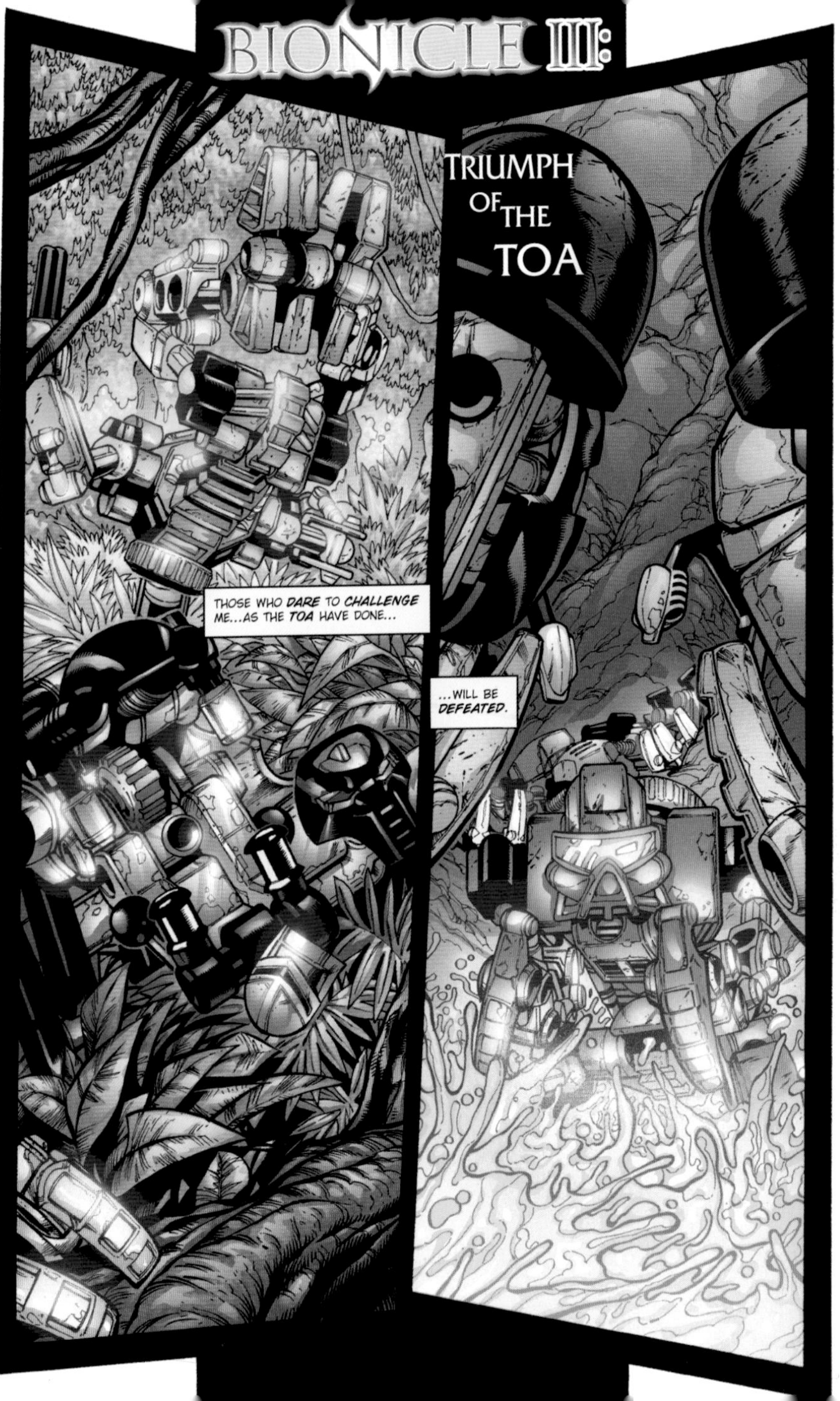
BIONICLE III:
TRIUMPH OF THE TOA
THOSE WHO DARE TO CHALLENGE ME...AS THE TOA HAVE DONE...
...WILL BE DEFEATED.

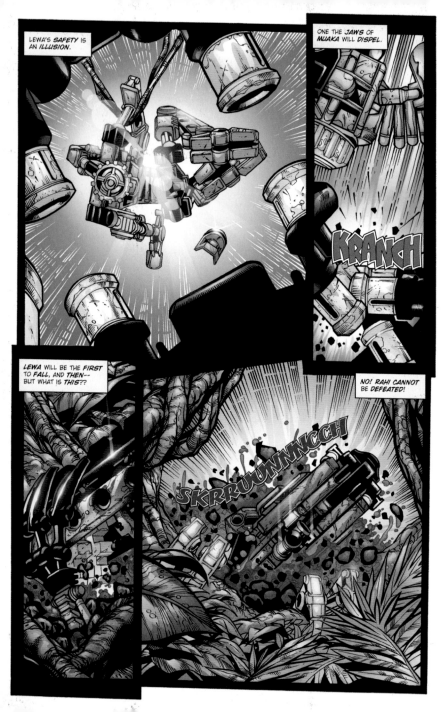

LEWA'S *SAFETY* IS AN *ILLUSION*.

ONE THE *JAWS* OF MUAKA WILL *DISPEL*.

KRANCH

LEWA WILL BE THE *FIRST* TO *FALL*, AND THEN-- BUT WHAT IS *THIS*??

SKRRUUNNNCCH

NO! RAHI CANNOT BE *DEFEATED*!

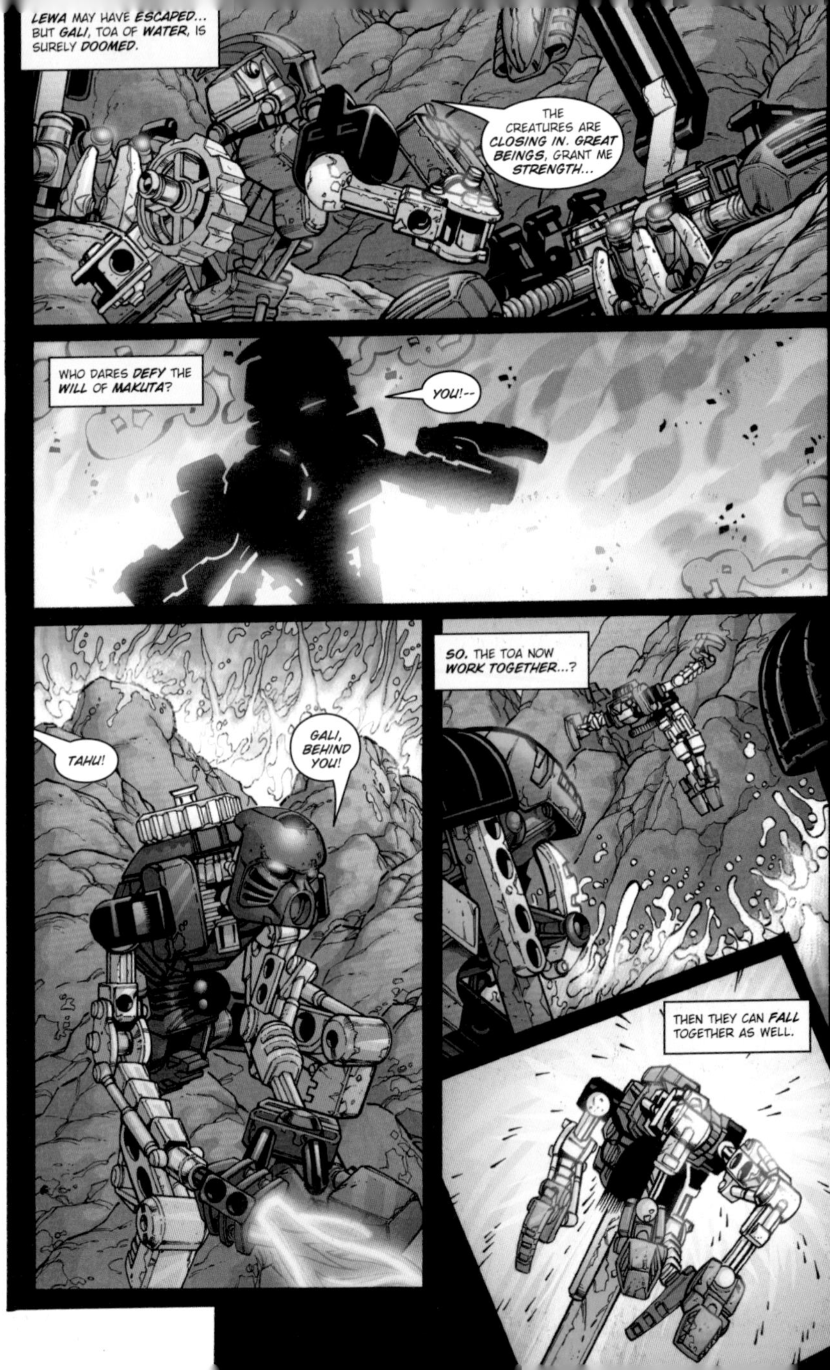
LEWA MAY HAVE ESCAPED... BUT GALI, TOA OF WATER, IS SURELY DOOMED.
THE CREATURES ARE CLOSING IN. GREAT BEINGS, GRANT ME STRENGTH...
WHO DARES DEFY THE WILL OF MAKUTA?
YOU!--
TAHU!
GALI, BEHIND YOU!
SO. THE TOA NOW WORK TOGETHER...?
THEN THEY CAN FALL TOGETHER AS WELL.

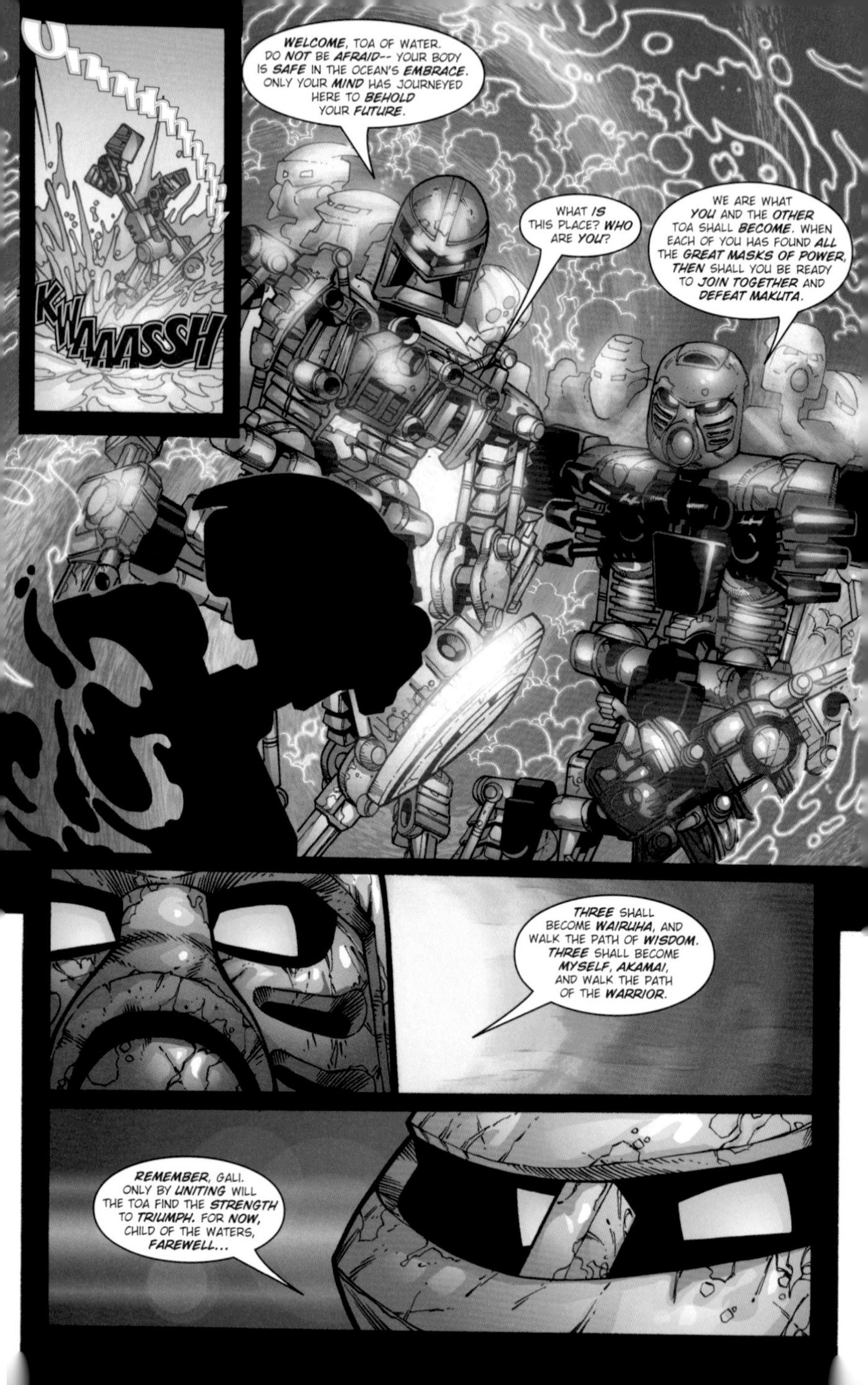
UNNNNNNNNNNNHH!
KWAAAASSH
WELCOME, TOA OF WATER. DO NOT BE AFRAID-- YOUR BODY IS SAFE IN THE OCEAN'S EMBRACE. ONLY YOUR MIND HAS JOURNEYED HERE TO BEHOLD YOUR FUTURE.
WHAT IS THIS PLACE? WHO ARE YOU?
WE ARE WHAT YOU AND THE OTHER TOA SHALL BECOME. WHEN EACH OF YOU HAS FOUND ALL THE GREAT MASKS OF POWER, THEN SHALL YOU BE READY TO JOIN TOGETHER AND DEFEAT MAKUTA.
THREE SHALL BECOME WAIRUHA, AND WALK THE PATH OF WISDOM. THREE SHALL BECOME MYSELF, AKAMAI, AND WALK THE PATH OF THE WARRIOR.
REMEMBER, GALI. ONLY BY UNITING WILL THE TOA FIND THE STRENGTH TO TRIUMPH. FOR NOW, CHILD OF THE WATERS, FAREWELL...

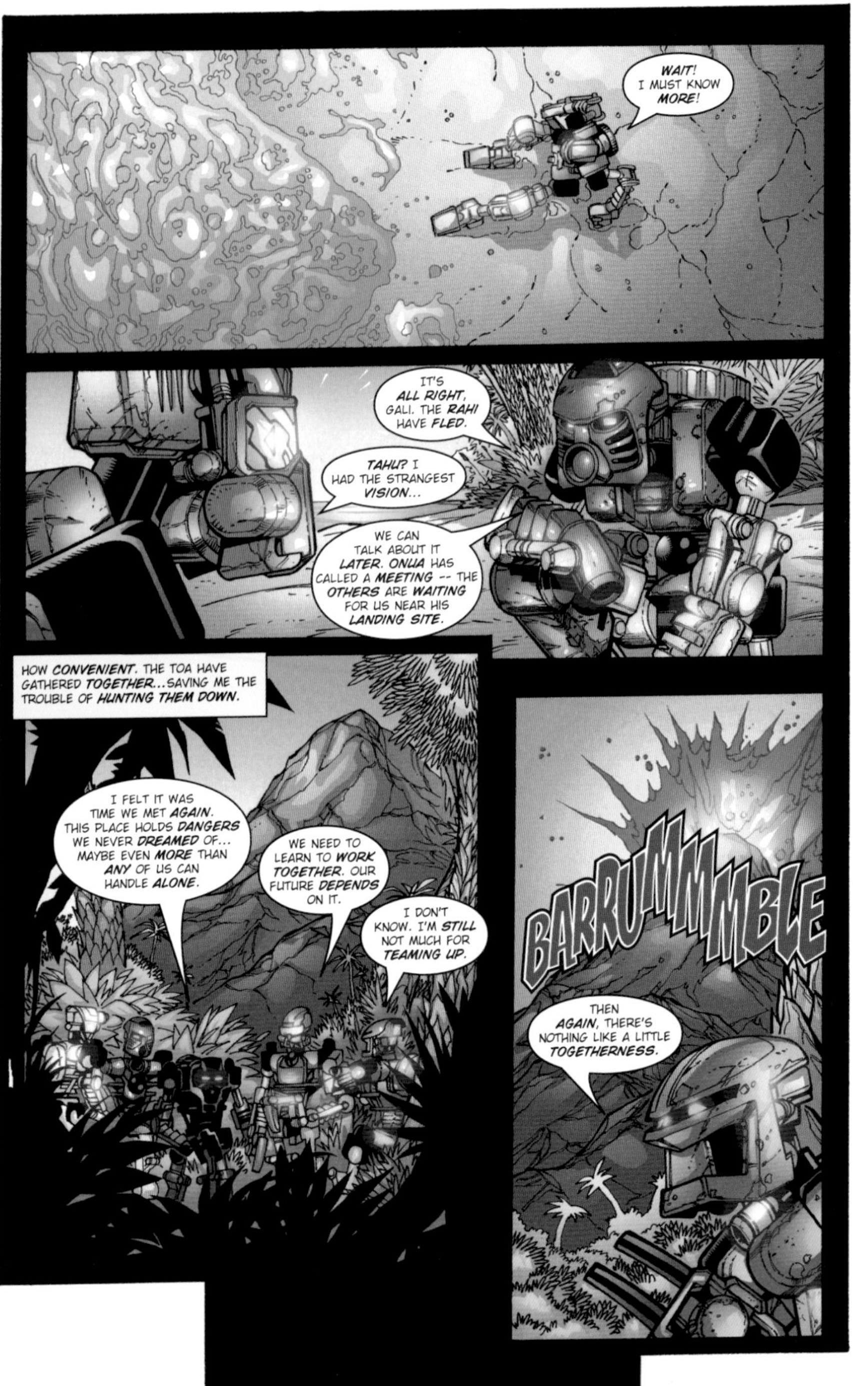
WAIT! I MUST KNOW MORE!
IT'S ALL RIGHT, GALI. THE RAHI HAVE FLED.
TAHU? I HAD THE STRANGEST VISION...
WE CAN TALK ABOUT IT LATER. ONUA HAS CALLED A MEETING -- THE OTHERS ARE WAITING FOR US NEAR HIS LANDING SITE.
HOW CONVENIENT. THE TOA HAVE GATHERED TOGETHER...SAVING ME THE TROUBLE OF HUNTING THEM DOWN.
I FELT IT WAS TIME WE MET AGAIN. THIS PLACE HOLDS DANGERS WE NEVER DREAMED OF... MAYBE EVEN MORE THAN ANY OF US CAN HANDLE ALONE.
WE NEED TO LEARN TO WORK TOGETHER. OUR FUTURE DEPENDS ON IT.
I DON'T KNOW. I'M STILL NOT MUCH FOR TEAMING UP.
BARRUMMMBLE
THEN AGAIN, THERE'S NOTHING LIKE A LITTLE TOGETHERNESS.

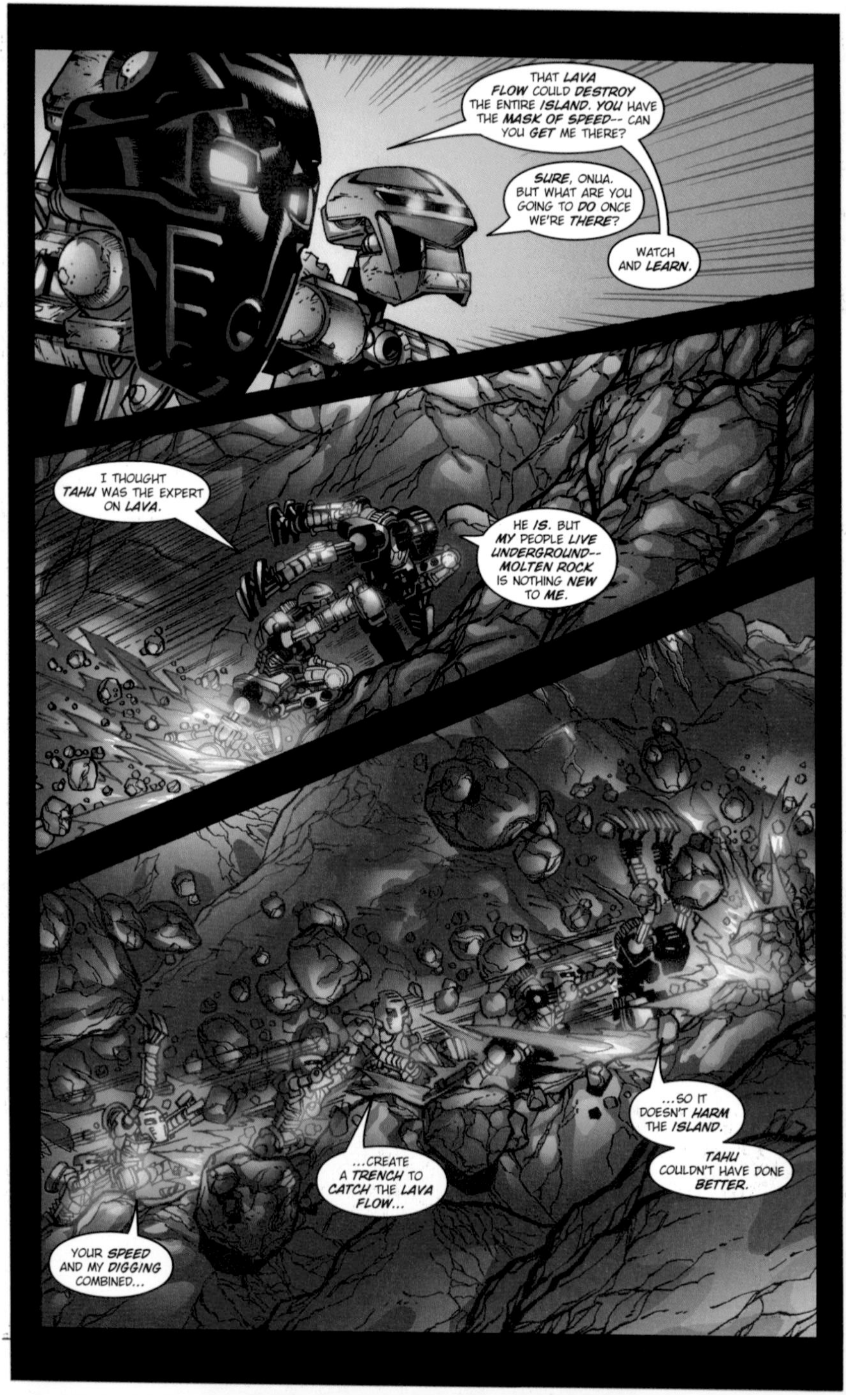

THAT LAVA FLOW COULD DESTROY THE ENTIRE ISLAND. YOU HAVE THE MASK OF SPEED-- CAN YOU GET ME THERE?
SURE, ONUA. BUT WHAT ARE YOU GOING TO DO ONCE WE'RE THERE?
WATCH AND LEARN.
I THOUGHT TAHU WAS THE EXPERT ON LAVA.
HE IS. BUT MY PEOPLE LIVE UNDERGROUND-- MOLTEN ROCK IS NOTHING NEW TO ME.
YOUR SPEED AND MY DIGGING COMBINED...
...CREATE A TRENCH TO CATCH THE LAVA FLOW...
...SO IT DOESN'T HARM THE ISLAND.
TAHU COULDN'T HAVE DONE BETTER.

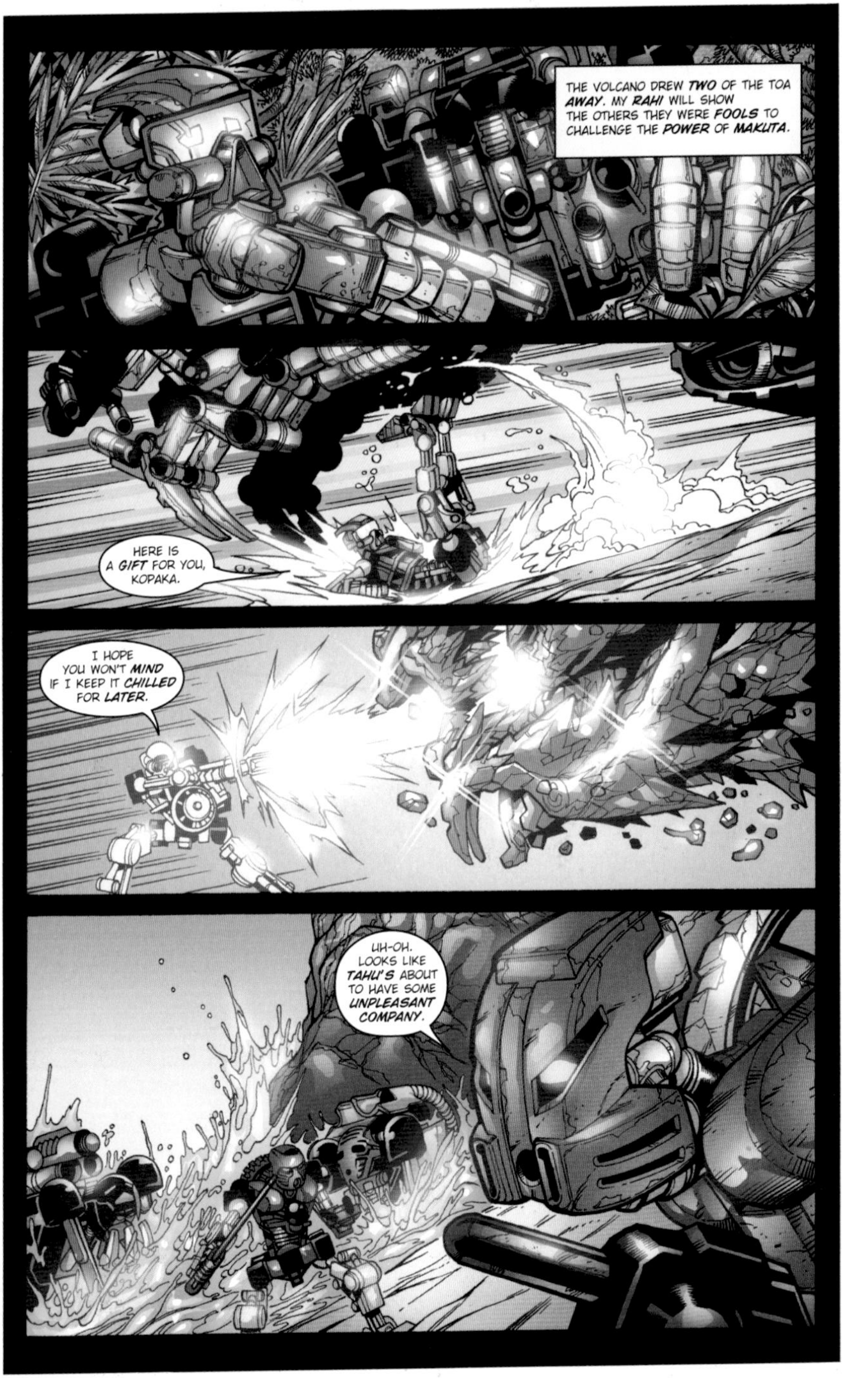
THE VOLCANO DREW TWO OF THE TOA AWAY. MY RAHI WILL SHOW THE OTHERS THEY WERE FOOLS TO CHALLENGE THE POWER OF MAKUTA.
HERE IS A GIFT FOR YOU, KOPAKA.
I HOPE YOU WON'T MIND IF I KEEP IT CHILLED FOR LATER.
UH-OH. LOOKS LIKE TAHU'S ABOUT TO HAVE SOME UNPLEASANT COMPANY.

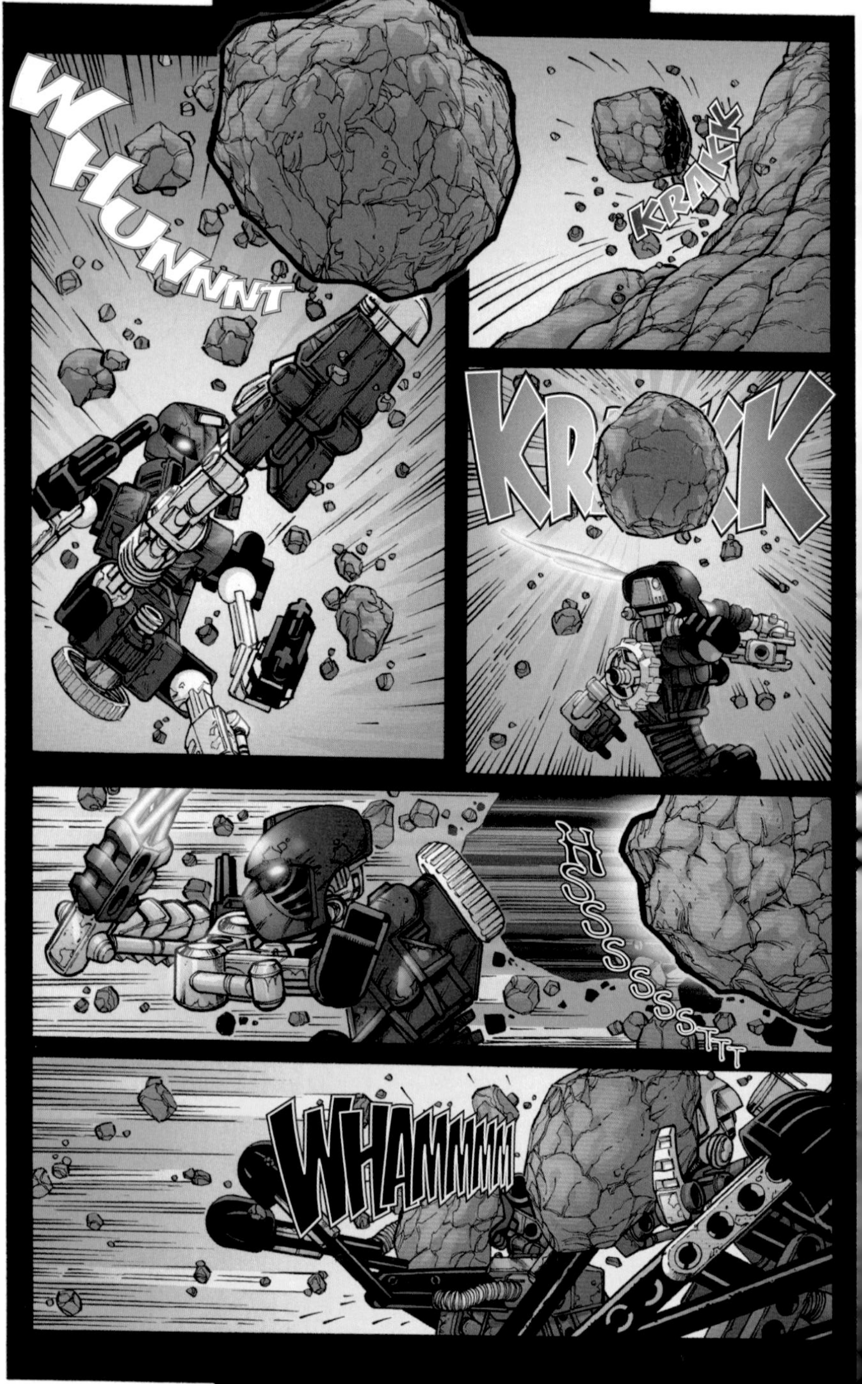

WHUNNNNT
KRAKK
KRAKK
HSSSSSSSTTT
WHAMMMMM

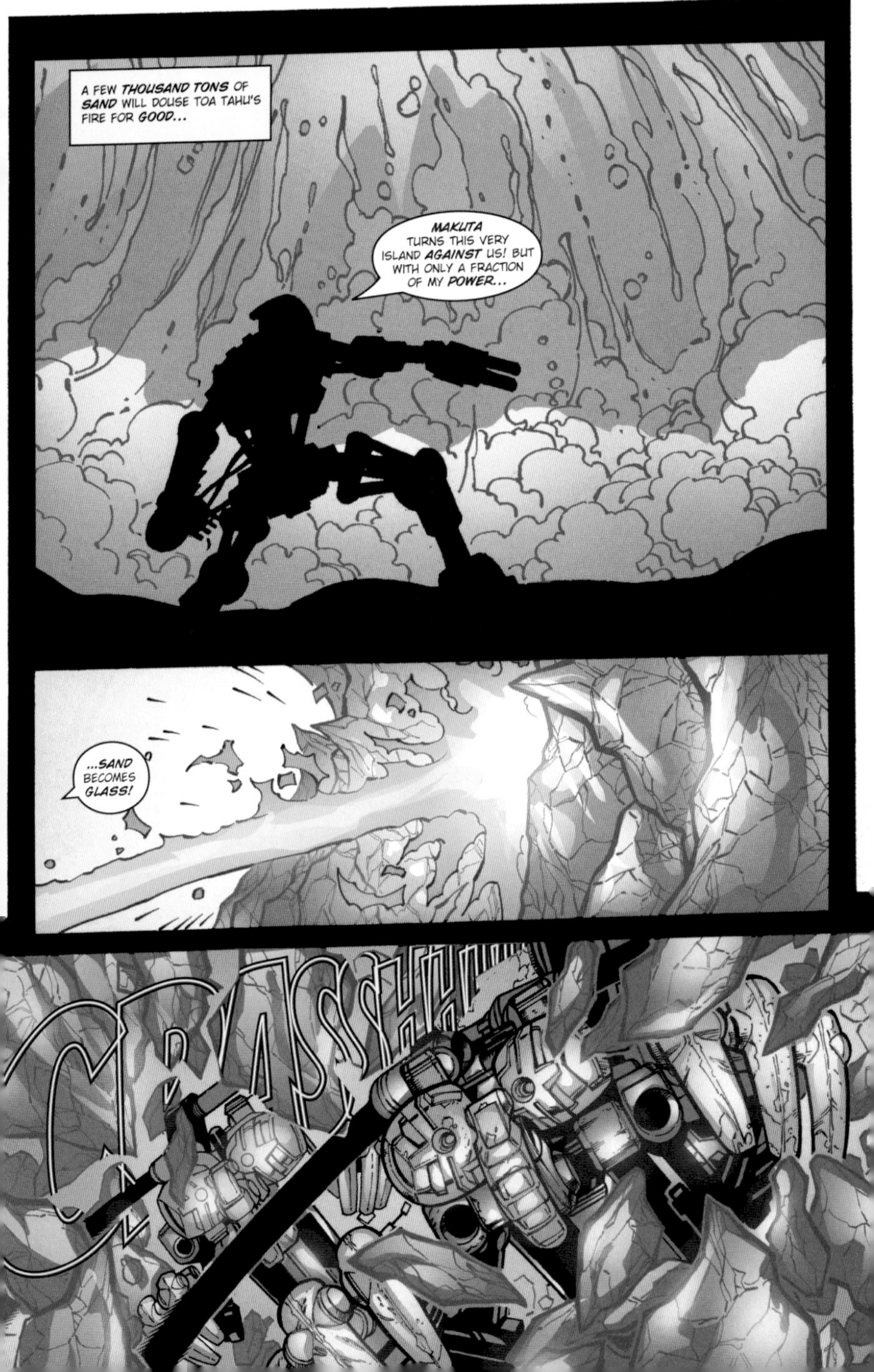
A FEW THOUSAND TONS OF SAND WILL DOUSE TOA TAHU'S FIRE FOR GOOD...
MAKUTA TURNS THIS VERY ISLAND AGAINST US! BUT WITH ONLY A FRACTION OF MY POWER...
...SAND BECOMES GLASS!

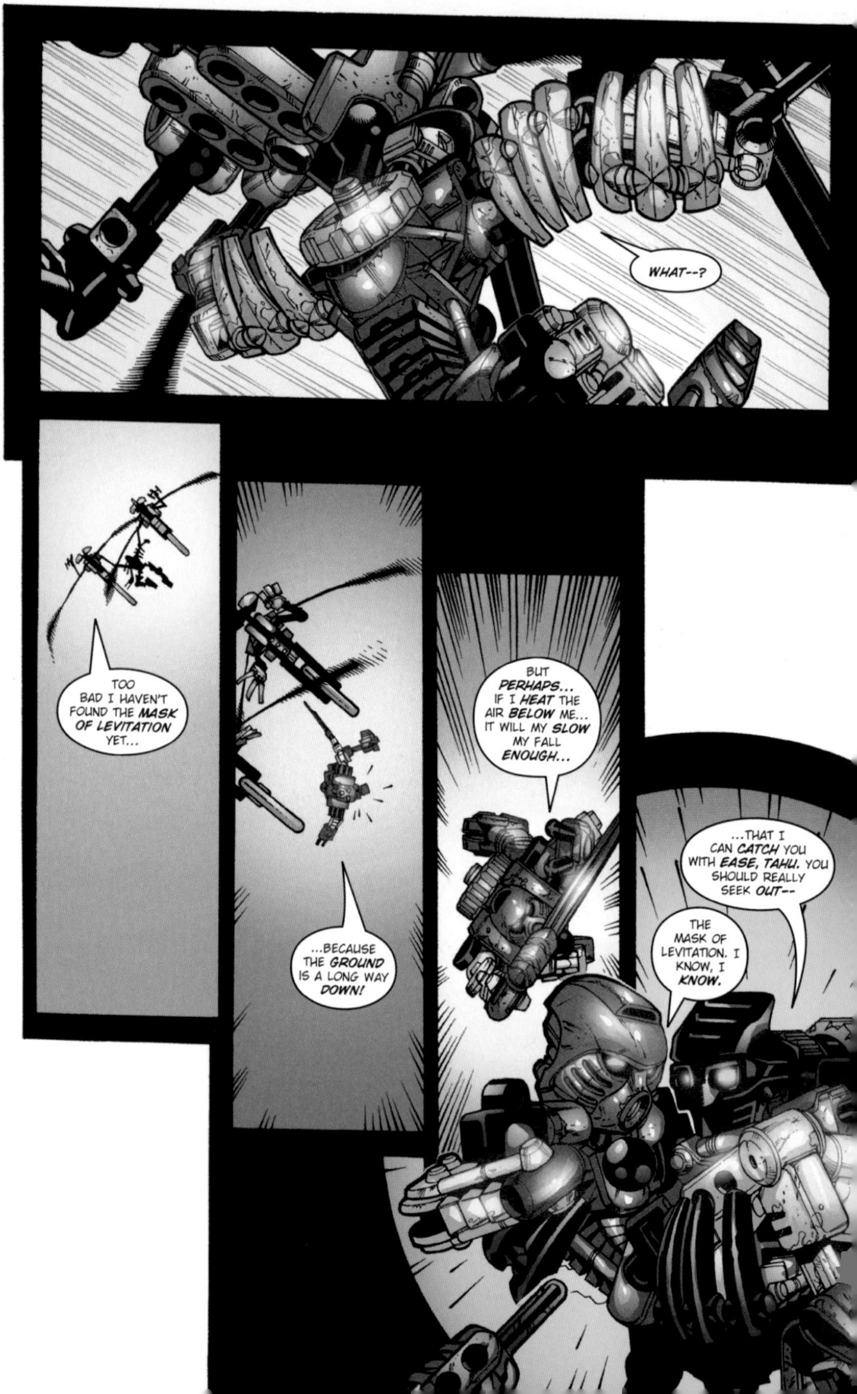
WHAT--?
TOO BAD I HAVEN'T FOUND THE **MASK OF LEVITATION** YET...
...BECAUSE THE **GROUND** IS A LONG WAY **DOWN!**
BUT **PERHAPS...** IF I **HEAT** THE AIR **BELOW** ME... IT WILL MY **SLOW** MY FALL **ENOUGH...**
...THAT I CAN **CATCH** YOU WITH **EASE, TAHU.** YOU SHOULD REALLY SEEK **OUT--**
THE MASK OF LEVITATION. I KNOW, I **KNOW.**

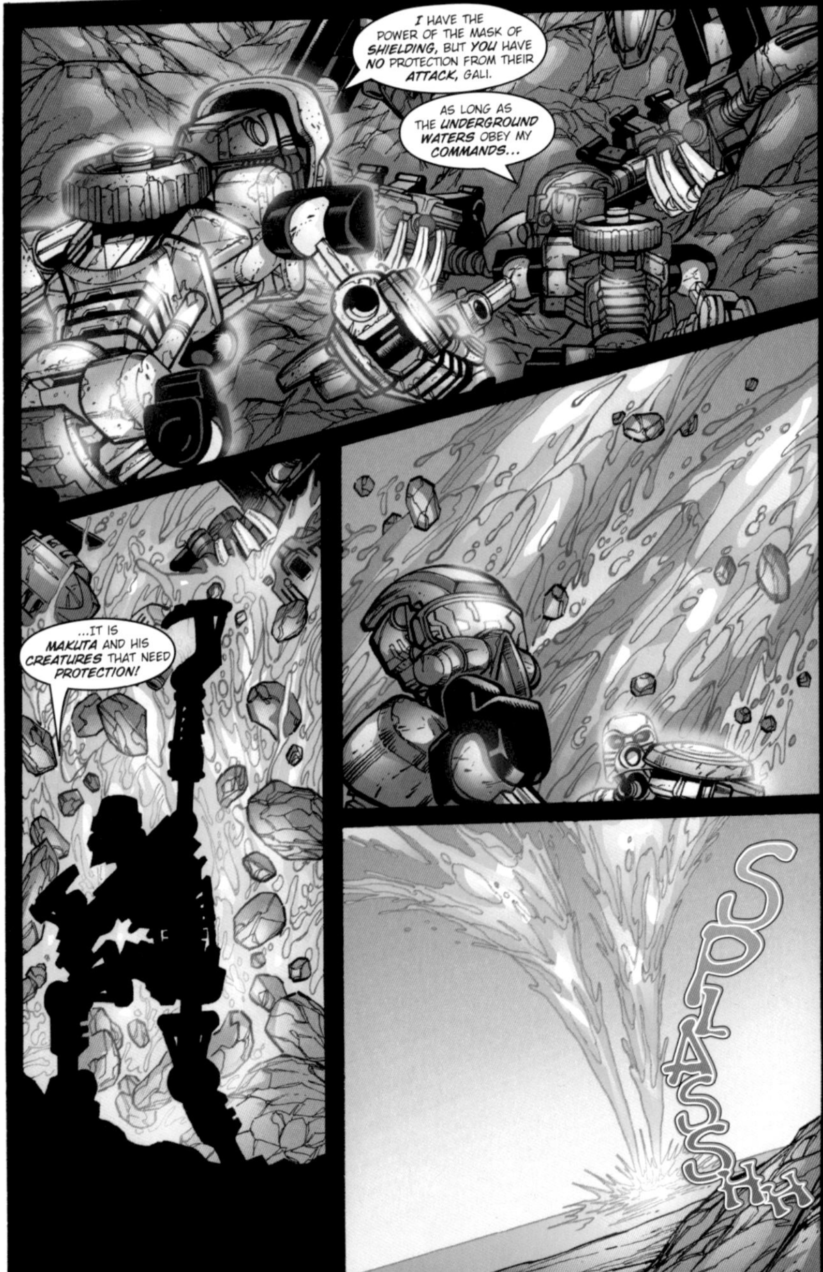
I HAVE THE POWER OF THE MASK OF SHIELDING, BUT YOU HAVE NO PROTECTION FROM THEIR ATTACK, GALI.
AS LONG AS THE UNDERGROUND WATERS OBEY MY COMMANDS...
...IT IS MAKUTA AND HIS CREATURES THAT NEED PROTECTION!
SPLASHH

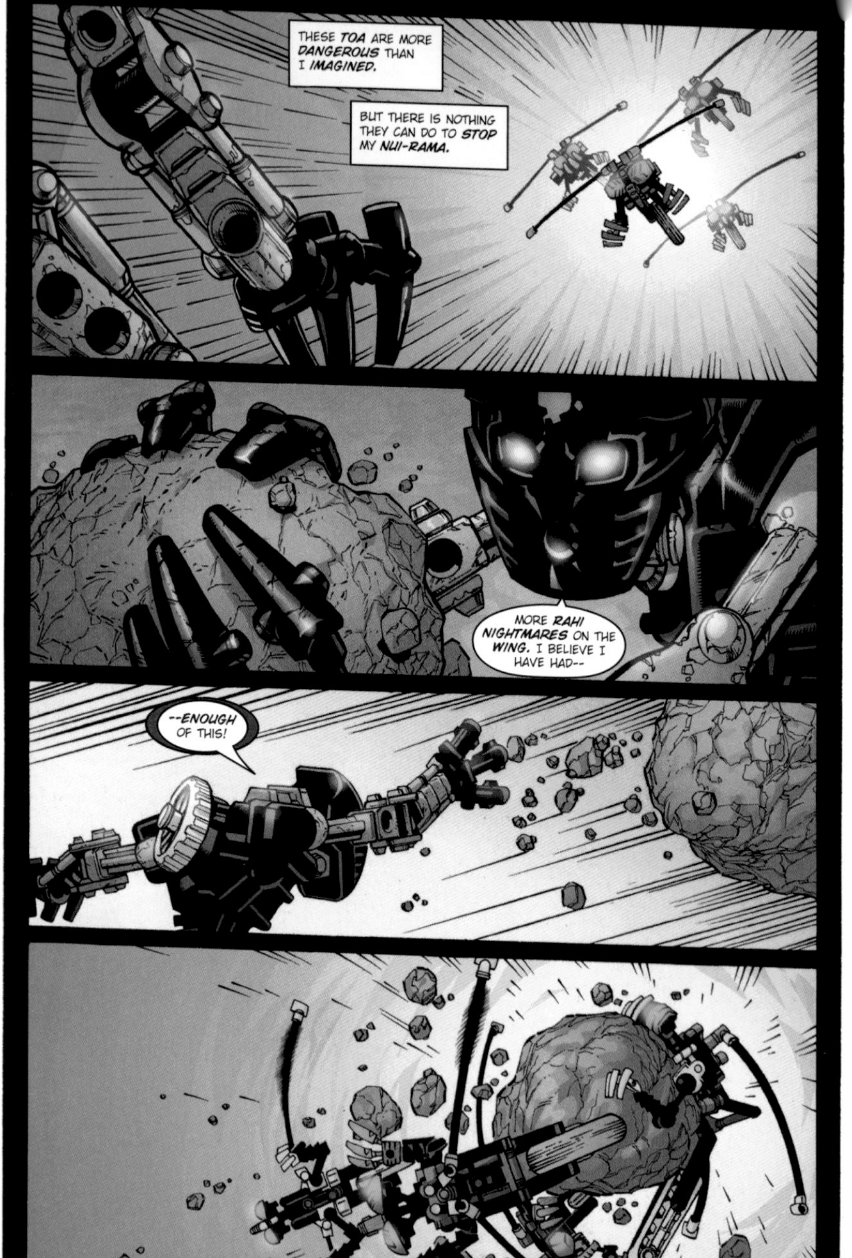
THESE TOA ARE MORE DANGEROUS THAN I IMAGINED.
BUT THERE IS NOTHING THEY CAN DO TO STOP MY NUI-RAMA.
MORE RAHI NIGHTMARES ON THE WING. I BELIEVE I HAVE HAD--
--ENOUGH OF THIS!

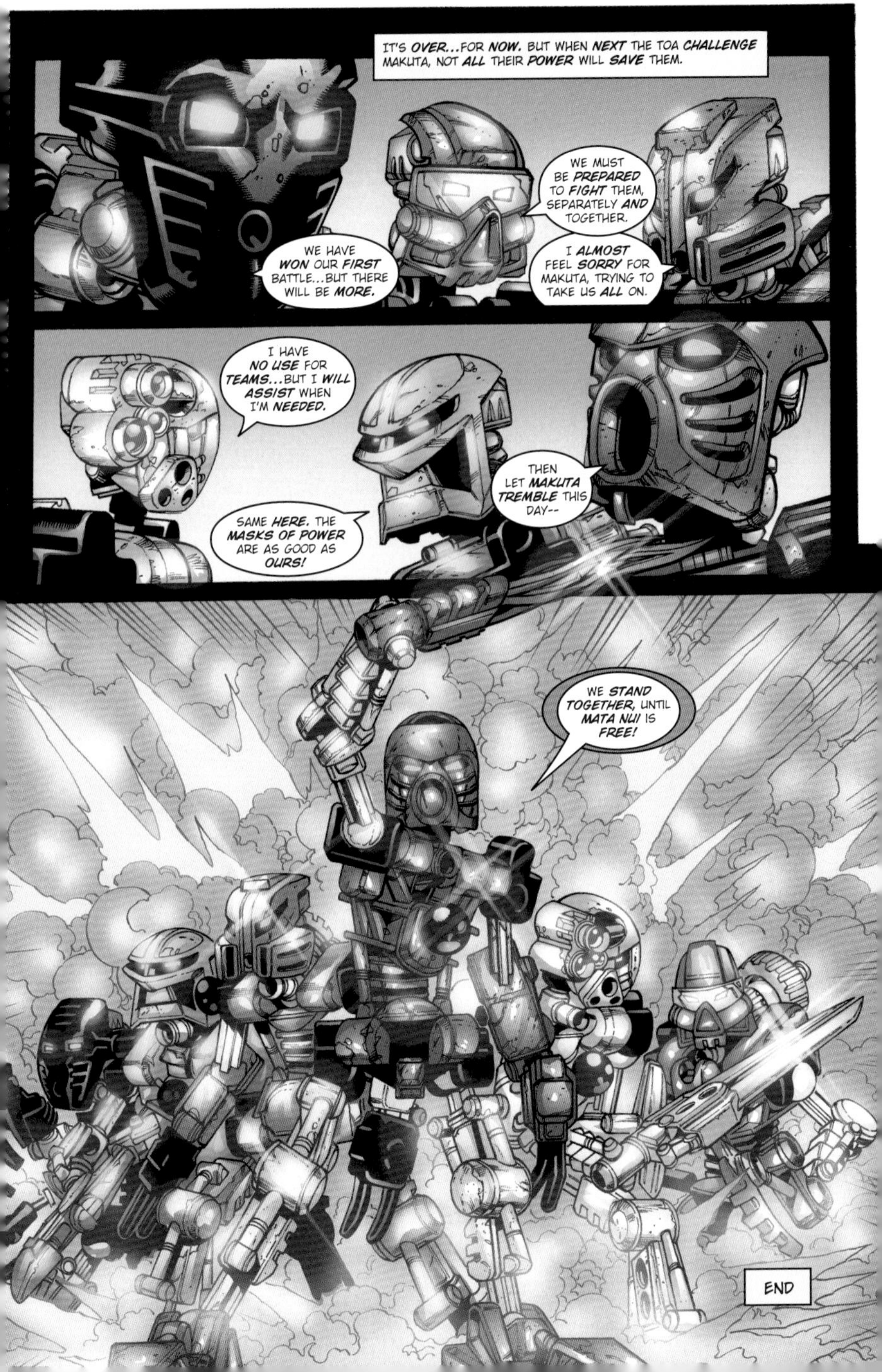
IT'S OVER...FOR NOW. BUT WHEN NEXT THE TOA CHALLENGE MAKUTA, NOT ALL THEIR POWER WILL SAVE THEM.
WE MUST BE PREPARED TO FIGHT THEM, SEPARATELY AND TOGETHER.
WE HAVE WON OUR FIRST BATTLE...BUT THERE WILL BE MORE.
I ALMOST FEEL SORRY FOR MAKUTA, TRYING TO TAKE US ALL ON.
I HAVE NO USE FOR TEAMS...BUT I WILL ASSIST WHEN I'M NEEDED.
SAME HERE. THE MASKS OF POWER ARE AS GOOD AS OURS!
THEN LET MAKUTA TREMBLE THIS DAY--
WE STAND TOGETHER, UNTIL MATA NUI IS FREE!
END

# THE BOHROK SAGA
# CHAPTER ONE

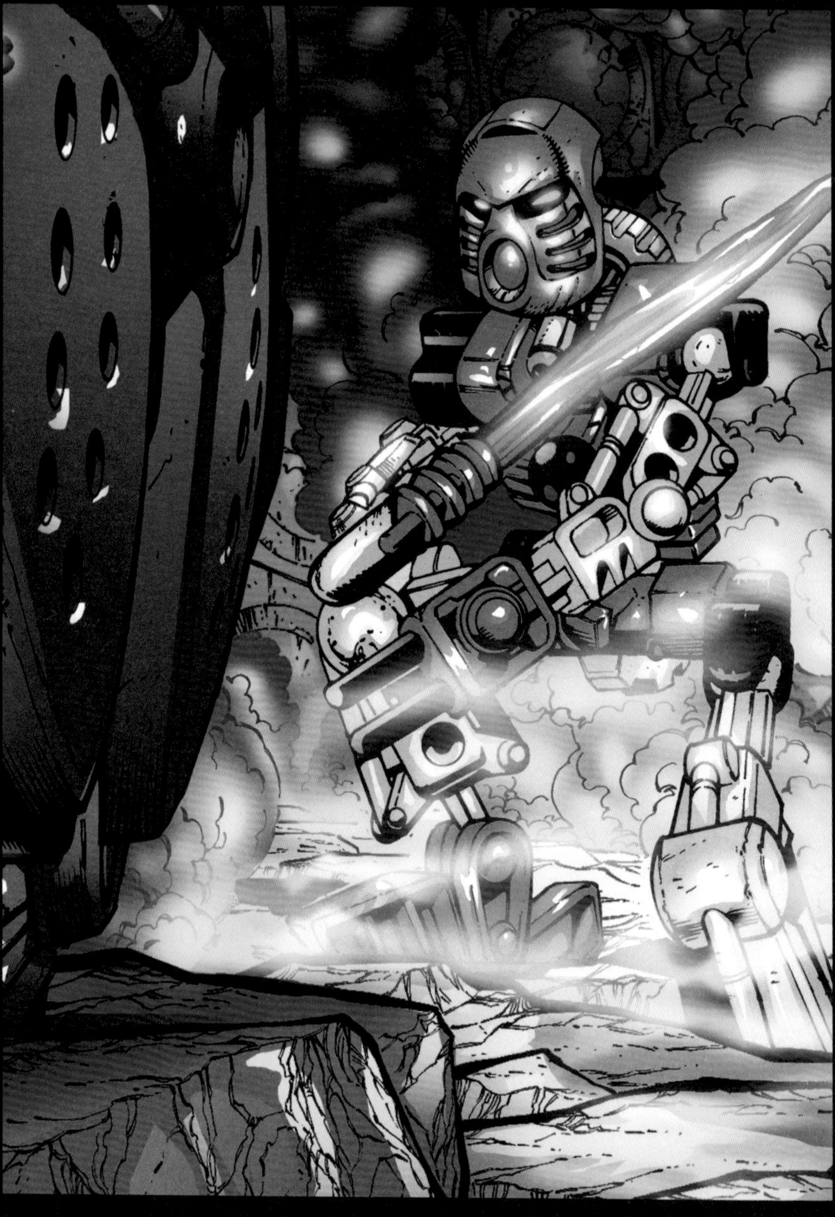

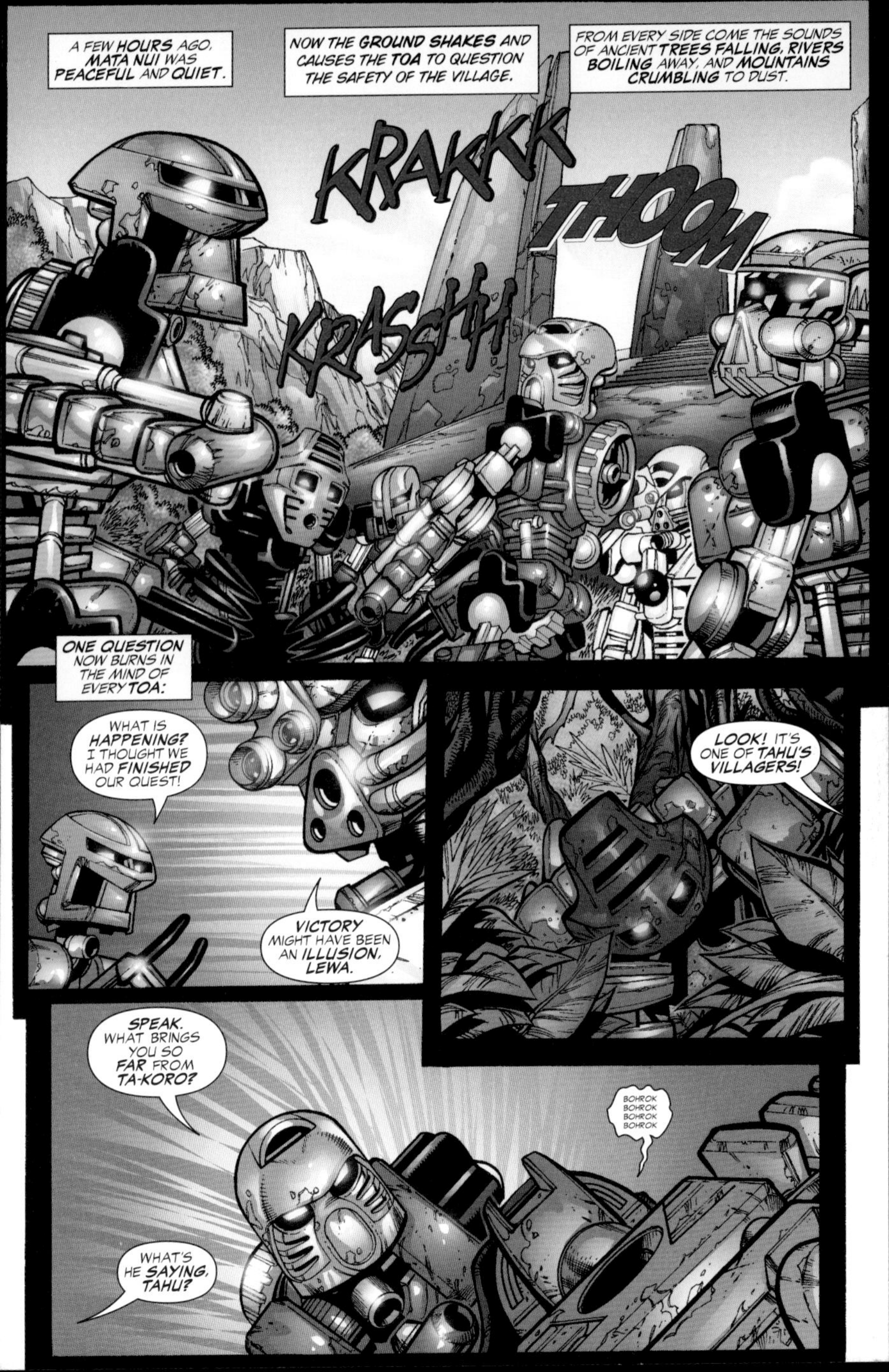
A FEW HOURS AGO, MATA NUI WAS PEACEFUL AND QUIET.
NOW THE GROUND SHAKES AND CAUSES THE TOA TO QUESTION THE SAFETY OF THE VILLAGE.
FROM EVERY SIDE COME THE SOUNDS OF ANCIENT TREES FALLING, RIVERS BOILING AWAY, AND MOUNTAINS CRUMBLING TO DUST.
KRAKKK
THOOM
KRASSHH
ONE QUESTION NOW BURNS IN THE MIND OF EVERY TOA:
WHAT IS HAPPENING? I THOUGHT WE HAD FINISHED OUR QUEST!
VICTORY MIGHT HAVE BEEN AN ILLUSION, LEWA.
LOOK! IT'S ONE OF TAHU'S VILLAGERS!
SPEAK. WHAT BRINGS YOU SO FAR FROM TA-KORO?
BOHROK BOHROK BOHROK BOHROK
WHAT'S HE SAYING, TAHU?

ONE *WORD* -- OVER AND *OVER*:

BOHROK.

I WILL *RETURN* TO TA-KORO *IMMEDIATELY*.

WE SHALL *ALL* GO, *TAHU*.

IF THERE IS A *THREAT* TO YOUR *VILLAGE*, IT IS A THREAT TO *ALL OUR* PEOPLE.

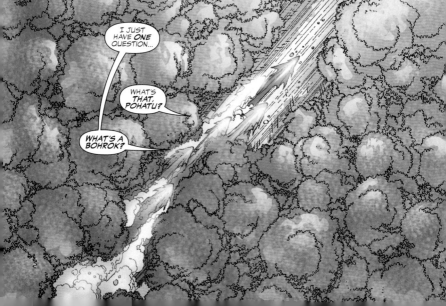

I JUST HAVE *ONE* QUESTION...

WHAT'S *THAT*, *POHATU*?

WHAT'S A *BOHROK*?

# THE BOHROK AWAKE

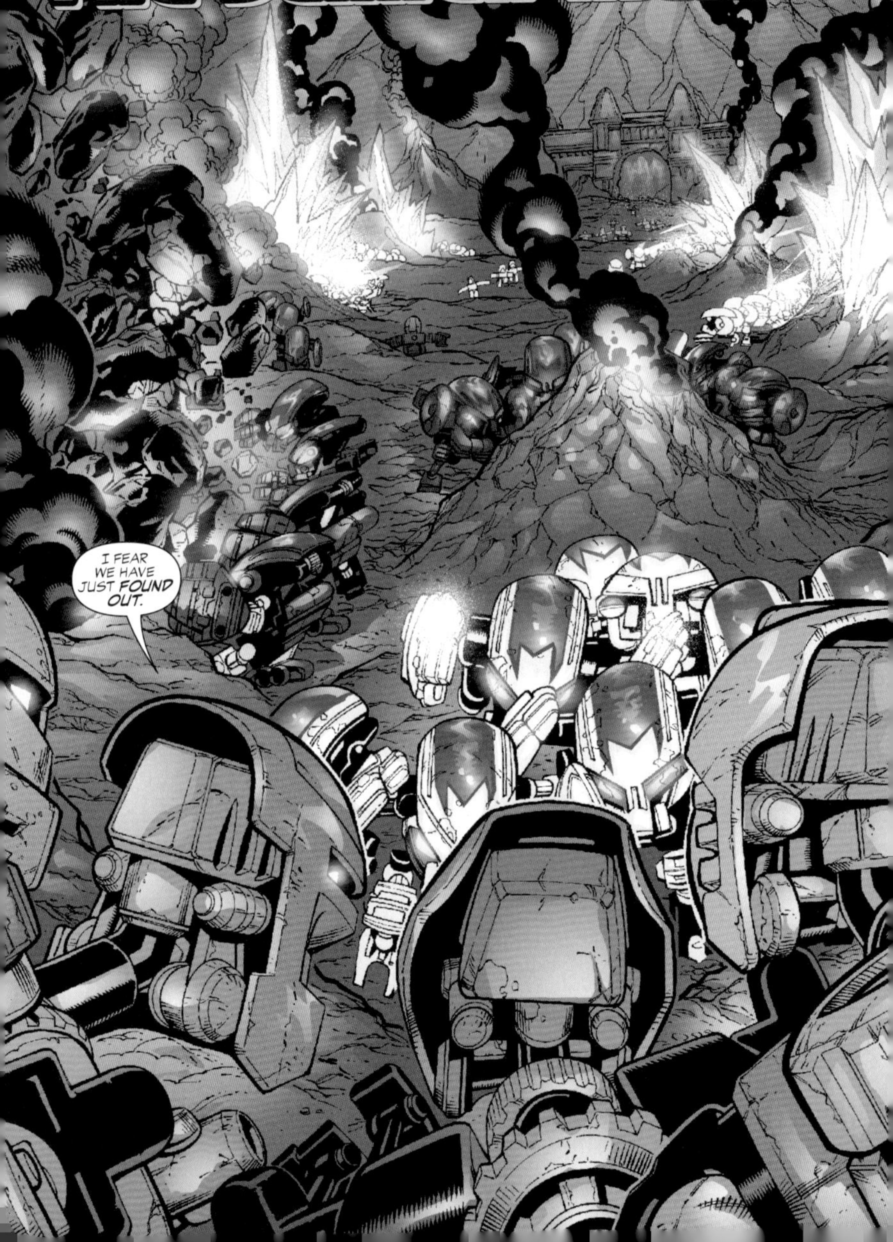
I FEAR WE HAVE JUST FOUND OUT.

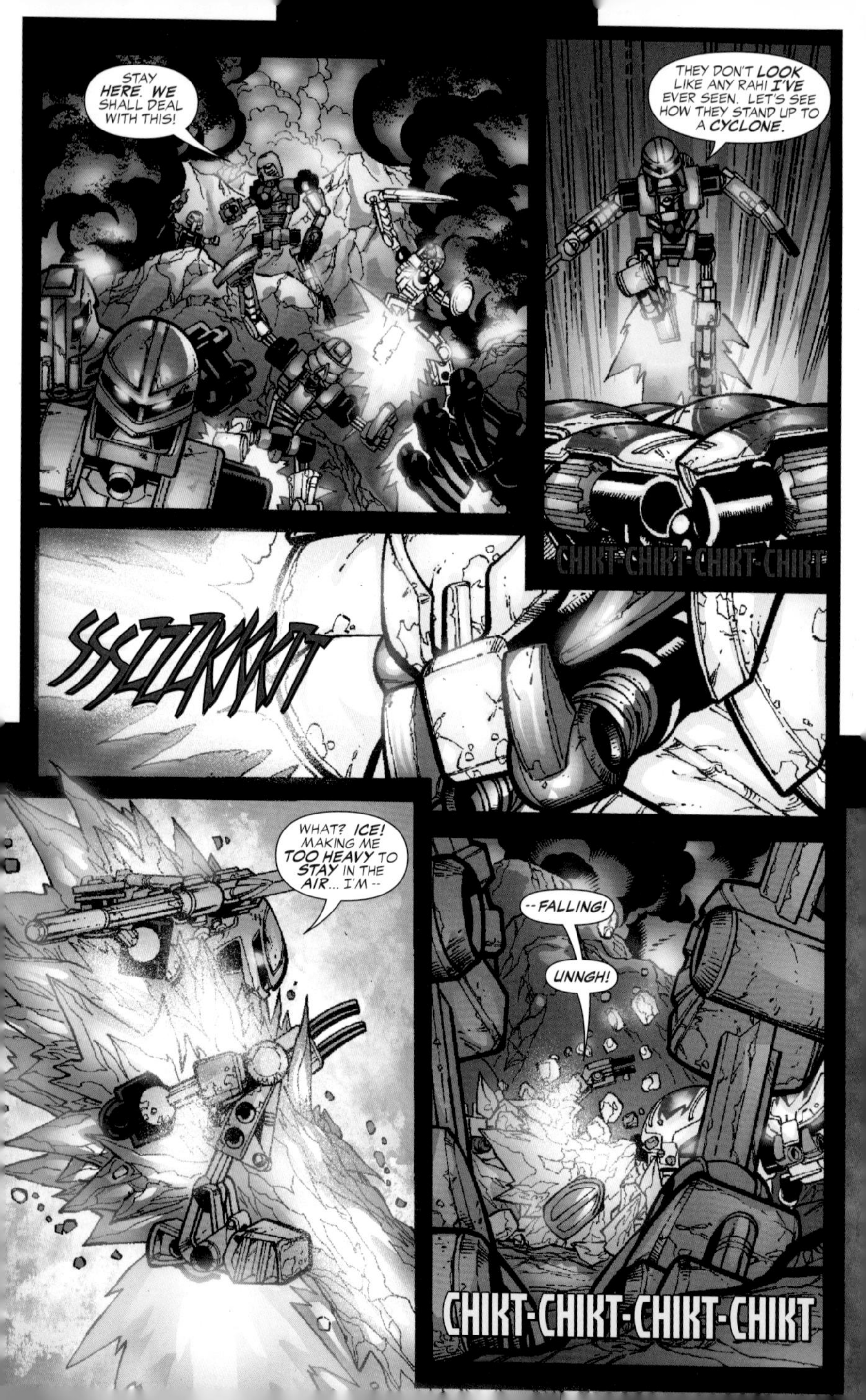
STAY HERE. WE SHALL DEAL WITH THIS!
THEY DON'T LOOK LIKE ANY RAHI I'VE EVER SEEN. LET'S SEE HOW THEY STAND UP TO A CYCLONE.
CHIKT-CHIKT-CHIKT-CHIKT
SSSZZZRKKKT
WHAT? ICE! MAKING ME TOO HEAVY TO STAY IN THE AIR... I'M --
--FALLING!
UNNGH!
CHIKT-CHIKT-CHIKT-CHIKT

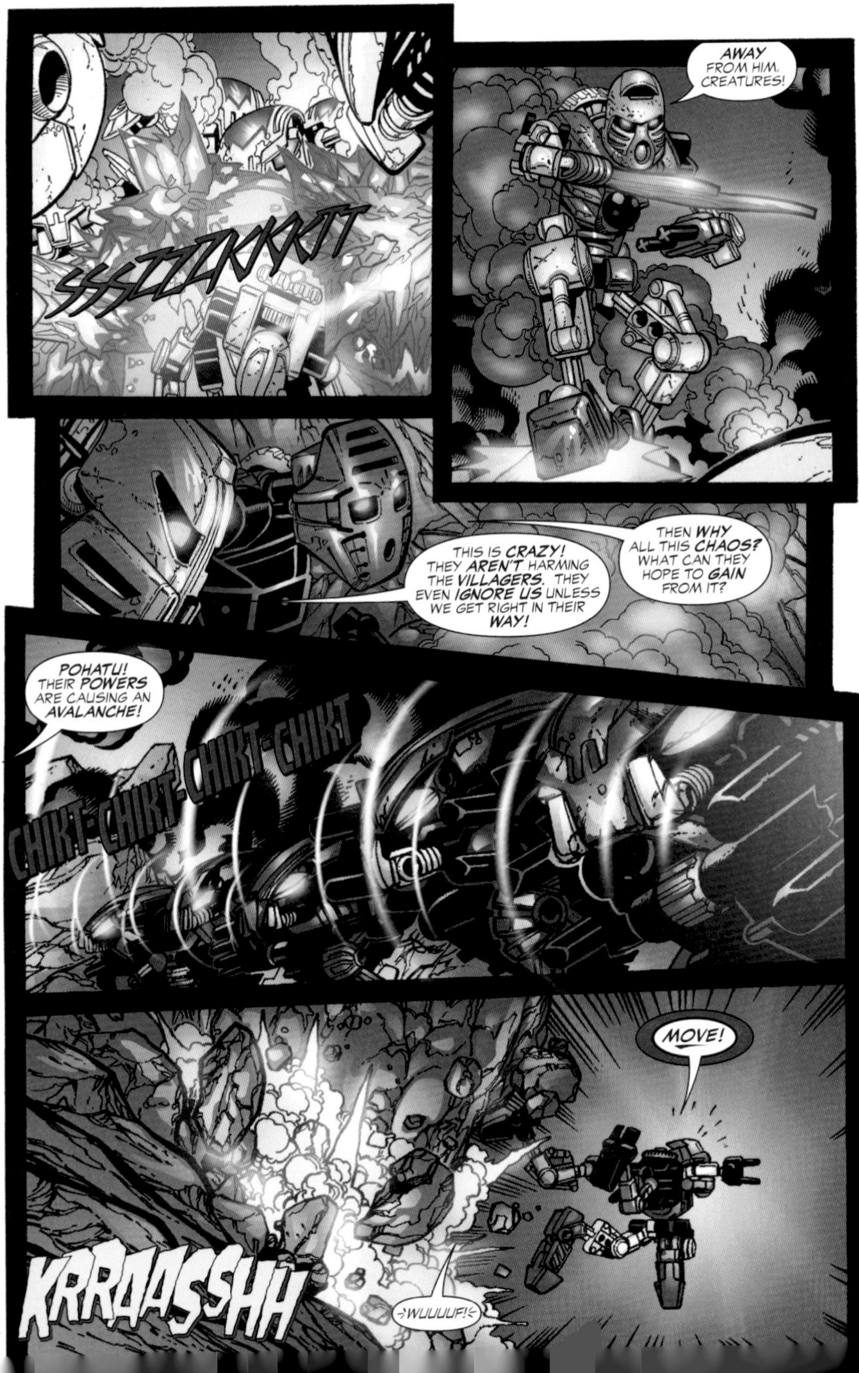
SSSZZZKKKTT
AWAY FROM HIM, CREATURES!
THIS IS CRAZY! THEY AREN'T HARMING THE VILLAGERS. THEY EVEN IGNORE US UNLESS WE GET RIGHT IN THEIR WAY!
THEN WHY ALL THIS CHAOS? WHAT CAN THEY HOPE TO GAIN FROM IT?
POHATU! THEIR POWERS ARE CAUSING AN AVALANCHE!
CHIKT-CHIKT-CHIKT-CHIKT
MOVE!
KRRAASSHH
WUUUUF!

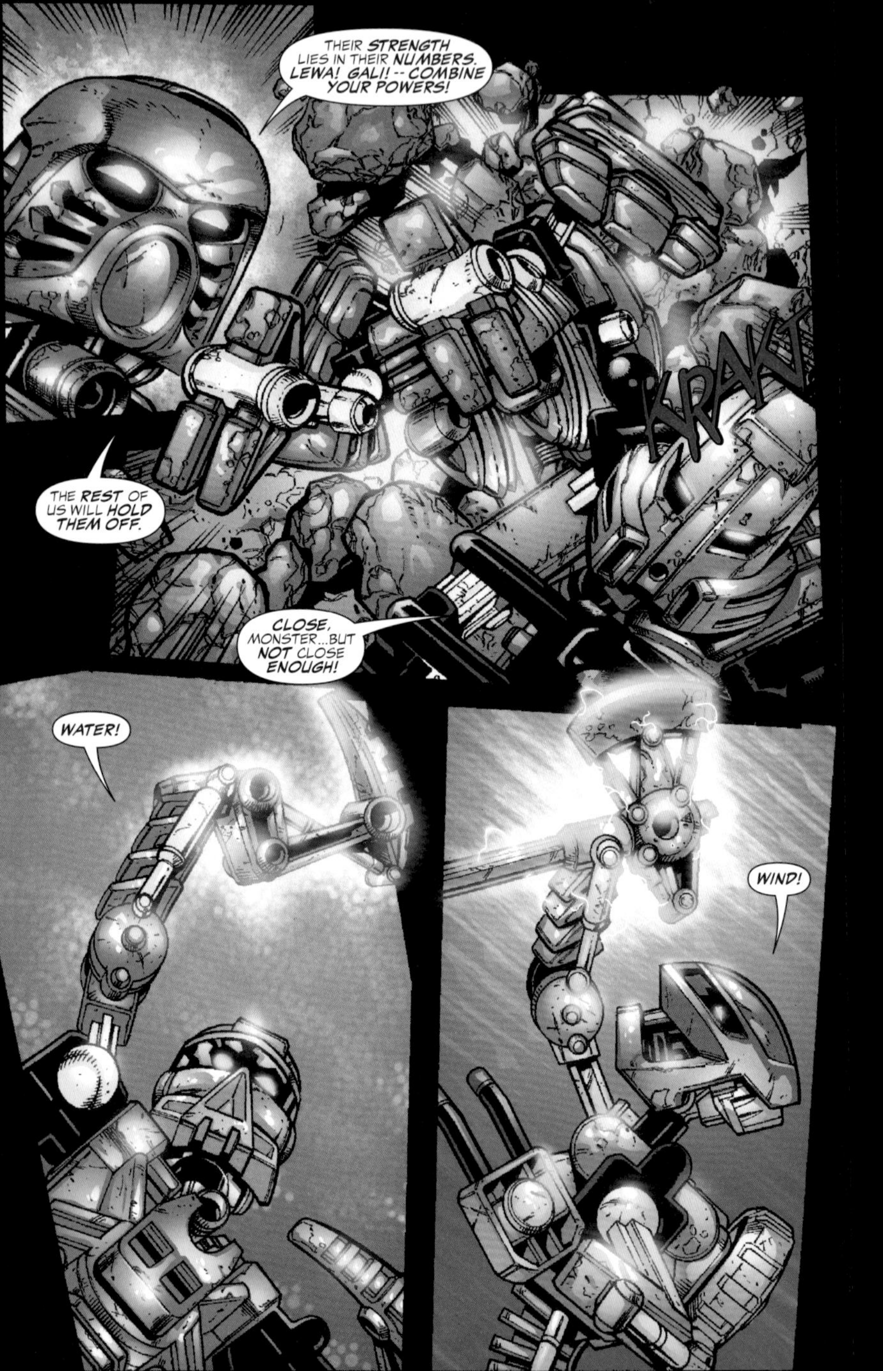
THEIR STRENGTH LIES IN THEIR NUMBERS. LEWA! GALI! -- COMBINE YOUR POWERS!
KRAKT
THE REST OF US WILL HOLD THEM OFF.
CLOSE, MONSTER...BUT NOT CLOSE ENOUGH!
WATER!
WIND!

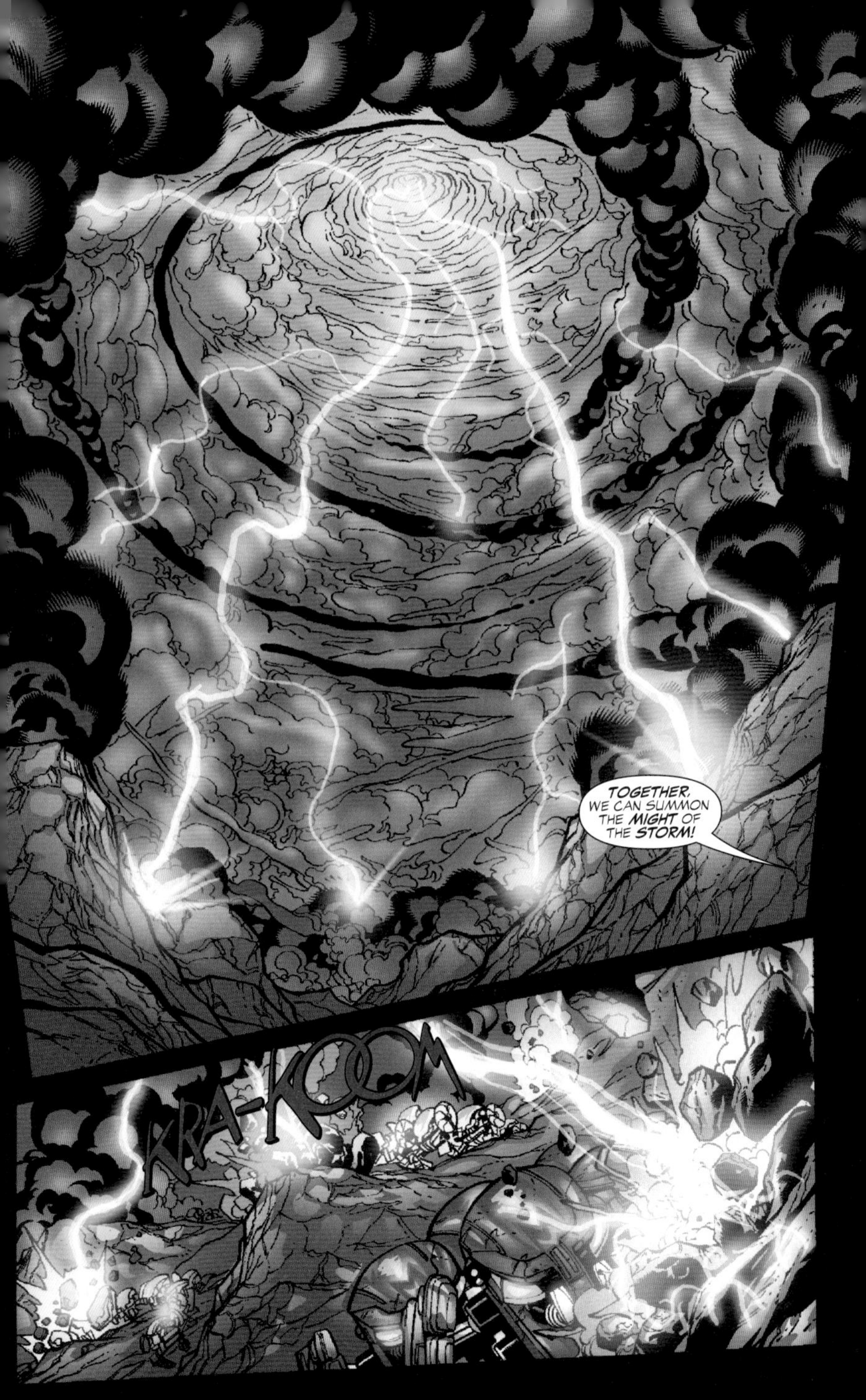
TOGETHER, WE CAN SUMMON THE MIGHT OF THE STORM!
KRA-KOOM

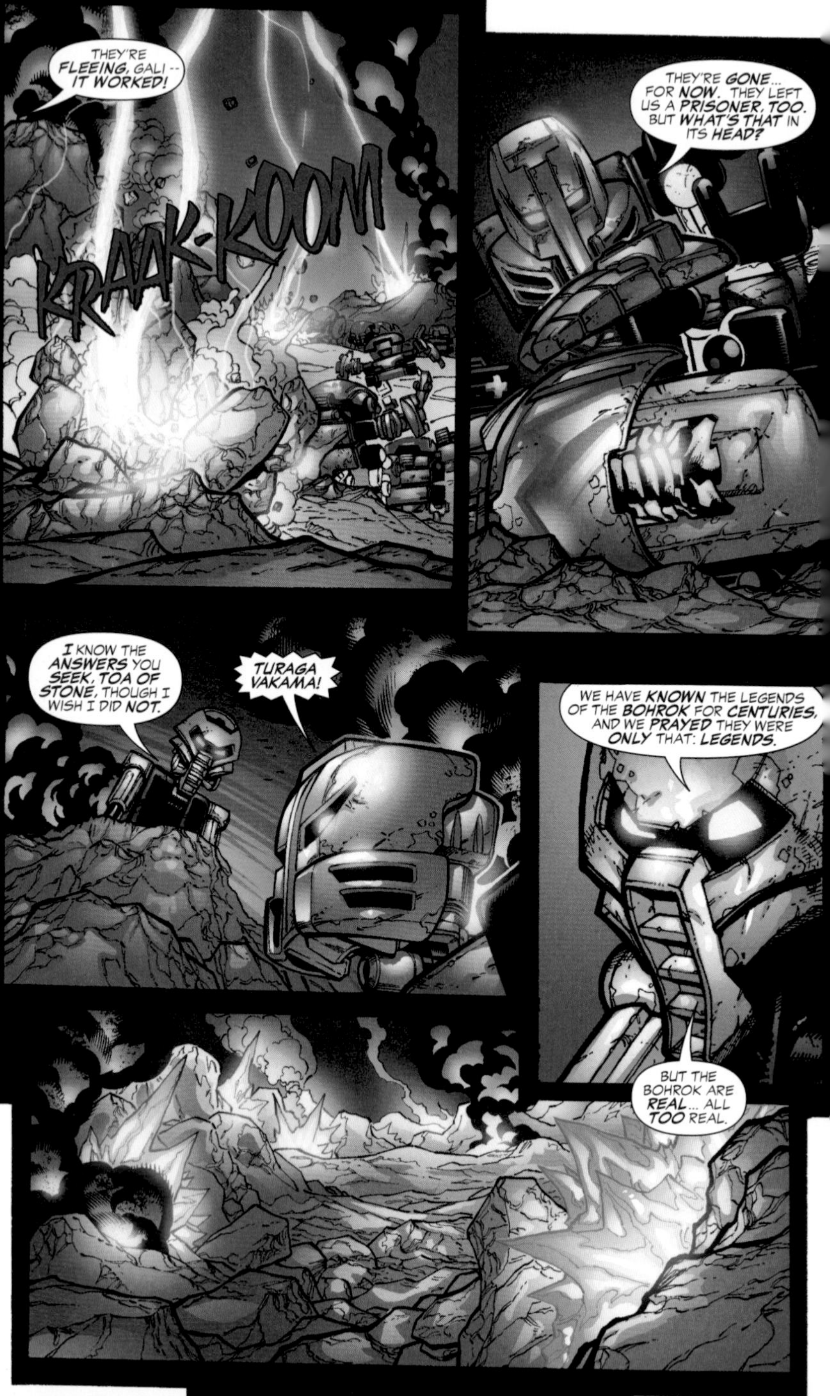
THEY'RE FLEEING, GALI -- IT WORKED!
KRAAK-KOOM
THEY'RE GONE... FOR NOW. THEY LEFT US A PRISONER, TOO. BUT WHAT'S THAT IN ITS HEAD?
I KNOW THE ANSWERS YOU SEEK, TOA OF STONE, THOUGH I WISH I DID NOT.
TURAGA VAKAMA!
WE HAVE KNOWN THE LEGENDS OF THE BOHROK FOR CENTURIES, AND WE PRAYED THEY WERE ONLY THAT: LEGENDS.
BUT THE BOHROK ARE REAL... ALL TOO REAL.

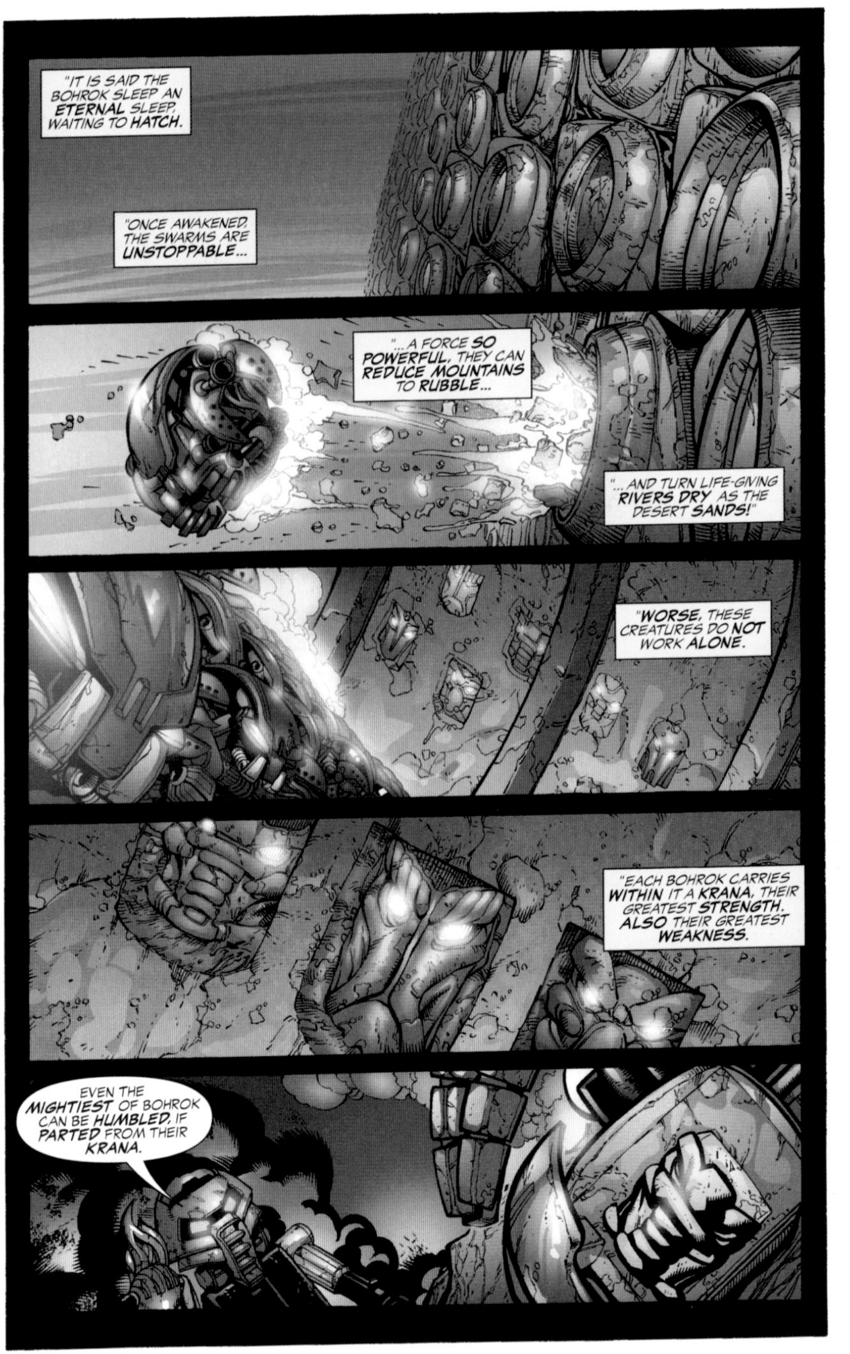
"IT IS SAID THE BOHROK SLEEP AN ETERNAL SLEEP, WAITING TO HATCH.
"ONCE AWAKENED, THE SWARMS ARE UNSTOPPABLE...
"...A FORCE SO POWERFUL, THEY CAN REDUCE MOUNTAINS TO RUBBLE...
"...AND TURN LIFE-GIVING RIVERS DRY AS THE DESERT SANDS!"
"WORSE, THESE CREATURES DO NOT WORK ALONE.
"EACH BOHROK CARRIES WITHIN IT A KRANA, THEIR GREATEST STRENGTH. ALSO THEIR GREATEST WEAKNESS.
EVEN THE MIGHTIEST OF BOHROK CAN BE HUMBLED, IF PARTED FROM THEIR KRANA.

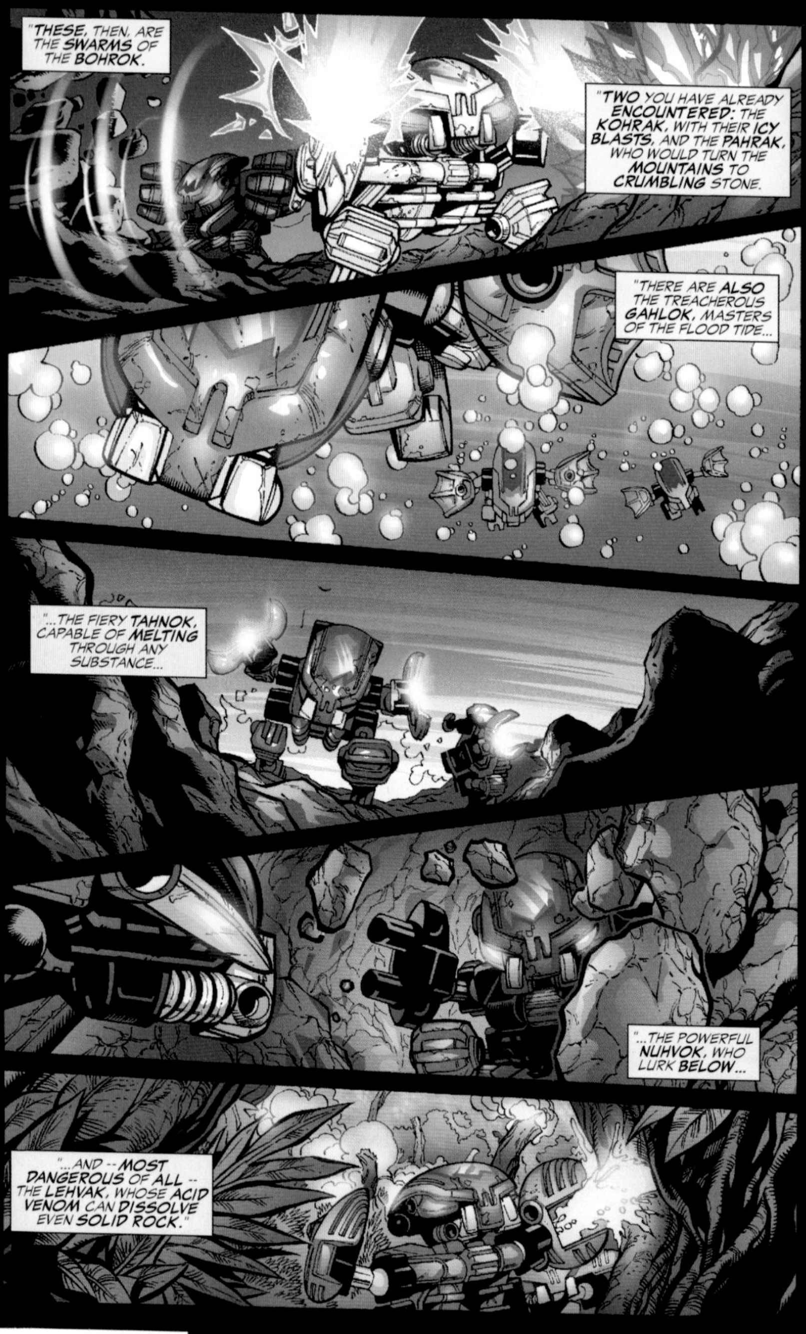
"THESE, THEN, ARE THE SWARMS OF THE BOHROK.
"TWO YOU HAVE ALREADY ENCOUNTERED: THE KOHRAK, WITH THEIR ICY BLASTS, AND THE PAHRAK, WHO WOULD TURN THE MOUNTAINS TO CRUMBLING STONE.
"THERE ARE ALSO THE TREACHEROUS GAHLOK, MASTERS OF THE FLOOD TIDE...
"...THE FIERY TAHNOK, CAPABLE OF MELTING THROUGH ANY SUBSTANCE...
"...THE POWERFUL NUHVOK, WHO LURK BELOW...
"...AND -- MOST DANGEROUS OF ALL -- THE LEHVAK, WHOSE ACID VENOM CAN DISSOLVE EVEN SOLID ROCK."

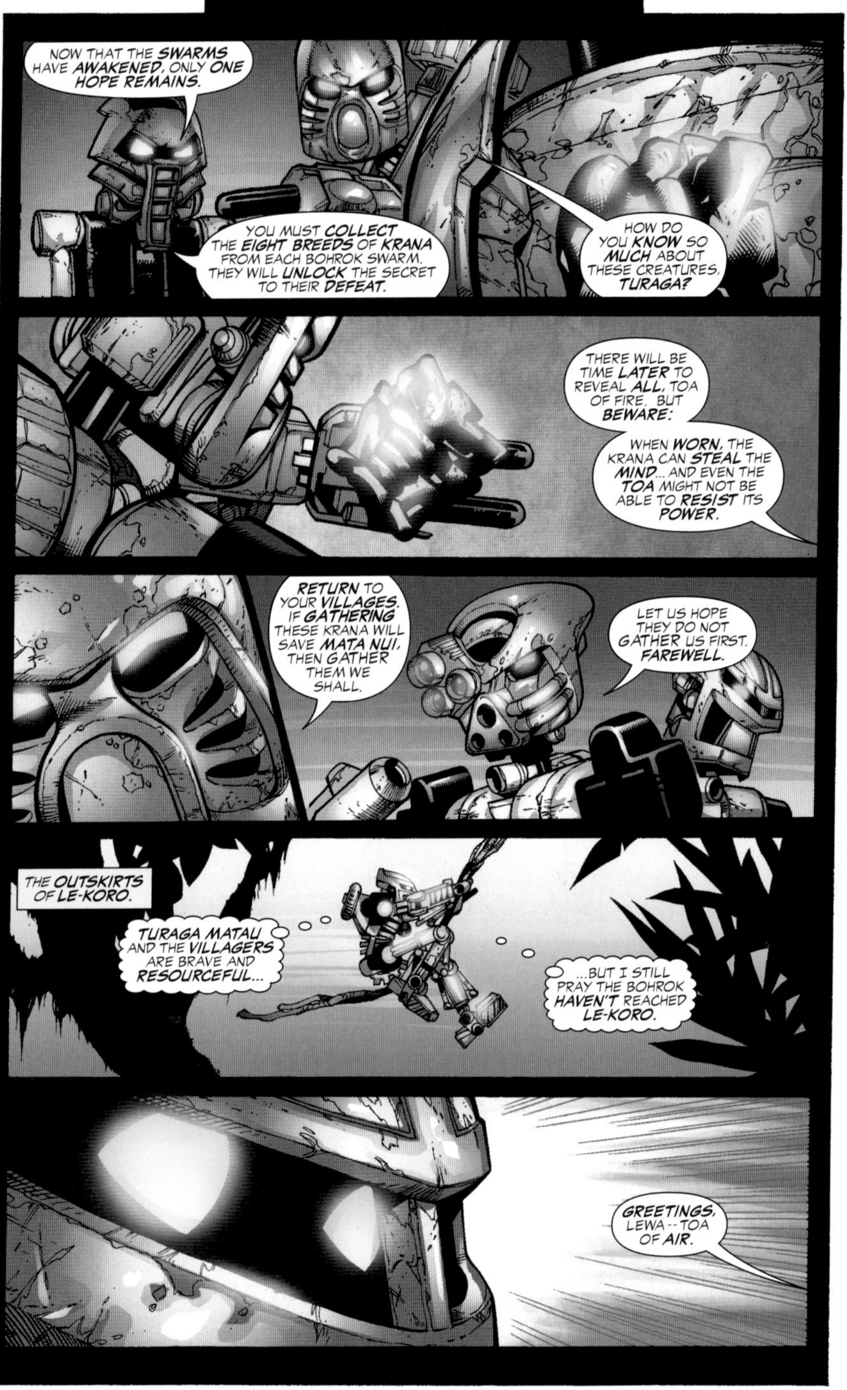
NOW THAT THE SWARMS HAVE AWAKENED, ONLY ONE HOPE REMAINS.
YOU MUST COLLECT THE EIGHT BREEDS OF KRANA FROM EACH BOHROK SWARM. THEY WILL UNLOCK THE SECRET TO THEIR DEFEAT.
HOW DO YOU KNOW SO MUCH ABOUT THESE CREATURES, TURAGA?
THERE WILL BE TIME LATER TO REVEAL ALL, TOA OF FIRE. BUT BEWARE:
WHEN WORN, THE KRANA CAN STEAL THE MIND... AND EVEN THE TOA MIGHT NOT BE ABLE TO RESIST ITS POWER.
RETURN TO YOUR VILLAGES. IF GATHERING THESE KRANA WILL SAVE MATA NUI, THEN GATHER THEM WE SHALL.
LET US HOPE THEY DO NOT GATHER US FIRST. FAREWELL.
THE OUTSKIRTS OF LE-KORO.
TURAGA MATAU AND THE VILLAGERS ARE BRAVE AND RESOURCEFUL...
...BUT I STILL PRAY THE BOHROK HAVEN'T REACHED LE-KORO.
GREETINGS, LEWA--TOA OF AIR.

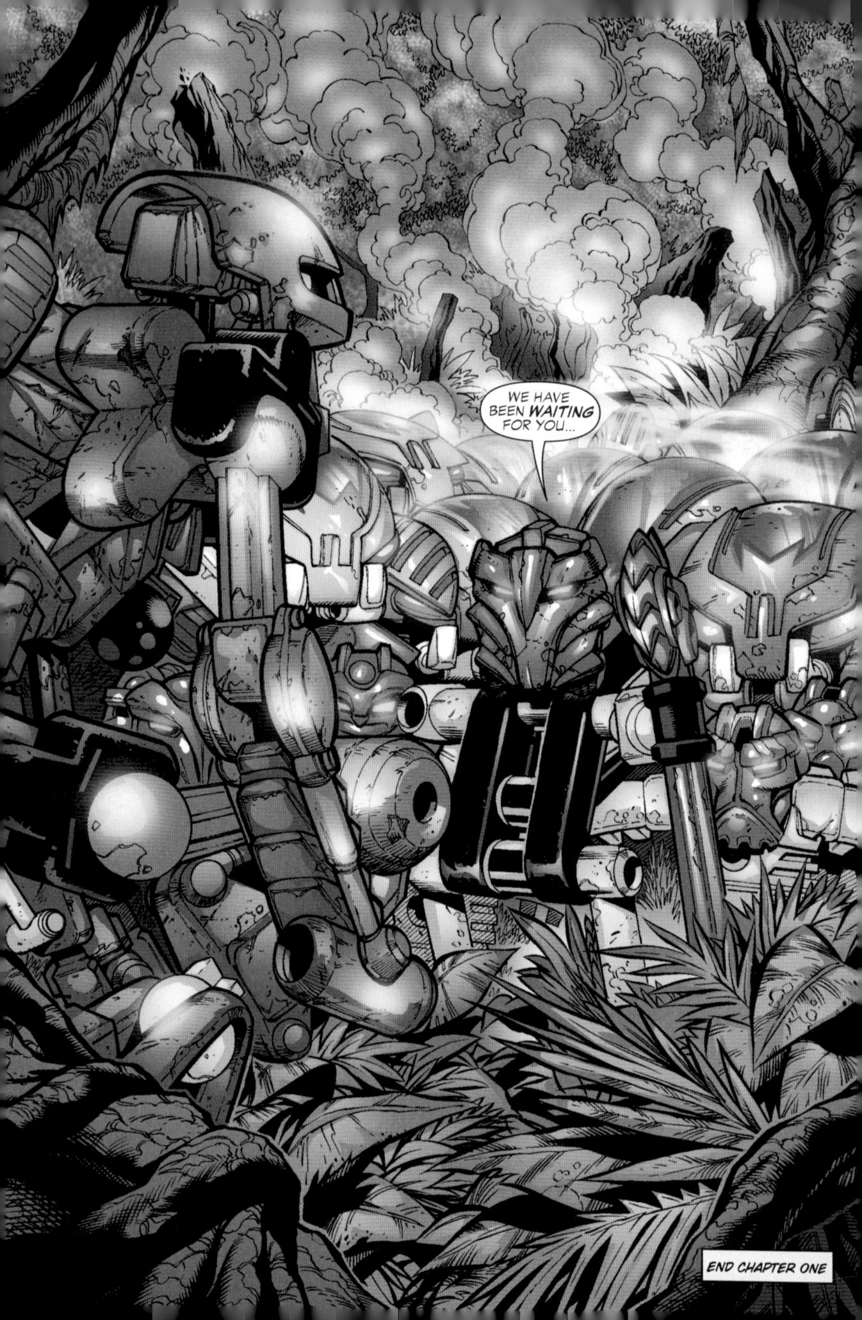
WE HAVE BEEN WAITING FOR YOU...
END CHAPTER ONE

# THE BOHROK SAGA
# CHAPTER TWO

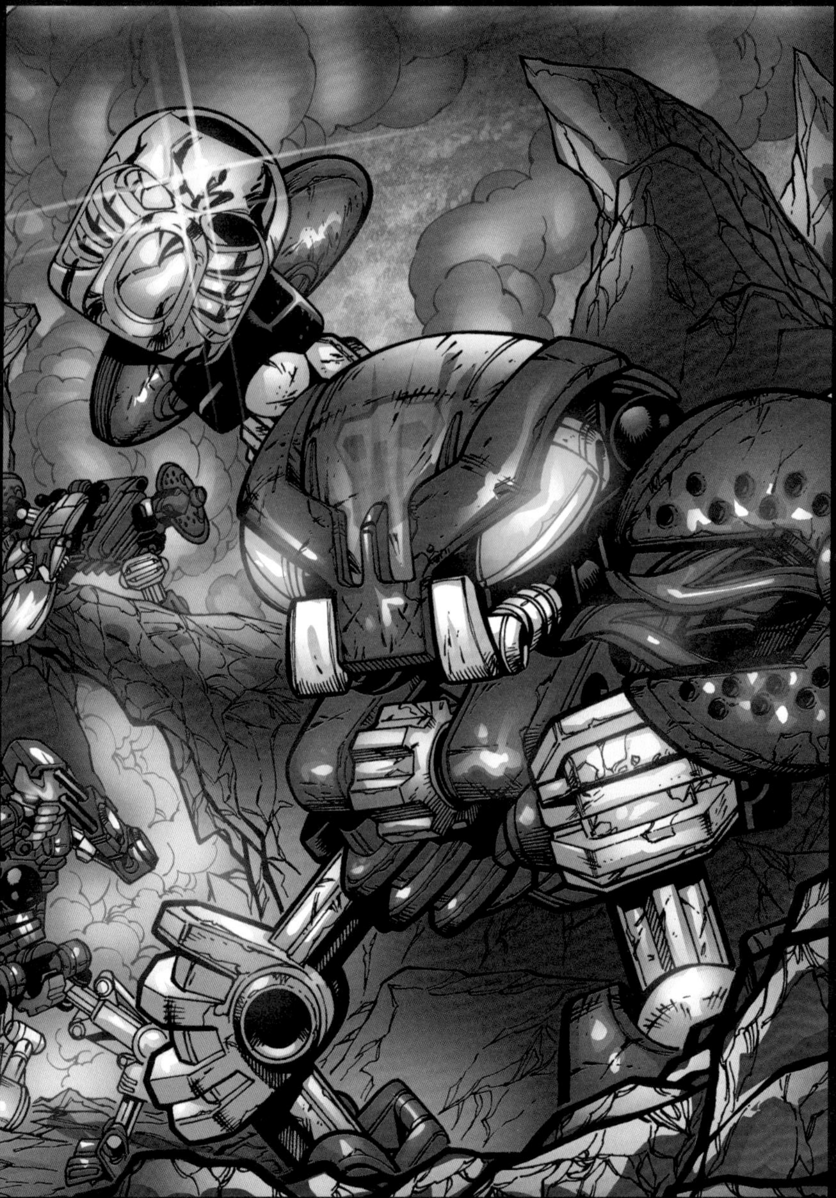

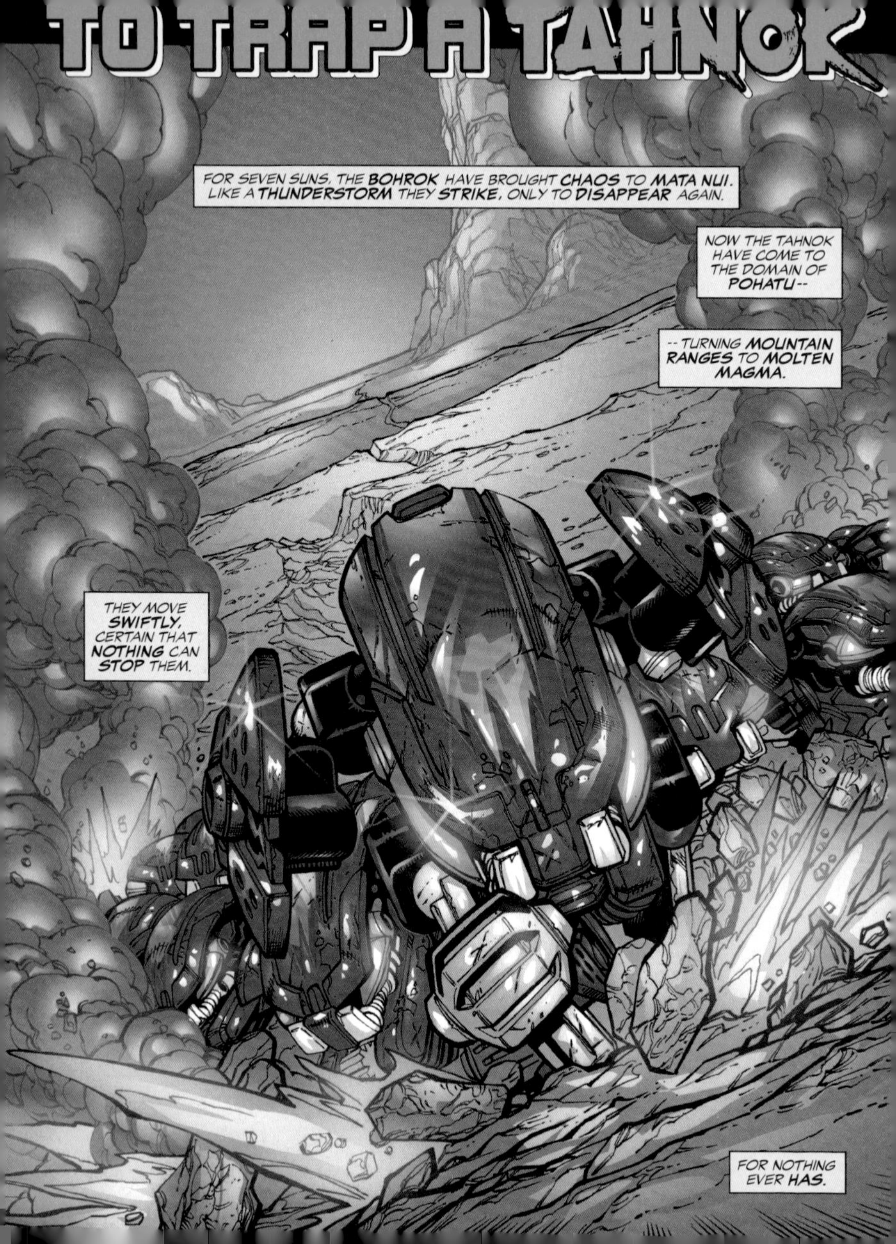
TO TRAP A TAHNOK
FOR SEVEN SUNS, THE BOHROK HAVE BROUGHT CHAOS TO MATA NUI. LIKE A THUNDERSTORM THEY STRIKE, ONLY TO DISAPPEAR AGAIN.
NOW THE TAHNOK HAVE COME TO THE DOMAIN OF POHATU--
--TURNING MOUNTAIN RANGES TO MOLTEN MAGMA.
THEY MOVE SWIFTLY, CERTAIN THAT NOTHING CAN STOP THEM.
FOR NOTHING EVER HAS.

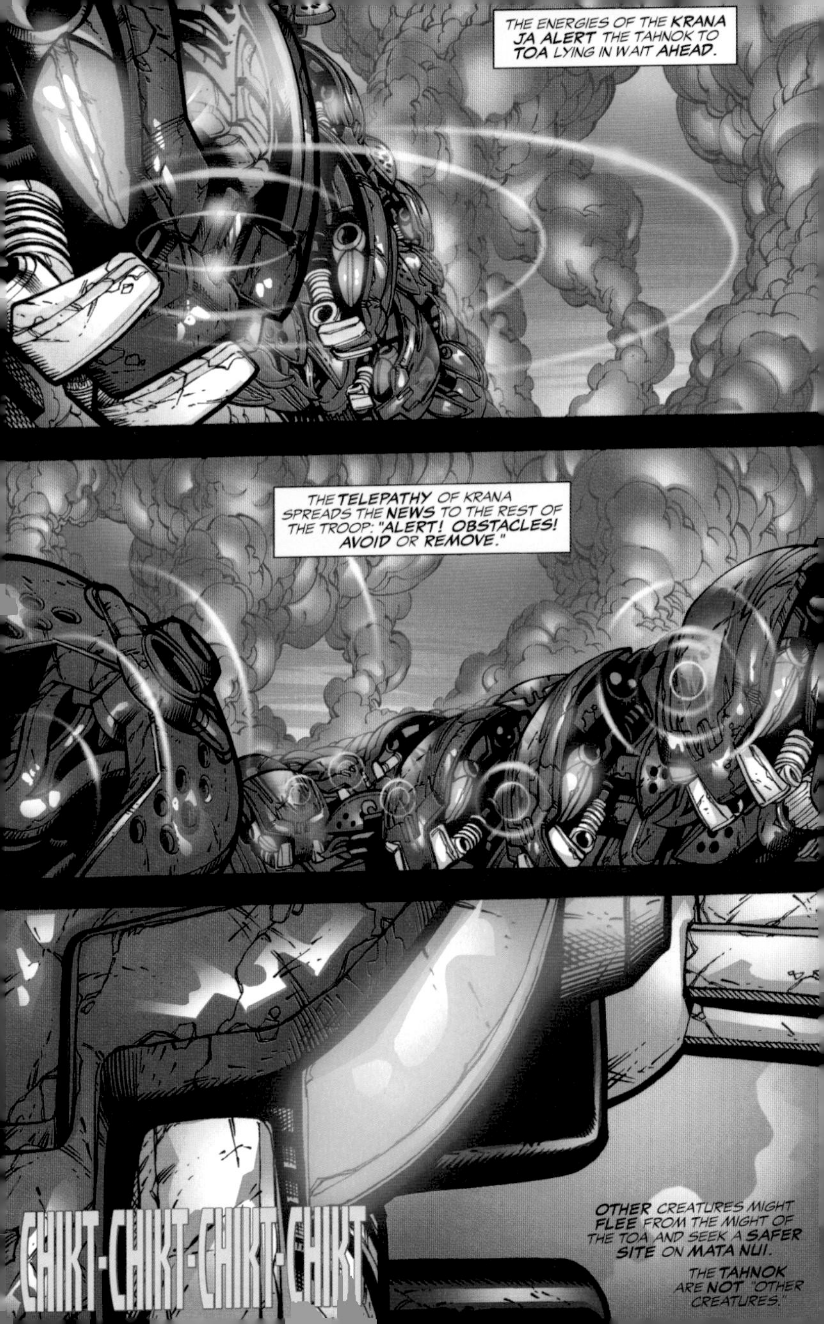
THE ENERGIES OF THE KRANA JA ALERT THE TAHNOK TO TOA LYING IN WAIT AHEAD.
THE TELEPATHY OF KRANA SPREADS THE NEWS TO THE REST OF THE TROOP: "ALERT! OBSTACLES! AVOID OR REMOVE."
CHIKT-CHIKT-CHIKT-CHIKT
OTHER CREATURES MIGHT FLEE FROM THE MIGHT OF THE TOA AND SEEK A SAFER SITE ON MATA NUI.
THE TAHNOK ARE NOT "OTHER CREATURES."

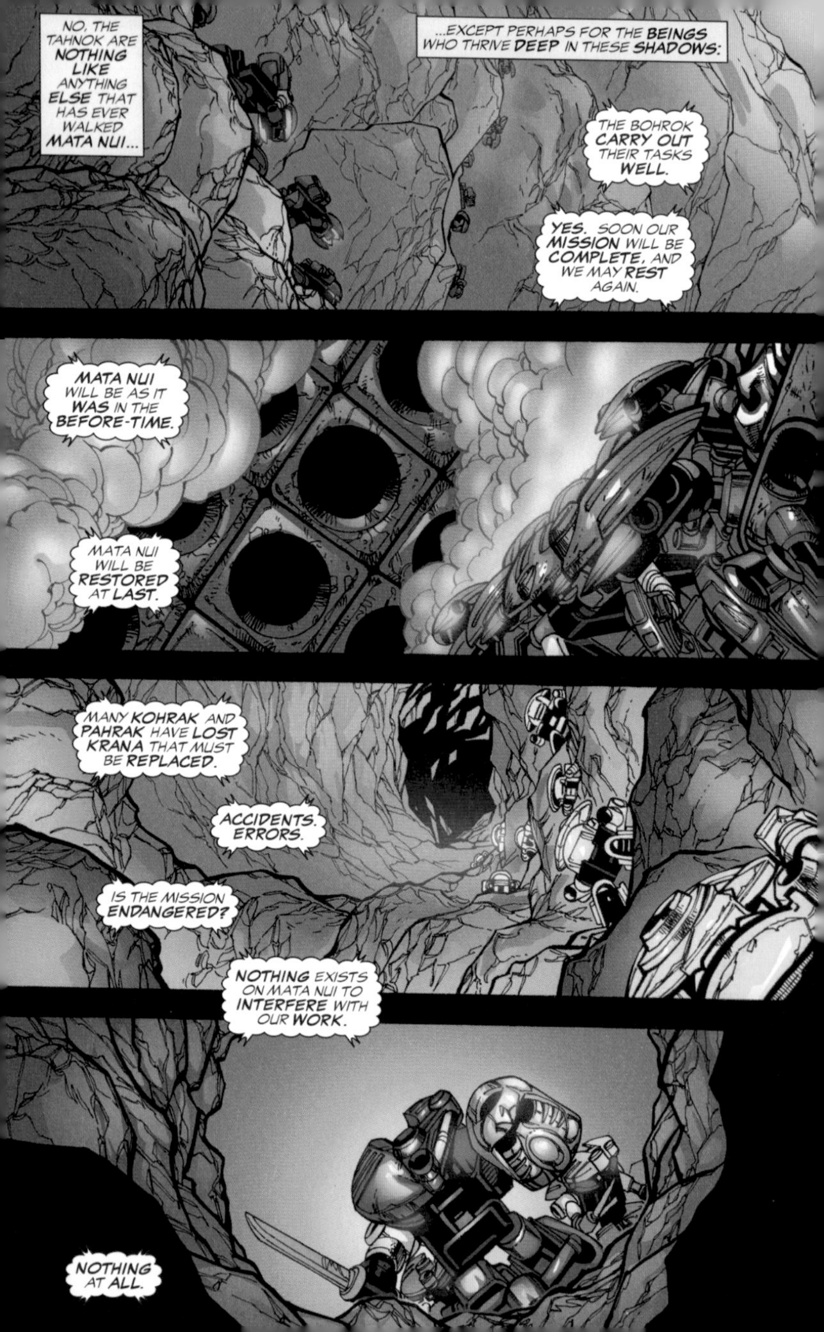
NO, THE TAHNOK ARE NOTHING LIKE ANYTHING ELSE THAT HAS EVER WALKED MATA NUI...
...EXCEPT PERHAPS FOR THE BEINGS WHO THRIVE DEEP IN THESE SHADOWS:
THE BOHROK CARRY OUT THEIR TASKS WELL.
YES. SOON OUR MISSION WILL BE COMPLETE, AND WE MAY REST AGAIN.
MATA NUI WILL BE AS IT WAS IN THE BEFORE-TIME.
MATA NUI WILL BE RESTORED AT LAST.
MANY KOHRAK AND PAHRAK HAVE LOST KRANA THAT MUST BE REPLACED.
ACCIDENTS. ERRORS.
IS THE MISSION ENDANGERED?
NOTHING EXISTS ON MATA NUI TO INTERFERE WITH OUR WORK.
NOTHING AT ALL.

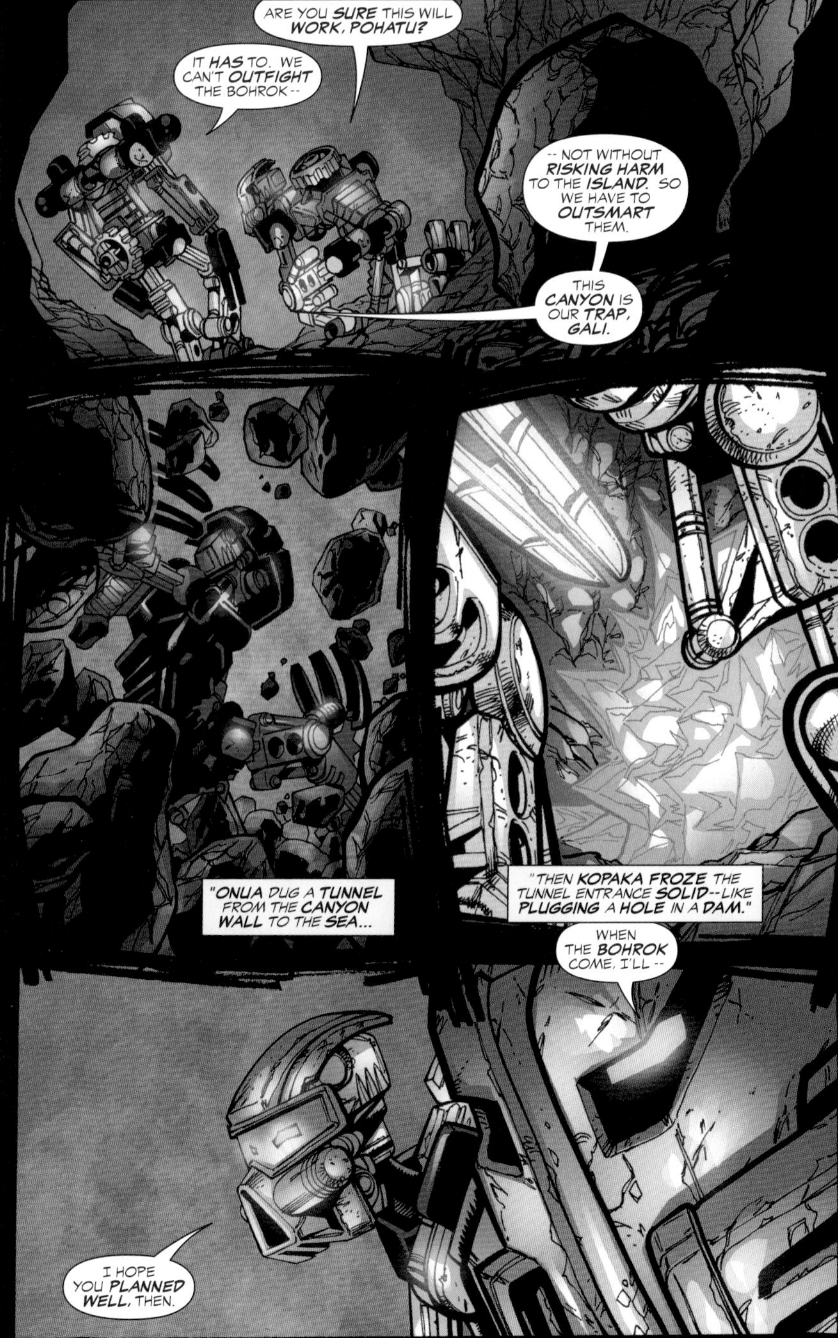

ARE YOU SURE THIS WILL WORK, POHATU?
IT HAS TO. WE CAN'T OUTFIGHT THE BOHROK --
-- NOT WITHOUT RISKING HARM TO THE ISLAND. SO WE HAVE TO OUTSMART THEM.
THIS CANYON IS OUR TRAP, GALI.
"ONUA DUG A TUNNEL FROM THE CANYON WALL TO THE SEA...
"THEN KOPAKA FROZE THE TUNNEL ENTRANCE SOLID--LIKE PLUGGING A HOLE IN A DAM."
WHEN THE BOHROK COME, I'LL --
I HOPE YOU PLANNED WELL, THEN.

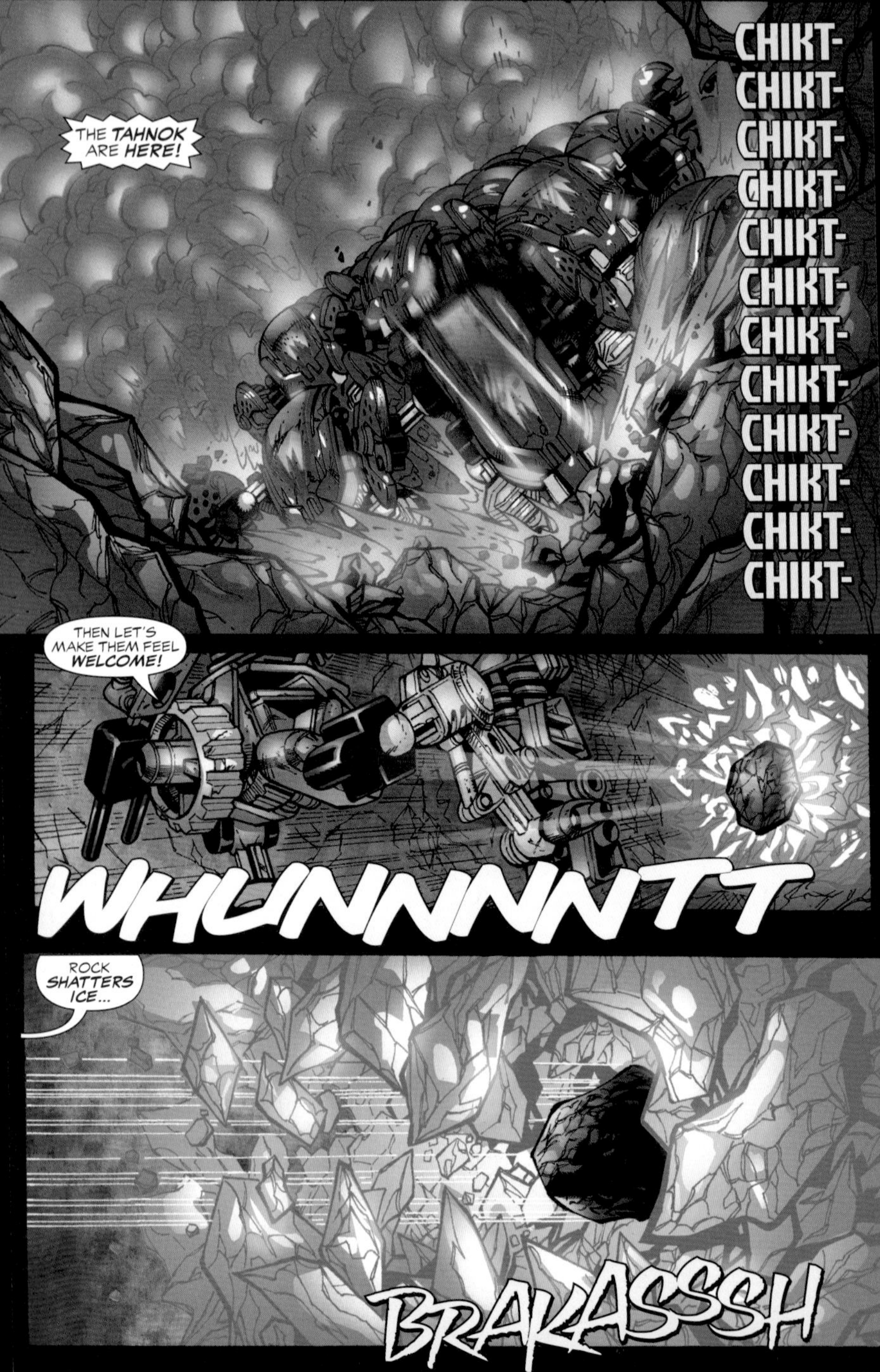
THE TAHNOK ARE HERE!
CHIKT-
CHIKT-
CHIKT-
CHIKT-
CHIKT-
CHIKT-
CHIKT-
CHIKT-
CHIKT-
CHIKT-
CHIKT-
CHIKT-
THEN LET'S MAKE THEM FEEL WELCOME!
WHUNNNNTT
ROCK SHATTERS ICE...
BRAKASSSH

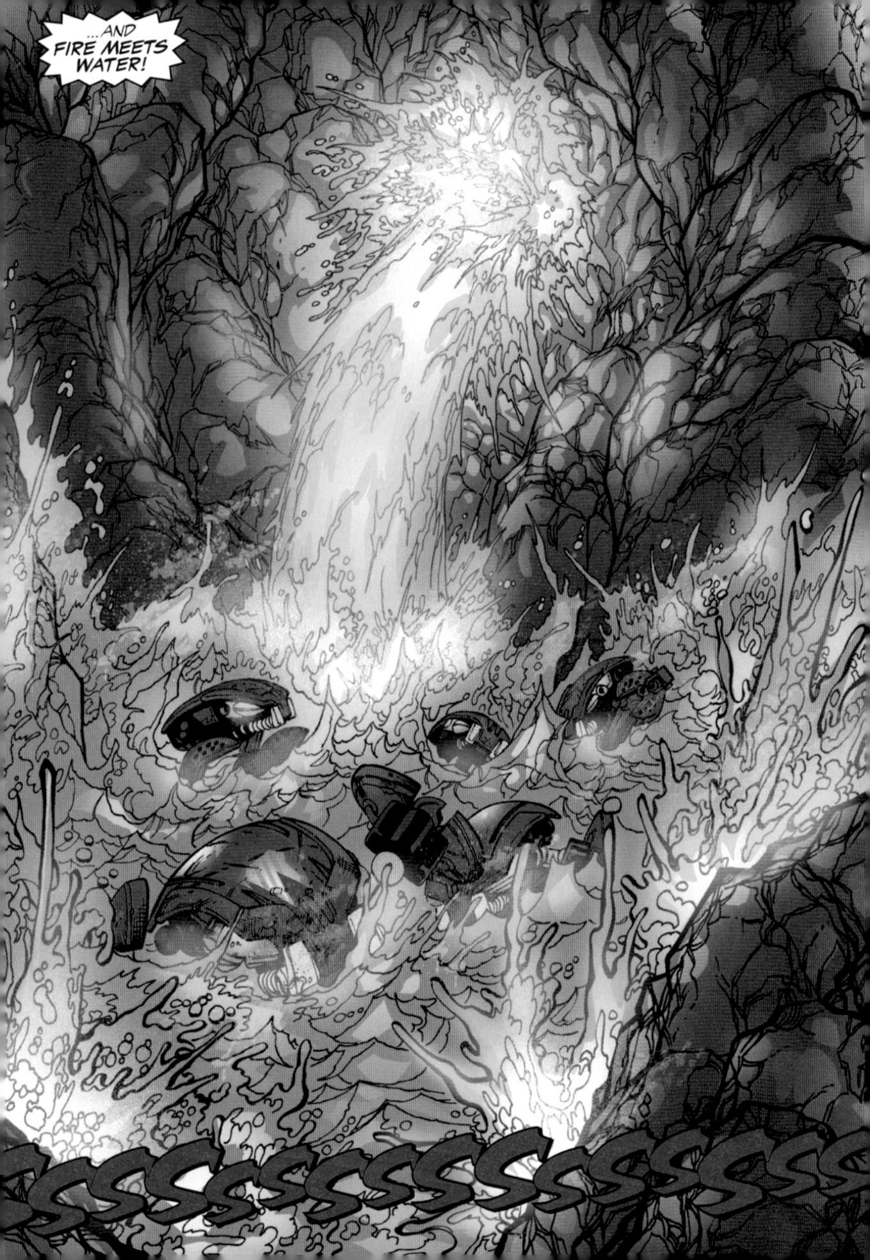
...AND FIRE MEETS WATER!
SSSSSSSSSSSSSSSS

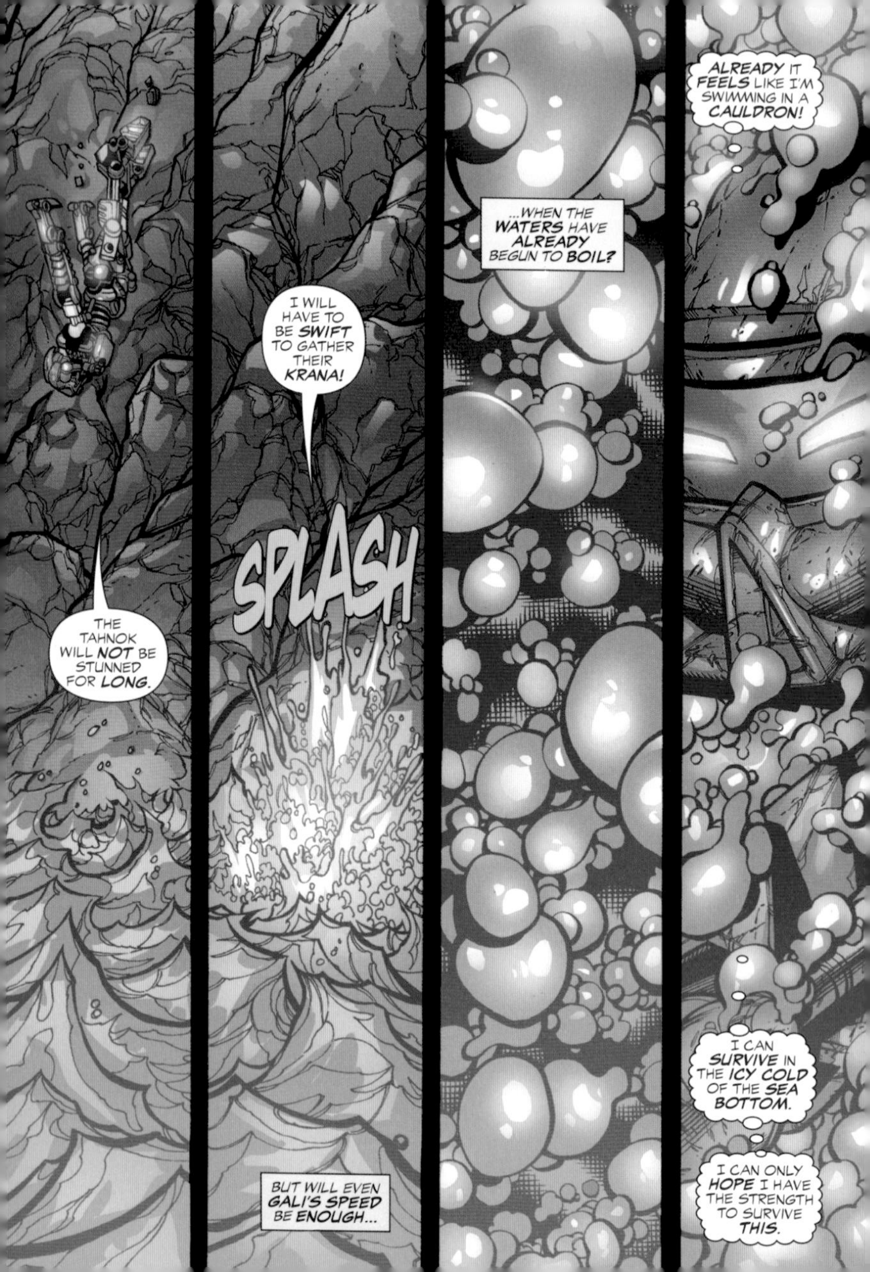
THE TAHNOK WILL NOT BE STUNNED FOR LONG.
I WILL HAVE TO BE SWIFT TO GATHER THEIR KRANA!
SPLASH
BUT WILL EVEN GALI'S SPEED BE ENOUGH...
...WHEN THE WATERS HAVE ALREADY BEGUN TO BOIL?
ALREADY IT FEELS LIKE I'M SWIMMING IN A CAULDRON!
I CAN SURVIVE IN THE ICY COLD OF THE SEA BOTTOM.
I CAN ONLY HOPE I HAVE THE STRENGTH TO SURVIVE THIS.

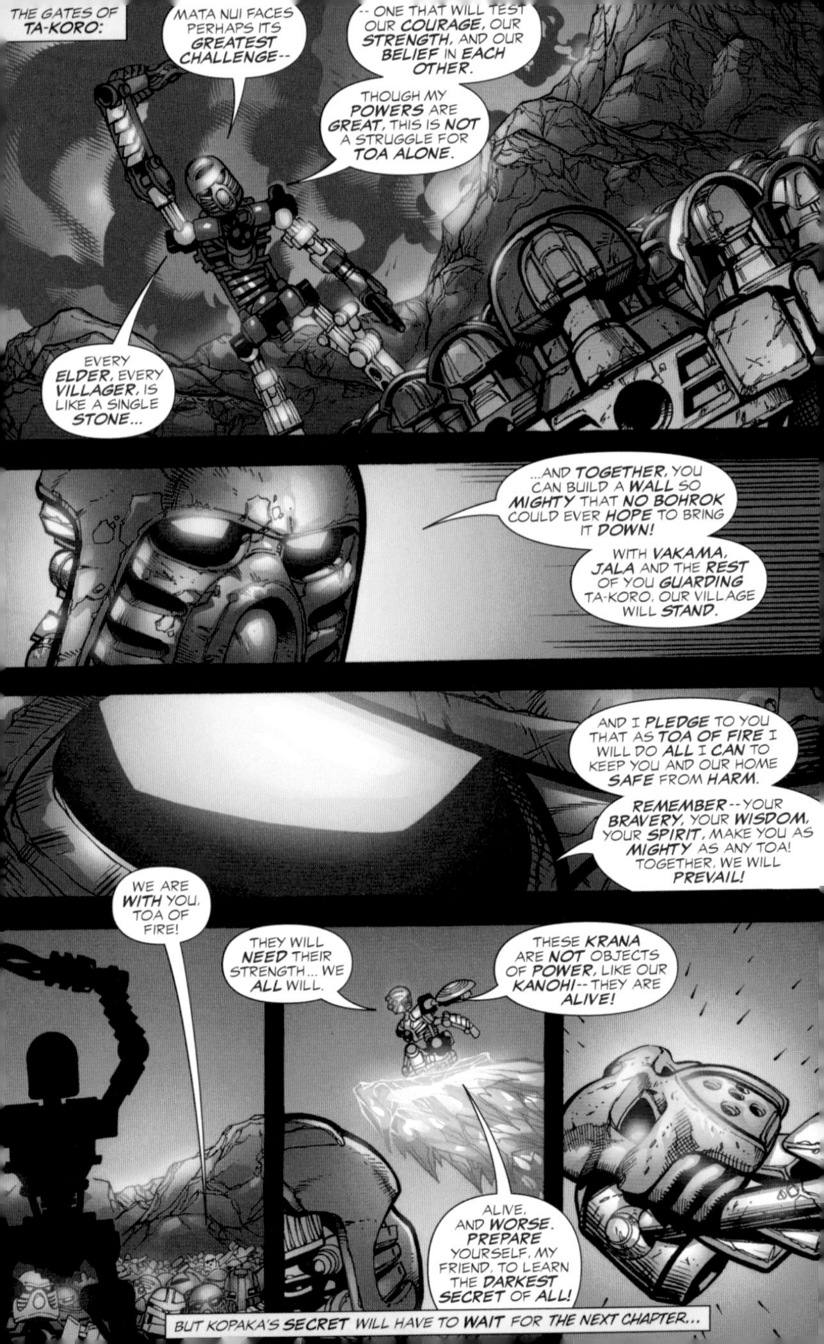
THE GATES OF TA-KORO:
MATA NUI FACES PERHAPS ITS GREATEST CHALLENGE--
-- ONE THAT WILL TEST OUR COURAGE, OUR STRENGTH, AND OUR BELIEF IN EACH OTHER.
THOUGH MY POWERS ARE GREAT, THIS IS NOT A STRUGGLE FOR TOA ALONE.
EVERY ELDER, EVERY VILLAGER, IS LIKE A SINGLE STONE...
...AND TOGETHER, YOU CAN BUILD A WALL SO MIGHTY THAT NO BOHROK COULD EVER HOPE TO BRING IT DOWN!
WITH VAKAMA, JALA AND THE REST OF YOU GUARDING TA-KORO, OUR VILLAGE WILL STAND.
AND I PLEDGE TO YOU THAT AS TOA OF FIRE I WILL DO ALL I CAN TO KEEP YOU AND OUR HOME SAFE FROM HARM.
REMEMBER--YOUR BRAVERY, YOUR WISDOM, YOUR SPIRIT, MAKE YOU AS MIGHTY AS ANY TOA! TOGETHER, WE WILL PREVAIL!
WE ARE WITH YOU, TOA OF FIRE!
THEY WILL NEED THEIR STRENGTH... WE ALL WILL.
THESE KRANA ARE NOT OBJECTS OF POWER, LIKE OUR KANOHI-- THEY ARE ALIVE!
ALIVE, AND WORSE. PREPARE YOURSELF, MY FRIEND, TO LEARN THE DARKEST SECRET OF ALL!
BUT KOPAKA'S SECRET WILL HAVE TO WAIT FOR THE NEXT CHAPTER...

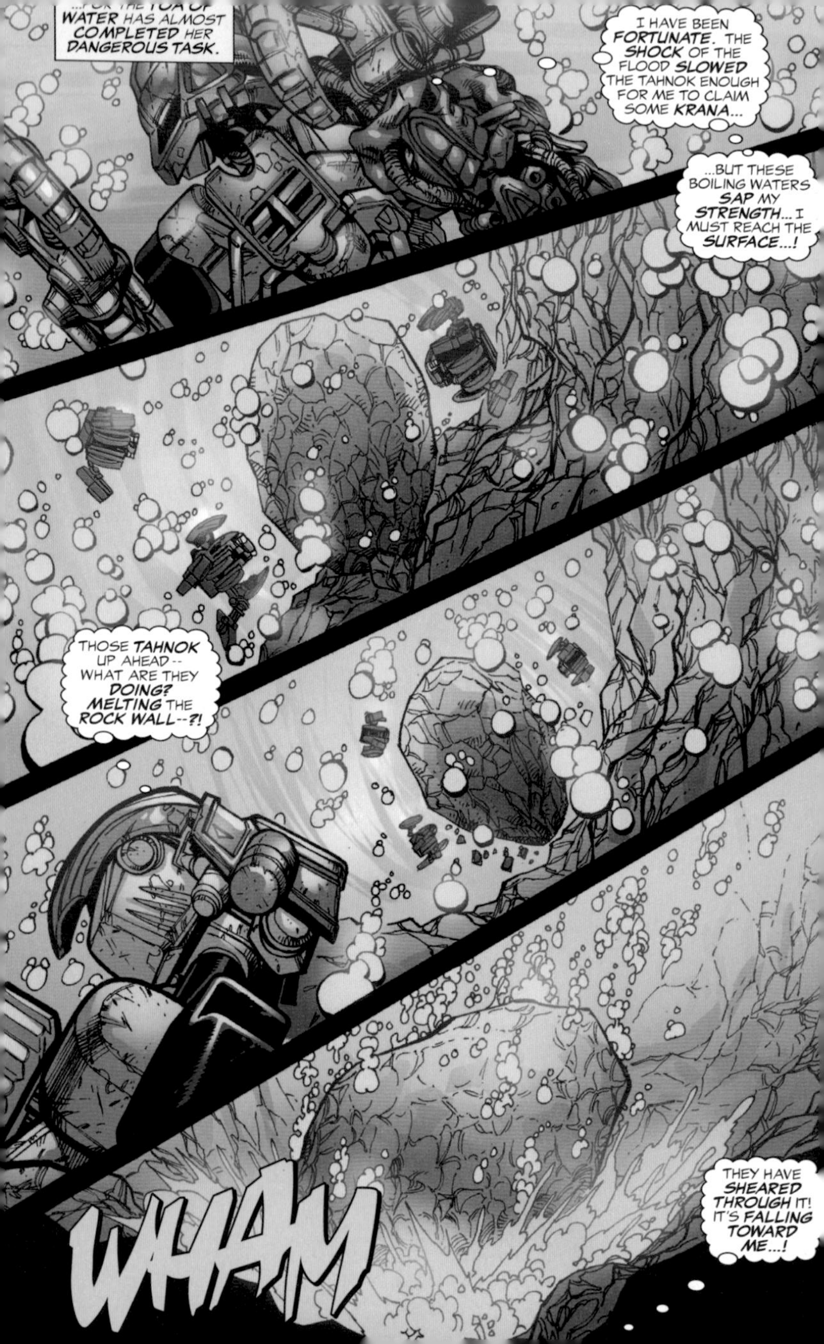
WATER HAS ALMOST COMPLETED HER DANGEROUS TASK.
I HAVE BEEN FORTUNATE. THE SHOCK OF THE FLOOD SLOWED THE TAHNOK ENOUGH FOR ME TO CLAIM SOME KRANA...
...BUT THESE BOILING WATERS SAP MY STRENGTH... I MUST REACH THE SURFACE...!
THOSE TAHNOK UP AHEAD -- WHAT ARE THEY DOING? MELTING THE ROCK WALL--?!
THEY HAVE SHEARED THROUGH IT! IT'S FALLING TOWARD ME...!
WHAM

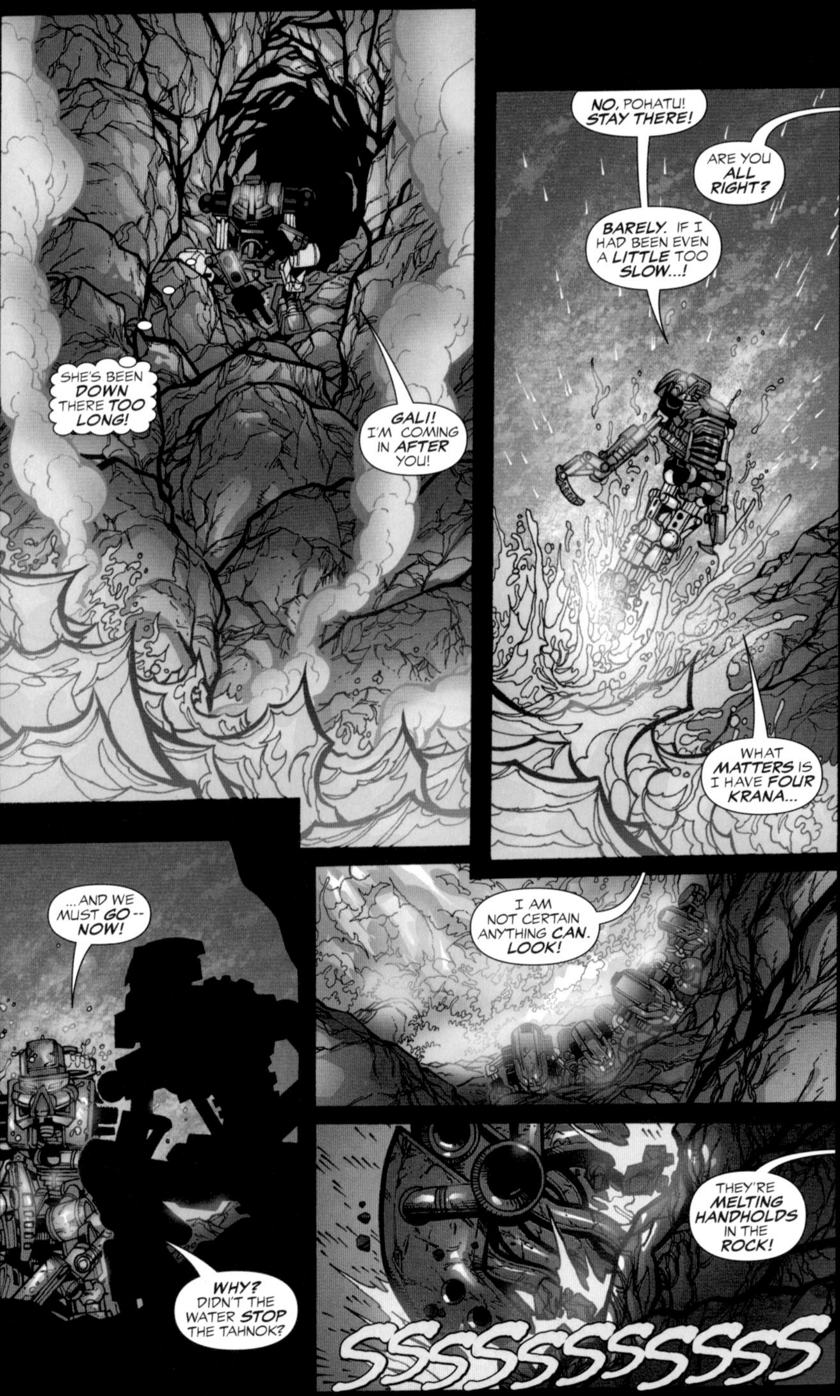
SHE'S BEEN DOWN THERE TOO LONG!
GALI! I'M COMING IN AFTER YOU!
NO, POHATU! STAY THERE!
ARE YOU ALL RIGHT?
BARELY. IF I HAD BEEN EVEN A LITTLE TOO SLOW...!
WHAT MATTERS IS I HAVE FOUR KRANA...
...AND WE MUST GO -- NOW!
WHY? DIDN'T THE WATER STOP THE TAHNOK?
I AM NOT CERTAIN ANYTHING CAN. LOOK!
THEY'RE MELTING HANDHOLDS IN THE ROCK!
SSSSSSSSSSSS

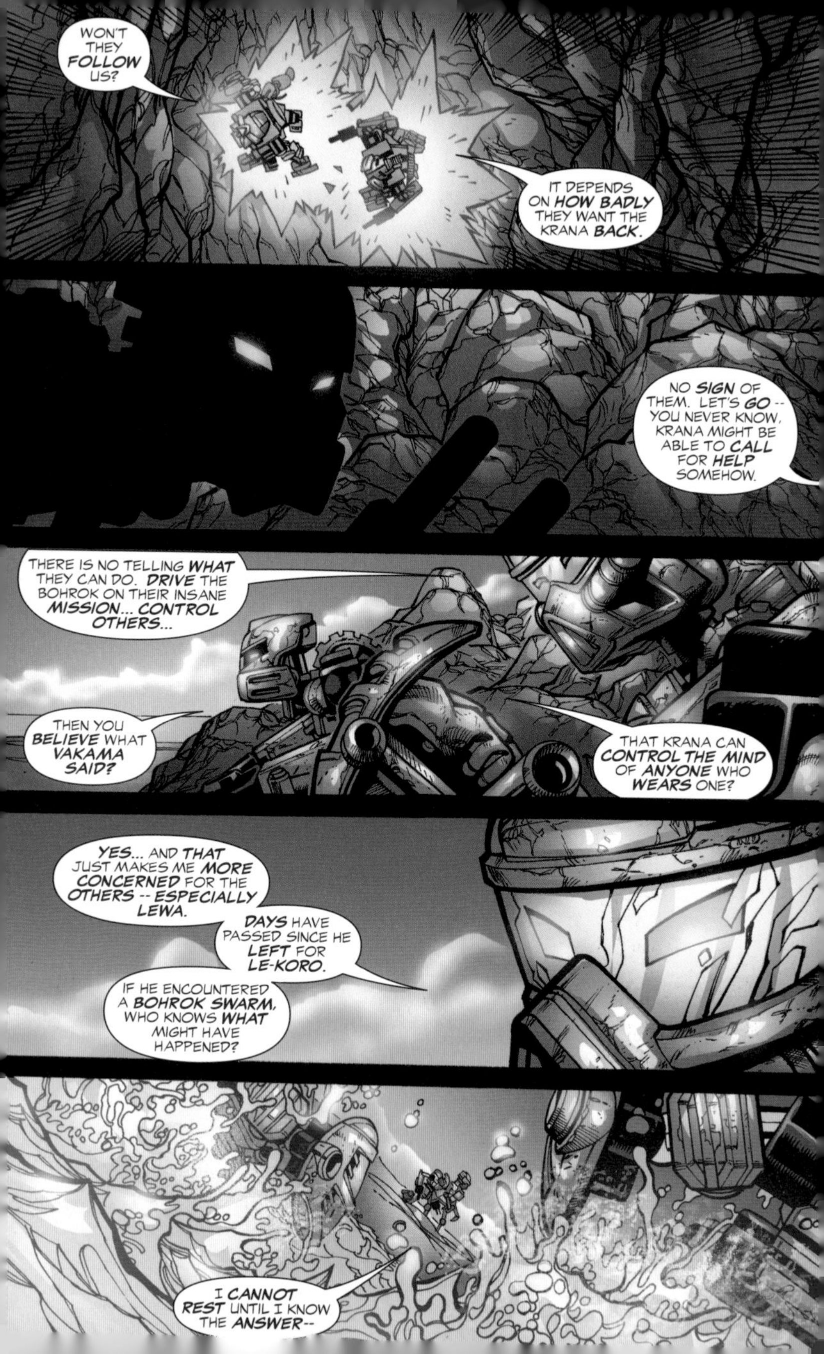
WON'T THEY FOLLOW US?
IT DEPENDS ON HOW BADLY THEY WANT THE KRANA BACK.
NO SIGN OF THEM. LET'S GO -- YOU NEVER KNOW, KRANA MIGHT BE ABLE TO CALL FOR HELP SOMEHOW.
THERE IS NO TELLING WHAT THEY CAN DO. DRIVE THE BOHROK ON THEIR INSANE MISSION... CONTROL OTHERS...
THEN YOU BELIEVE WHAT VAKAMA SAID?
THAT KRANA CAN CONTROL THE MIND OF ANYONE WHO WEARS ONE?
YES... AND THAT JUST MAKES ME MORE CONCERNED FOR THE OTHERS -- ESPECIALLY LEWA.
DAYS HAVE PASSED SINCE HE LEFT FOR LE-KORO.
IF HE ENCOUNTERED A BOHROK SWARM, WHO KNOWS WHAT MIGHT HAVE HAPPENED?
I CANNOT REST UNTIL I KNOW THE ANSWER--

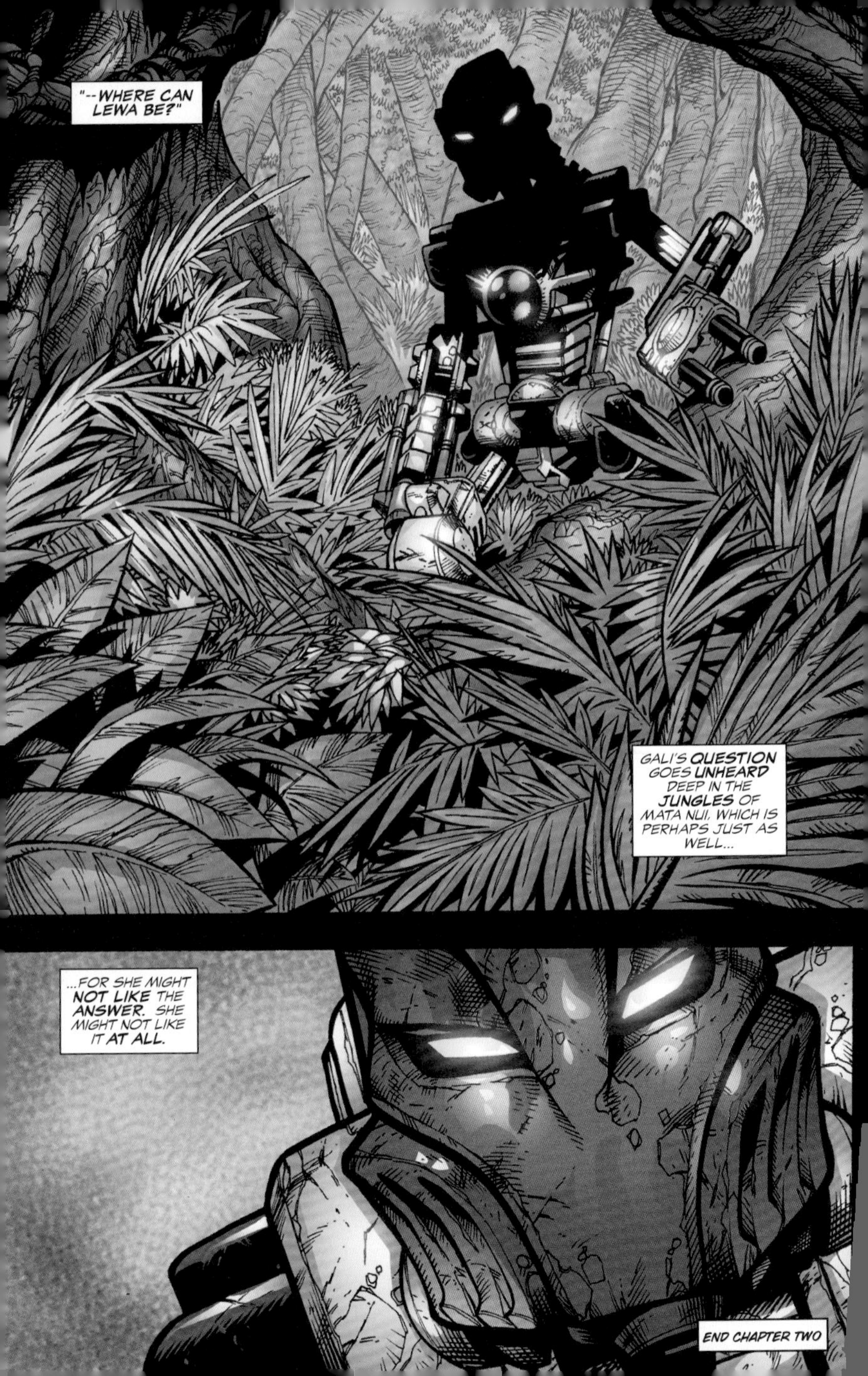
"--WHERE CAN LEWA BE?"
GALI'S QUESTION GOES UNHEARD DEEP IN THE JUNGLES OF MATA NUI, WHICH IS PERHAPS JUST AS WELL...
...FOR SHE MIGHT NOT LIKE THE ANSWER. SHE MIGHT NOT LIKE IT AT ALL.
END CHAPTER TWO

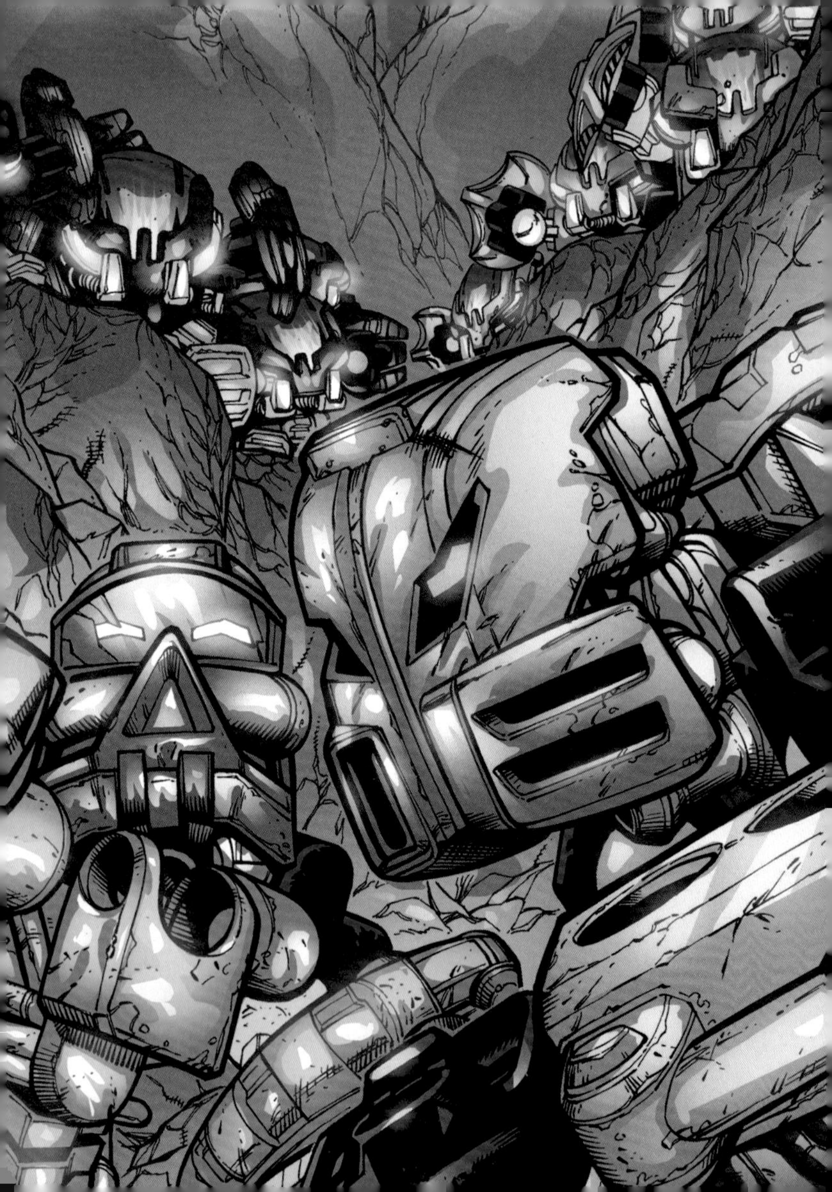

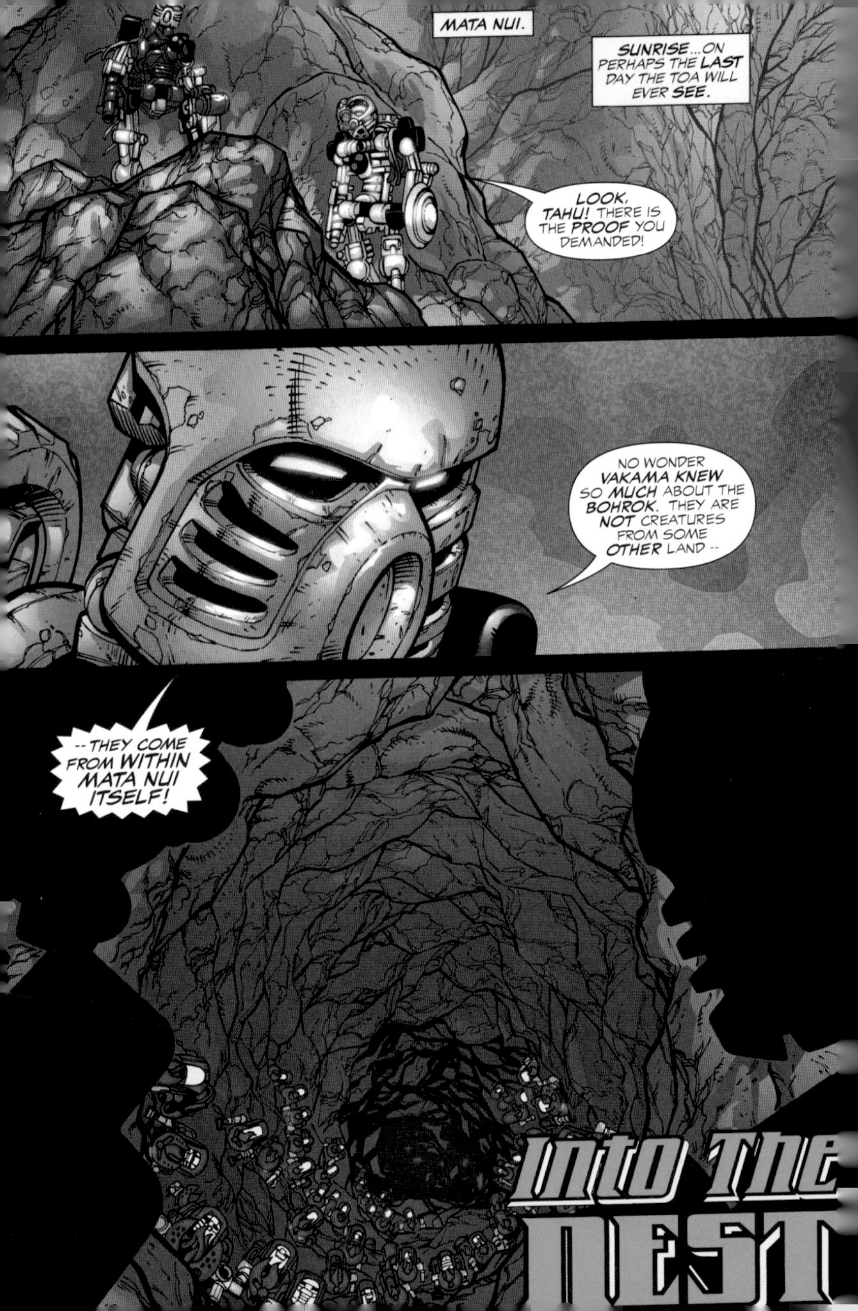
MATA NUI.
SUNRISE...ON PERHAPS THE LAST DAY THE TOA WILL EVER SEE.
LOOK, TAHU! THERE IS THE PROOF YOU DEMANDED!
NO WONDER VAKAMA KNEW SO MUCH ABOUT THE BOHROK. THEY ARE NOT CREATURES FROM SOME OTHER LAND --
-- THEY COME FROM WITHIN MATA NUI ITSELF!
INTO THE NEST

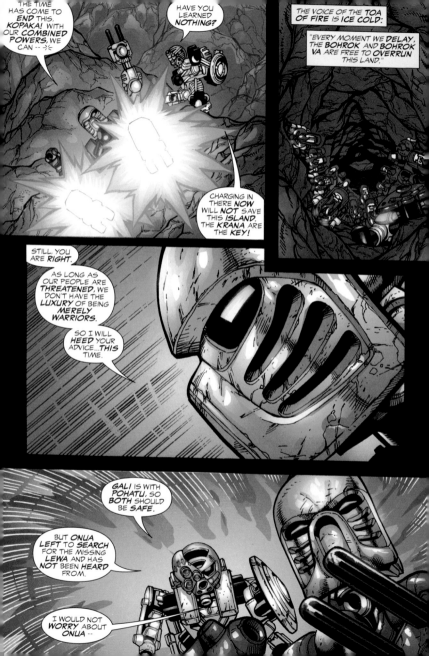

THE TIME HAS COME TO **END** THIS, **KOPAKA!** WITH OUR **COMBINED POWERS,** WE CAN -- ⚡

HAVE YOU LEARNED **NOTHING?**

THE VOICE OF THE **TOA OF FIRE** IS ICE COLD:

"EVERY MOMENT WE DELAY, THE **BOHROK** AND **BOHROK VA** ARE FREE TO OVERRUN THIS LAND."

**CHARGING IN THERE NOW** WILL **NOT** SAVE THIS **ISLAND.** THE **KRANA** ARE THE **KEY!**

STILL, YOU ARE **RIGHT.**

AS LONG AS OUR PEOPLE ARE **THREATENED,** WE DON'T HAVE THE **LUXURY** OF BEING **MERELY WARRIORS.**

SO I WILL **HEED** YOUR ADVICE...**THIS** TIME.

**GALI** IS WITH **POHATU,** SO **BOTH** SHOULD BE **SAFE.**

BUT **ONUA** **LEFT** TO **SEARCH** FOR THE MISSING **LEWA** AND HAS **NOT** BEEN **HEARD** FROM.

I WOULD NOT **WORRY** ABOUT **ONUA** --

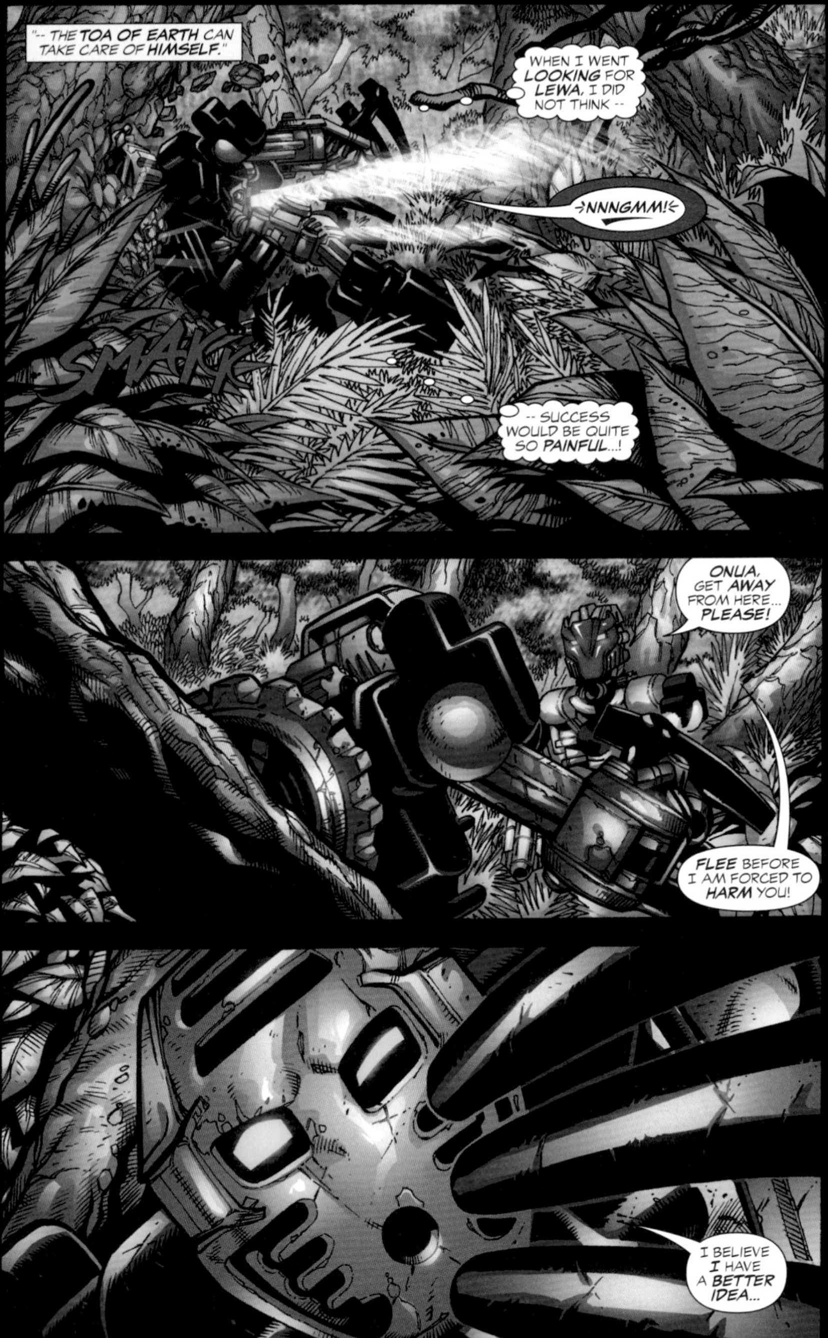
"-- THE TOA OF EARTH CAN TAKE CARE OF HIMSELF."
WHEN I WENT LOOKING FOR LEWA, I DID NOT THINK --
NNNGMM!
SMAKK
-- SUCCESS WOULD BE QUITE SO PAINFUL...!
ONUA, GET AWAY FROM HERE... PLEASE!
FLEE BEFORE I AM FORCED TO HARM YOU!
I BELIEVE I HAVE A BETTER IDEA...

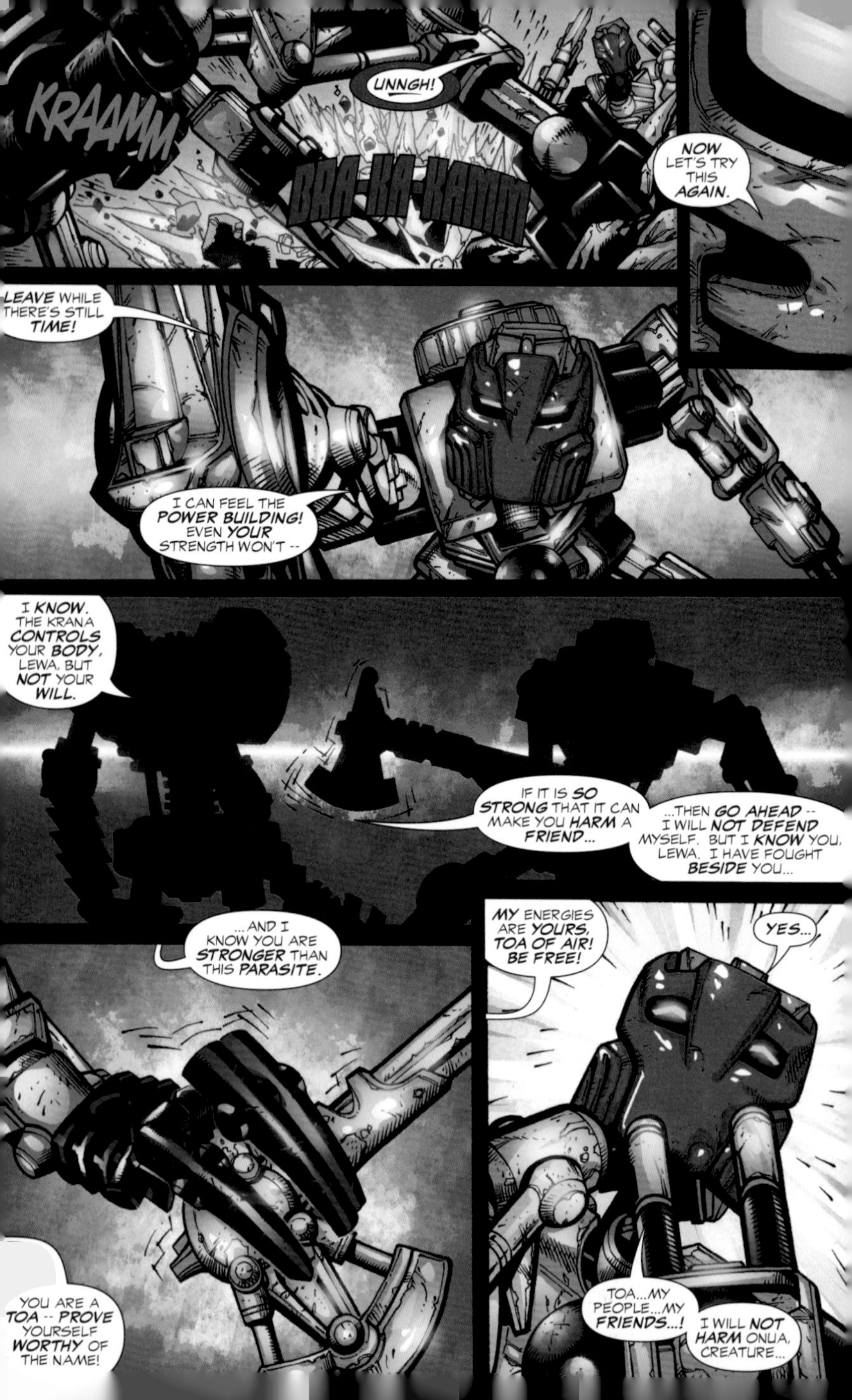
KRAAMM
UNNGH!
BRA-KA-KAMM
NOW LET'S TRY THIS AGAIN.
LEAVE WHILE THERE'S STILL TIME!
I CAN FEEL THE POWER BUILDING! EVEN YOUR STRENGTH WON'T --
I KNOW. THE KRANA CONTROLS YOUR BODY, LEWA, BUT NOT YOUR WILL.
IF IT IS SO STRONG THAT IT CAN MAKE YOU HARM A FRIEND...
...THEN GO AHEAD -- I WILL NOT DEFEND MYSELF. BUT I KNOW YOU, LEWA. I HAVE FOUGHT BESIDE YOU...
...AND I KNOW YOU ARE STRONGER THAN THIS PARASITE.
YOU ARE A TOA -- PROVE YOURSELF WORTHY OF THE NAME!
MY ENERGIES ARE YOURS, TOA OF AIR! BE FREE!
YES...
TOA...MY PEOPLE...MY FRIENDS...!
I WILL NOT HARM ONUA, CREATURE...

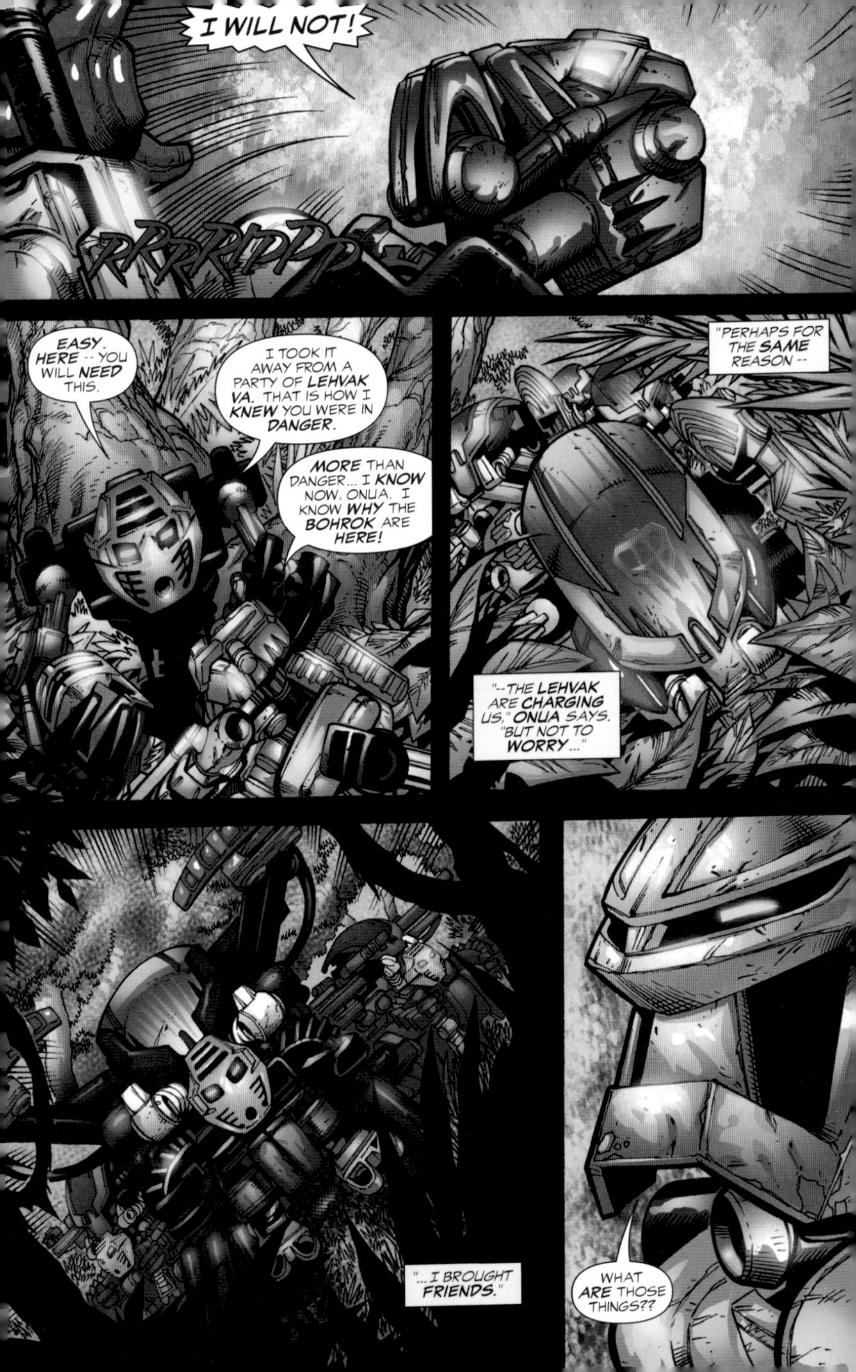
I WILL NOT!
RRRRIPPP
EASY. HERE -- YOU WILL NEED THIS.
I TOOK IT AWAY FROM A PARTY OF LEHVAK VA. THAT IS HOW I KNEW YOU WERE IN DANGER.
MORE THAN DANGER... I KNOW NOW, ONUA. I KNOW WHY THE BOHROK ARE HERE!
"PERHAPS FOR THE SAME REASON --
"--THE LEHVAK ARE CHARGING US," ONUA SAYS. "BUT NOT TO WORRY..."
"...I BROUGHT FRIENDS."
WHAT ARE THOSE THINGS??

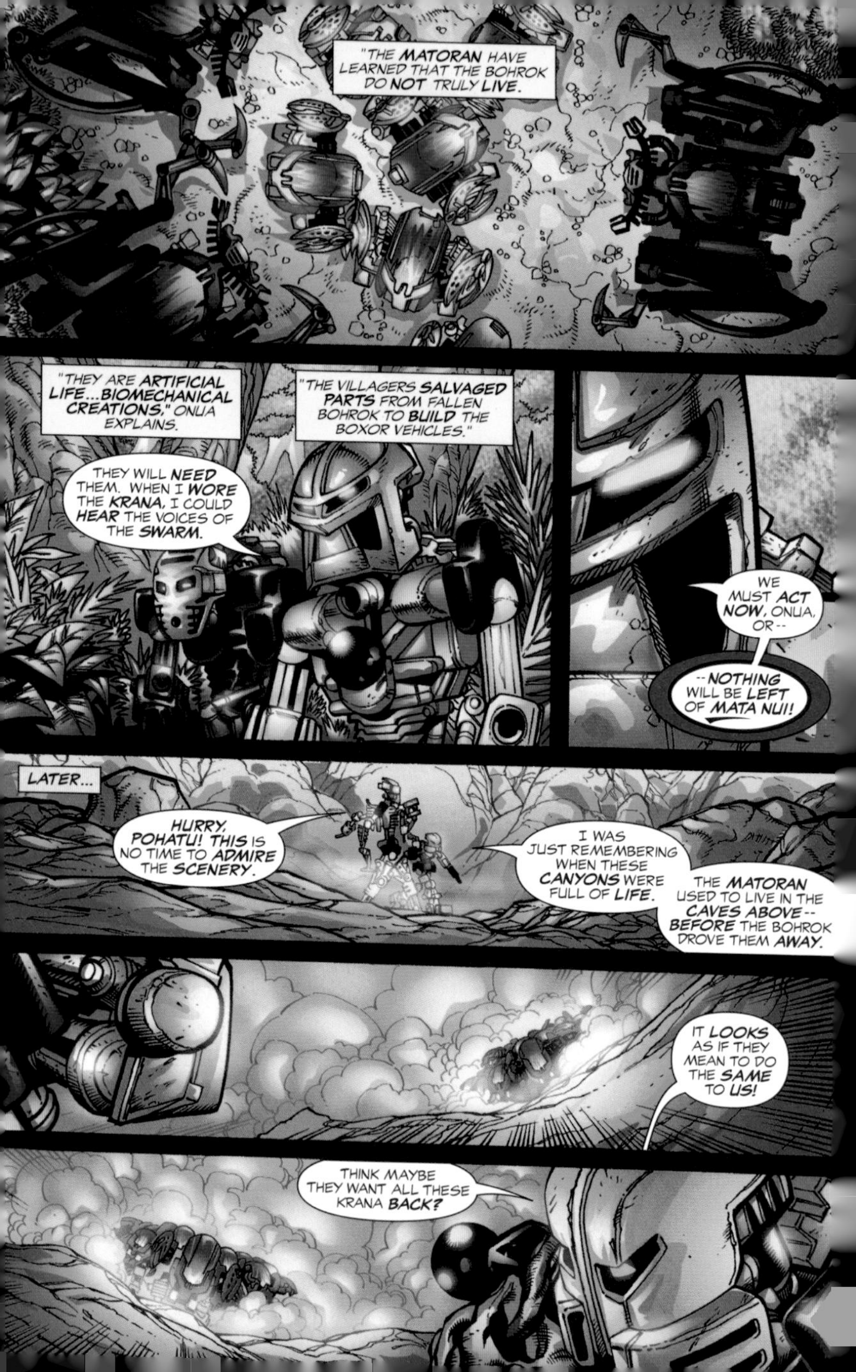
"THE MATORAN HAVE LEARNED THAT THE BOHROK DO NOT TRULY LIVE.
"THEY ARE ARTIFICIAL LIFE...BIOMECHANICAL CREATIONS," ONUA EXPLAINS.
"THE VILLAGERS SALVAGED PARTS FROM FALLEN BOHROK TO BUILD THE BOXOR VEHICLES."
THEY WILL NEED THEM. WHEN I WORE THE KRANA, I COULD HEAR THE VOICES OF THE SWARM.
WE MUST ACT NOW, ONUA, OR --
-- NOTHING WILL BE LEFT OF MATA NUI!
LATER...
HURRY, POHATU! THIS IS NO TIME TO ADMIRE THE SCENERY.
I WAS JUST REMEMBERING WHEN THESE CANYONS WERE FULL OF LIFE.
THE MATORAN USED TO LIVE IN THE CAVES ABOVE -- BEFORE THE BOHROK DROVE THEM AWAY.
IT LOOKS AS IF THEY MEAN TO DO THE SAME TO US!
THINK MAYBE THEY WANT ALL THESE KRANA BACK?

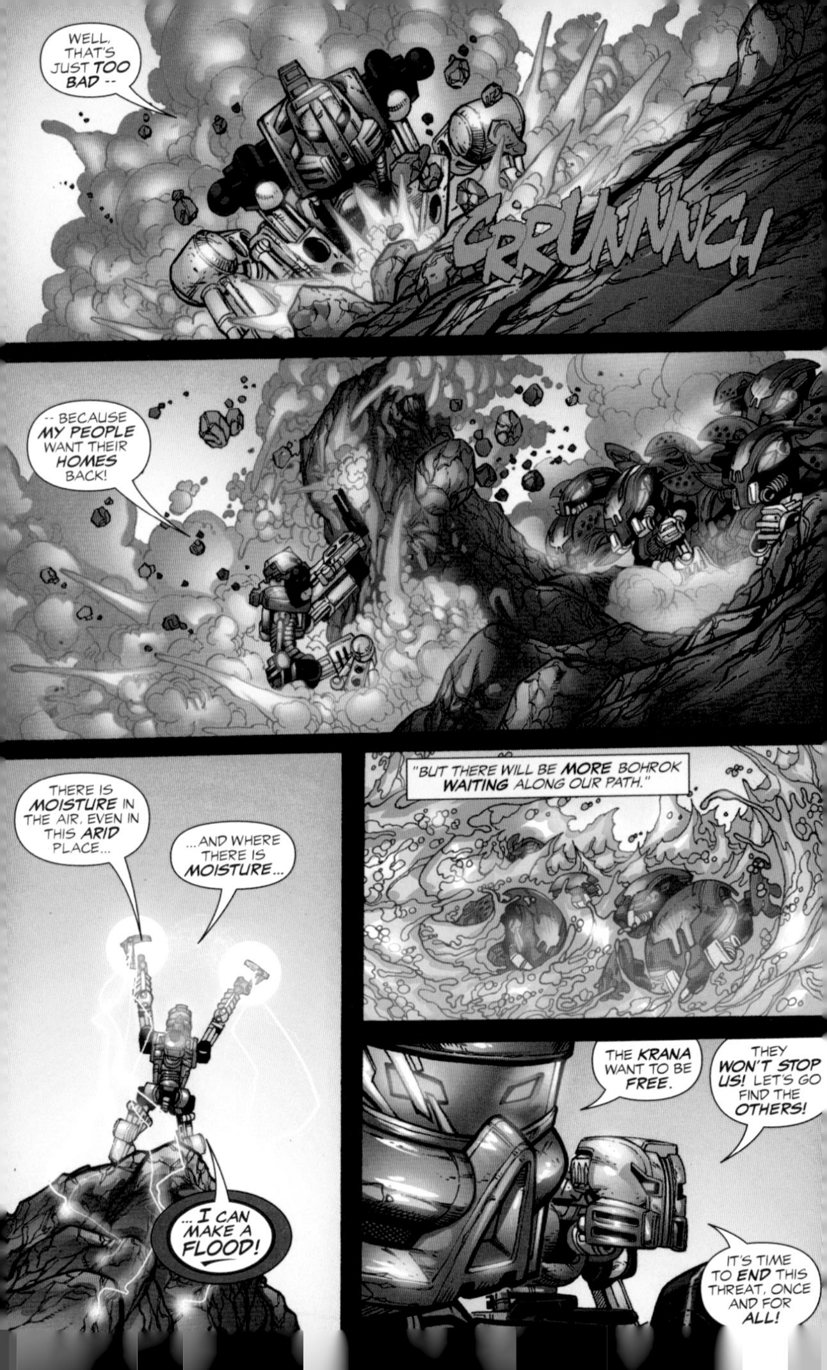
WELL, THAT'S JUST TOO BAD --
CRRUNNNCH
-- BECAUSE MY PEOPLE WANT THEIR HOMES BACK!
THERE IS MOISTURE IN THE AIR, EVEN IN THIS ARID PLACE...
...AND WHERE THERE IS MOISTURE...
...I CAN MAKE A FLOOD!
"BUT THERE WILL BE MORE BOHROK WAITING ALONG OUR PATH."
THE KRANA WANT TO BE FREE.
THEY WON'T STOP US! LET'S GO FIND THE OTHERS!
IT'S TIME TO END THIS THREAT, ONCE AND FOR ALL!

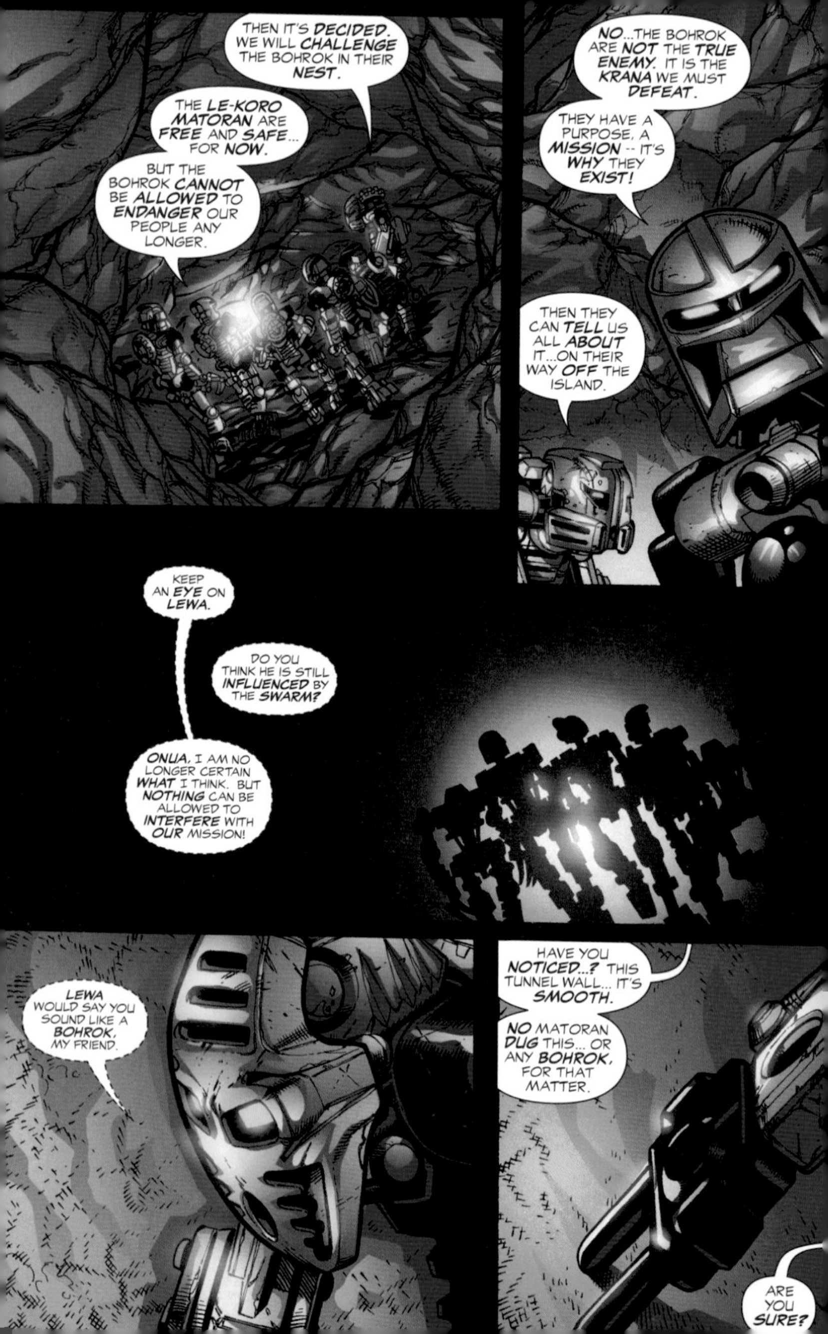
THEN IT'S DECIDED. WE WILL CHALLENGE THE BOHROK IN THEIR NEST.
THE LE-KORO MATORAN ARE FREE AND SAFE... FOR NOW.
BUT THE BOHROK CANNOT BE ALLOWED TO ENDANGER OUR PEOPLE ANY LONGER.
NO...THE BOHROK ARE NOT THE TRUE ENEMY. IT IS THE KRANA WE MUST DEFEAT.
THEY HAVE A PURPOSE, A MISSION -- IT'S WHY THEY EXIST!
THEN THEY CAN TELL US ALL ABOUT IT...ON THEIR WAY OFF THE ISLAND.
KEEP AN EYE ON LEWA.
DO YOU THINK HE IS STILL INFLUENCED BY THE SWARM?
ONUA, I AM NO LONGER CERTAIN WHAT I THINK. BUT NOTHING CAN BE ALLOWED TO INTERFERE WITH OUR MISSION!
LEWA WOULD SAY YOU SOUND LIKE A BOHROK, MY FRIEND.
HAVE YOU NOTICED...? THIS TUNNEL WALL... IT'S SMOOTH.
NO MATORAN DUG THIS... OR ANY BOHROK, FOR THAT MATTER.
ARE YOU SURE?

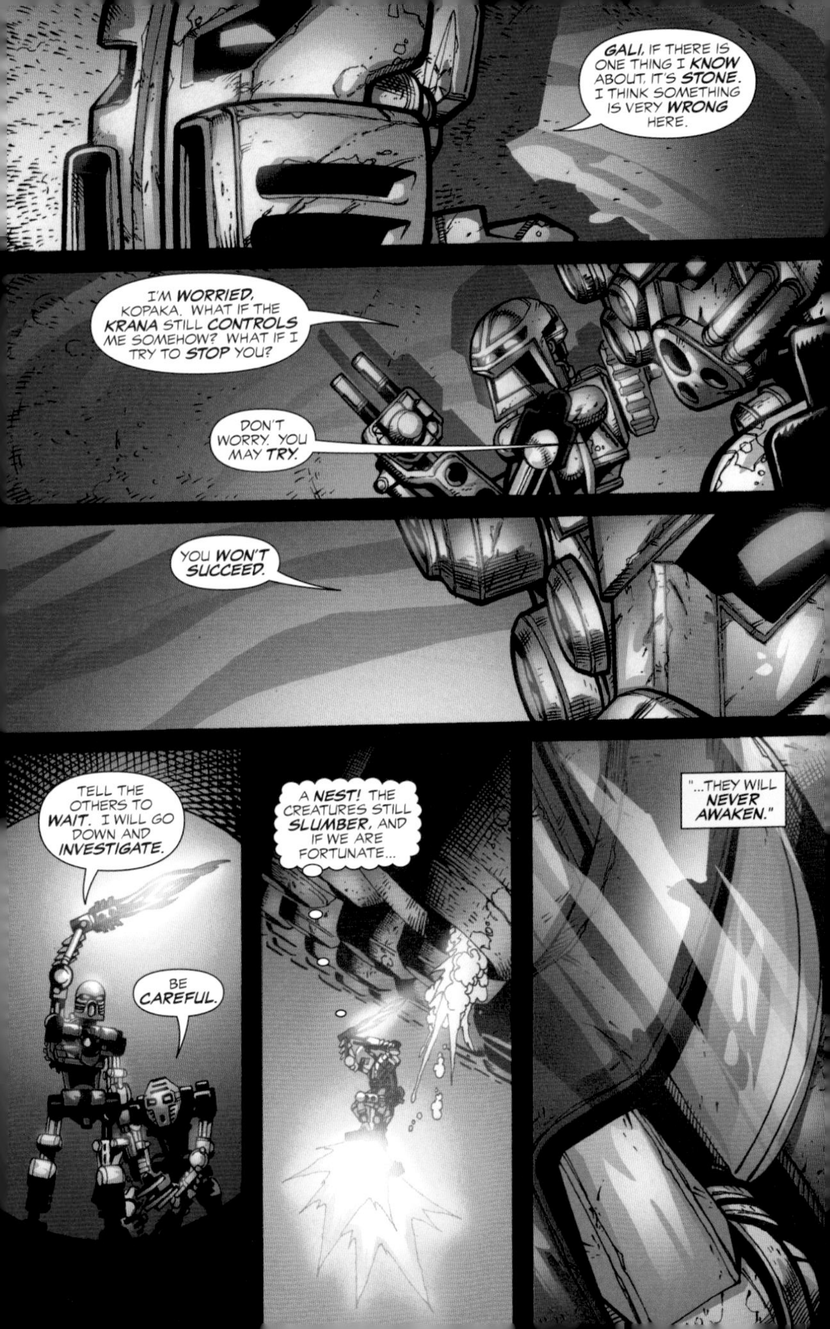
GALI, IF THERE IS ONE THING I KNOW ABOUT, IT'S STONE. I THINK SOMETHING IS VERY WRONG HERE.
I'M WORRIED, KOPAKA. WHAT IF THE KRANA STILL CONTROLS ME SOMEHOW? WHAT IF I TRY TO STOP YOU?
DON'T WORRY. YOU MAY TRY.
YOU WON'T SUCCEED.
TELL THE OTHERS TO WAIT. I WILL GO DOWN AND INVESTIGATE.
BE CAREFUL.
A NEST! THE CREATURES STILL SLUMBER, AND IF WE ARE FORTUNATE...
"...THEY WILL NEVER AWAKEN."

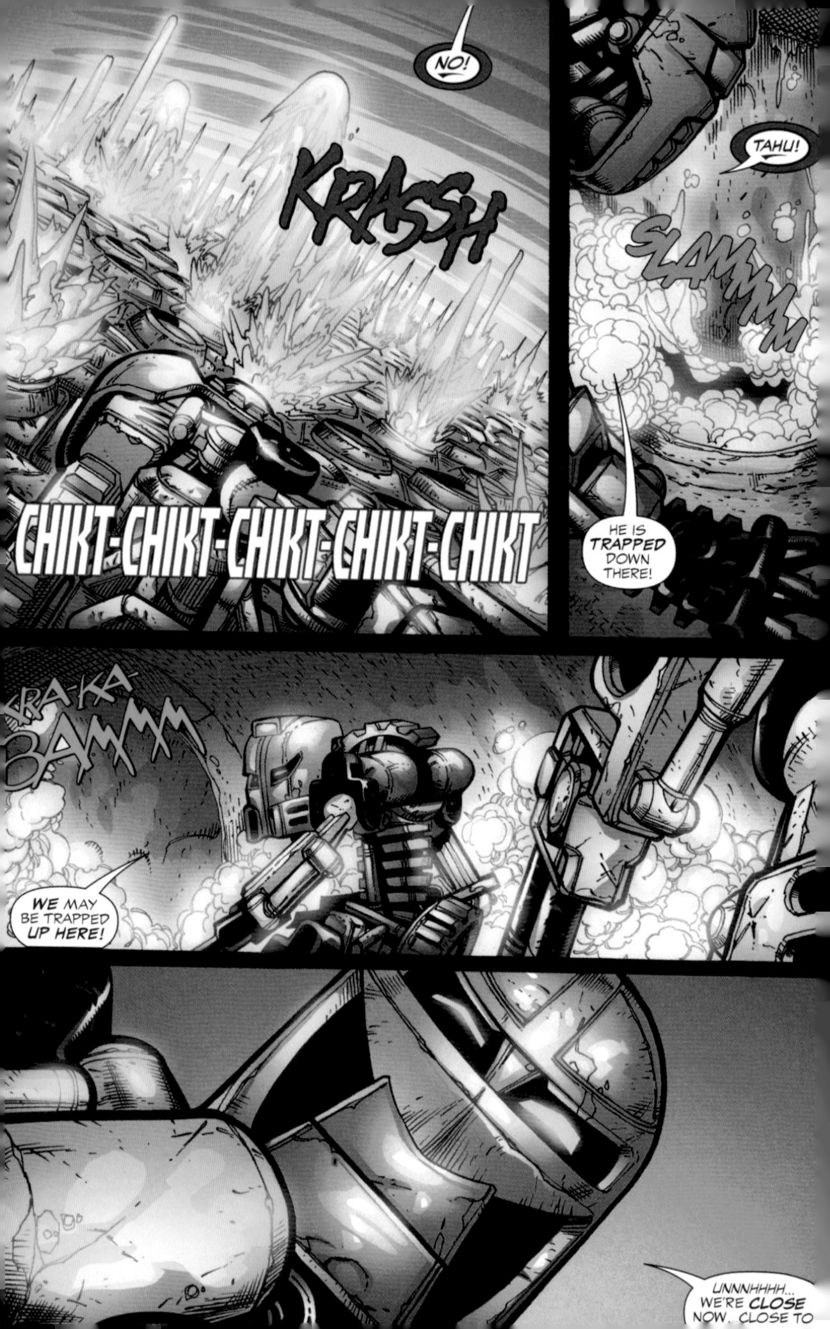
NO!
KRASH
CHIKT-CHIKT-CHIKT-CHIKT-CHIKT
TAHU!
SLAMMMM
HE IS TRAPPED DOWN THERE!
KRA-KA-BAMMM
WE MAY BE TRAPPED UP HERE!
UNNNHHHH... WE'RE CLOSE NOW.. CLOSE TO

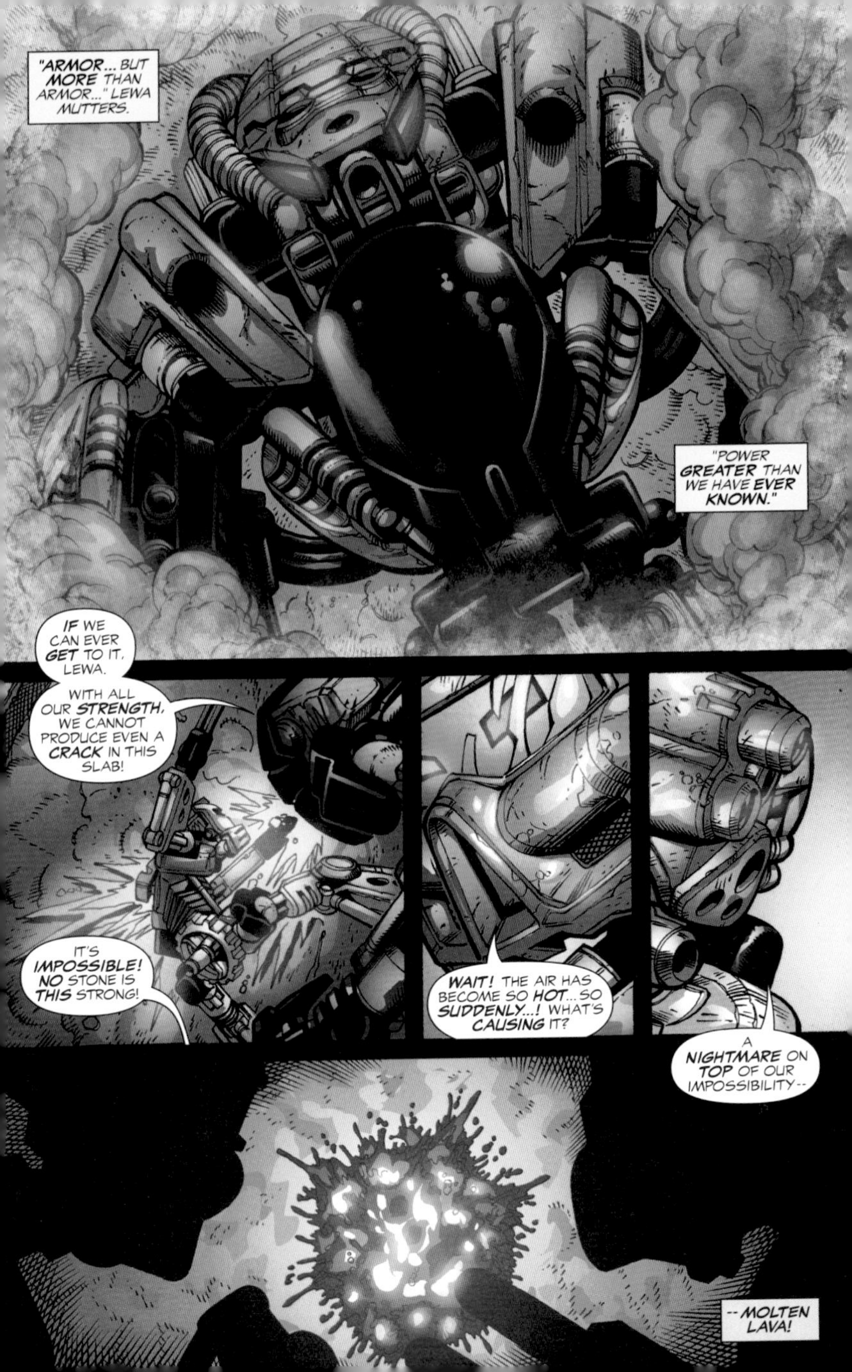
"ARMOR... BUT MORE THAN ARMOR..." LEWA MUTTERS.
"POWER GREATER THAN WE HAVE EVER KNOWN."
IF WE CAN EVER GET TO IT, LEWA.
WITH ALL OUR STRENGTH, WE CANNOT PRODUCE EVEN A CRACK IN THIS SLAB!
IT'S IMPOSSIBLE! NO STONE IS THIS STRONG!
WAIT! THE AIR HAS BECOME SO HOT... SO SUDDENLY...! WHAT'S CAUSING IT?
A NIGHTMARE ON TOP OF OUR IMPOSSIBILITY--
--MOLTEN LAVA!

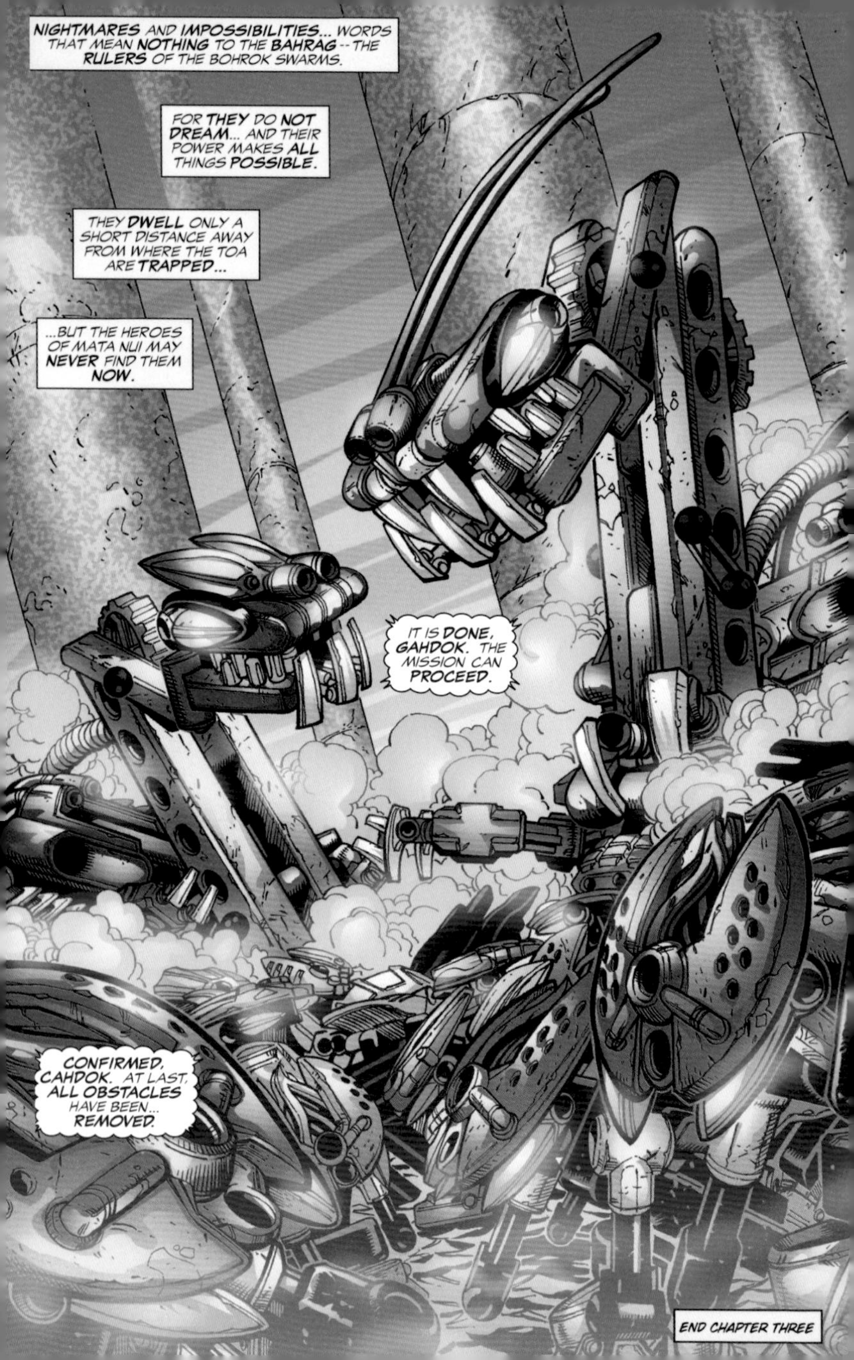
NIGHTMARES AND IMPOSSIBILITIES... WORDS THAT MEAN NOTHING TO THE BAHRAG -- THE RULERS OF THE BOHROK SWARMS.
FOR THEY DO NOT DREAM... AND THEIR POWER MAKES ALL THINGS POSSIBLE.
THEY DWELL ONLY A SHORT DISTANCE AWAY FROM WHERE THE TOA ARE TRAPPED...
...BUT THE HEROES OF MATA NUI MAY NEVER FIND THEM NOW.
IT IS DONE, GAHDOK. THE MISSION CAN PROCEED.
CONFIRMED, CAHDOK. AT LAST, ALL OBSTACLES HAVE BEEN... REMOVED.
END CHAPTER THREE

# THE BOHROK SAGA
# CHAPTER FOUR

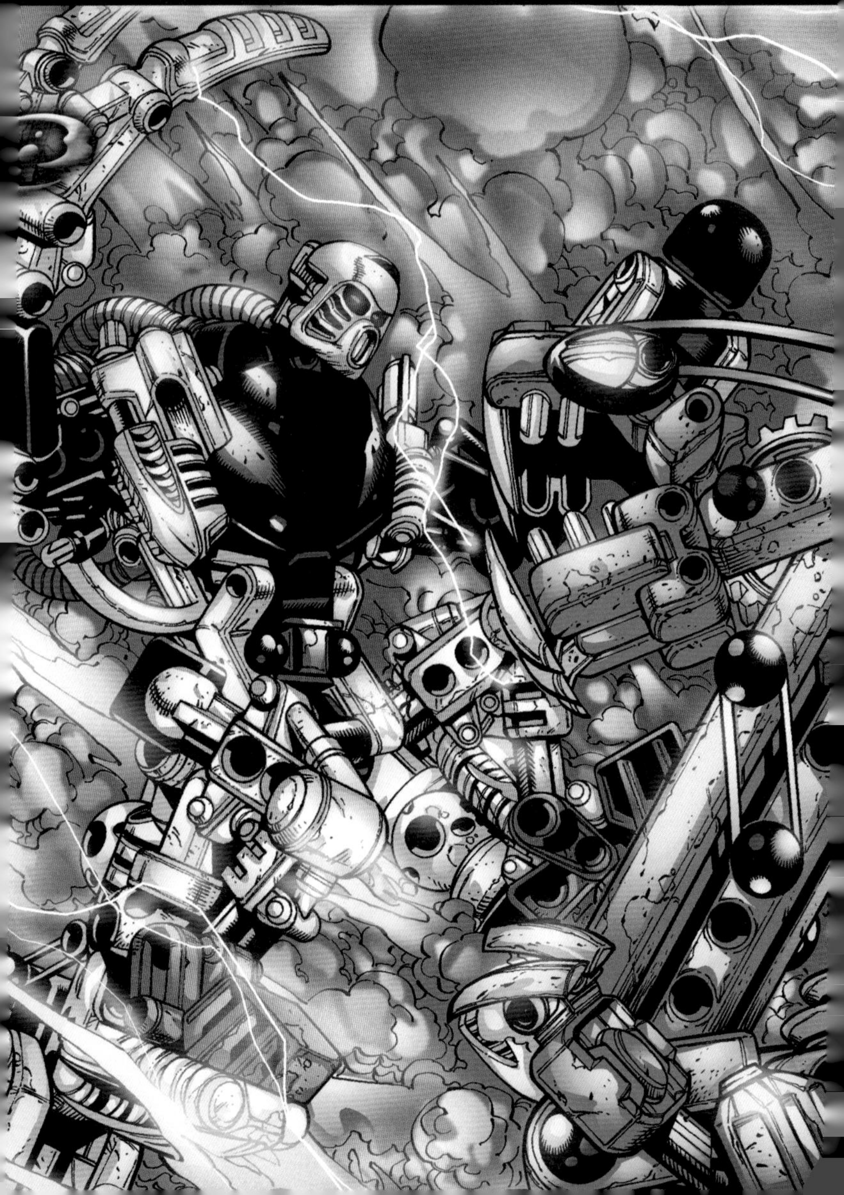

# WHAT LURKS BELOW

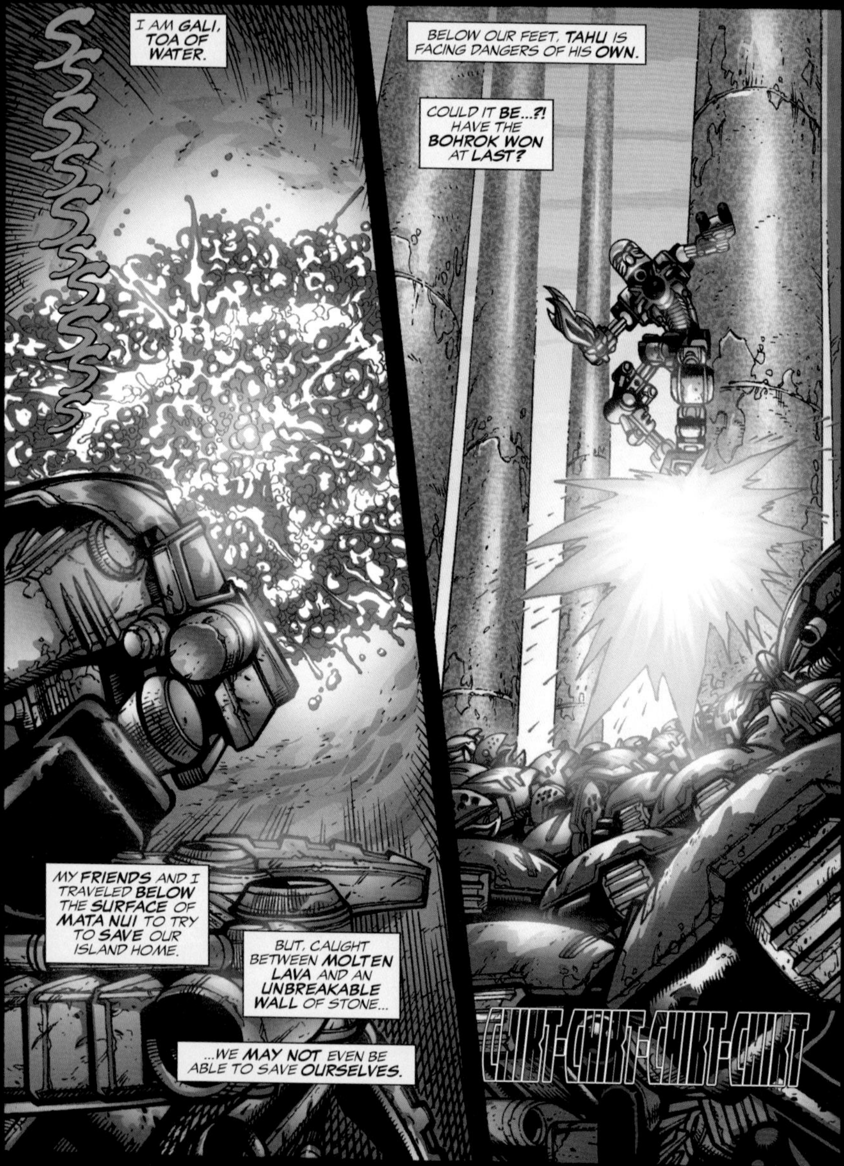
I AM GALI, TOA OF WATER.
MY FRIENDS AND I TRAVELED BELOW THE SURFACE OF MATA NUI TO TRY TO SAVE OUR ISLAND HOME.
BUT, CAUGHT BETWEEN MOLTEN LAVA AND AN UNBREAKABLE WALL OF STONE...
...WE MAY NOT EVEN BE ABLE TO SAVE OURSELVES.
BELOW OUR FEET, TAHU IS FACING DANGERS OF HIS OWN.
COULD IT BE...?! HAVE THE BOHROK WON AT LAST?
CHIKT-CHIKT-CHIKT-CHIKT

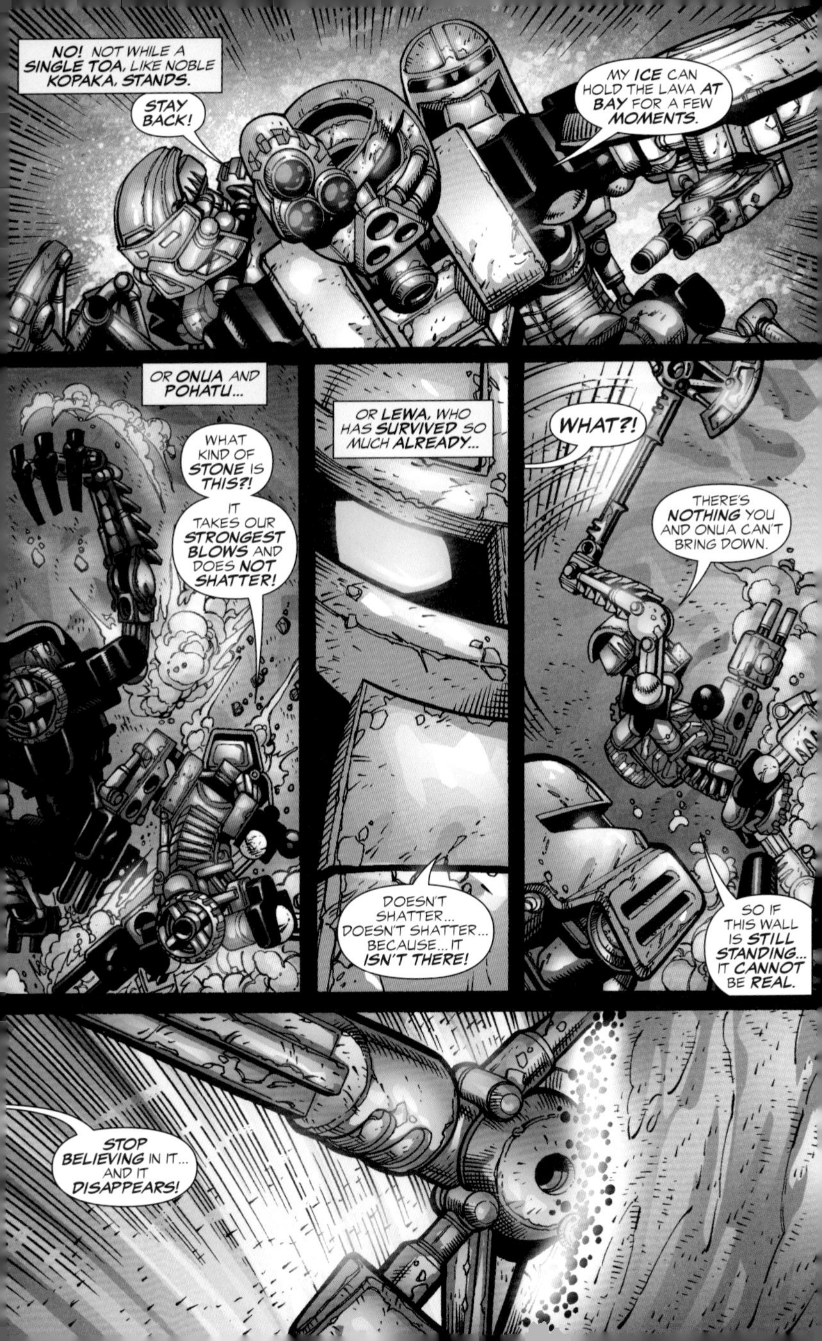
NO! NOT WHILE A SINGLE TOA, LIKE NOBLE KOPAKA, STANDS.
STAY BACK!
MY ICE CAN HOLD THE LAVA AT BAY FOR A FEW MOMENTS.
OR ONUA AND POHATU...
WHAT KIND OF STONE IS THIS?!
IT TAKES OUR STRONGEST BLOWS AND DOES NOT SHATTER!
OR LEWA, WHO HAS SURVIVED SO MUCH ALREADY...
DOESN'T SHATTER... DOESN'T SHATTER... BECAUSE... IT ISN'T THERE!
WHAT?!
THERE'S NOTHING YOU AND ONUA CAN'T BRING DOWN.
SO IF THIS WALL IS STILL STANDING... IT CANNOT BE REAL.
STOP BELIEVING IN IT... AND IT DISAPPEARS!

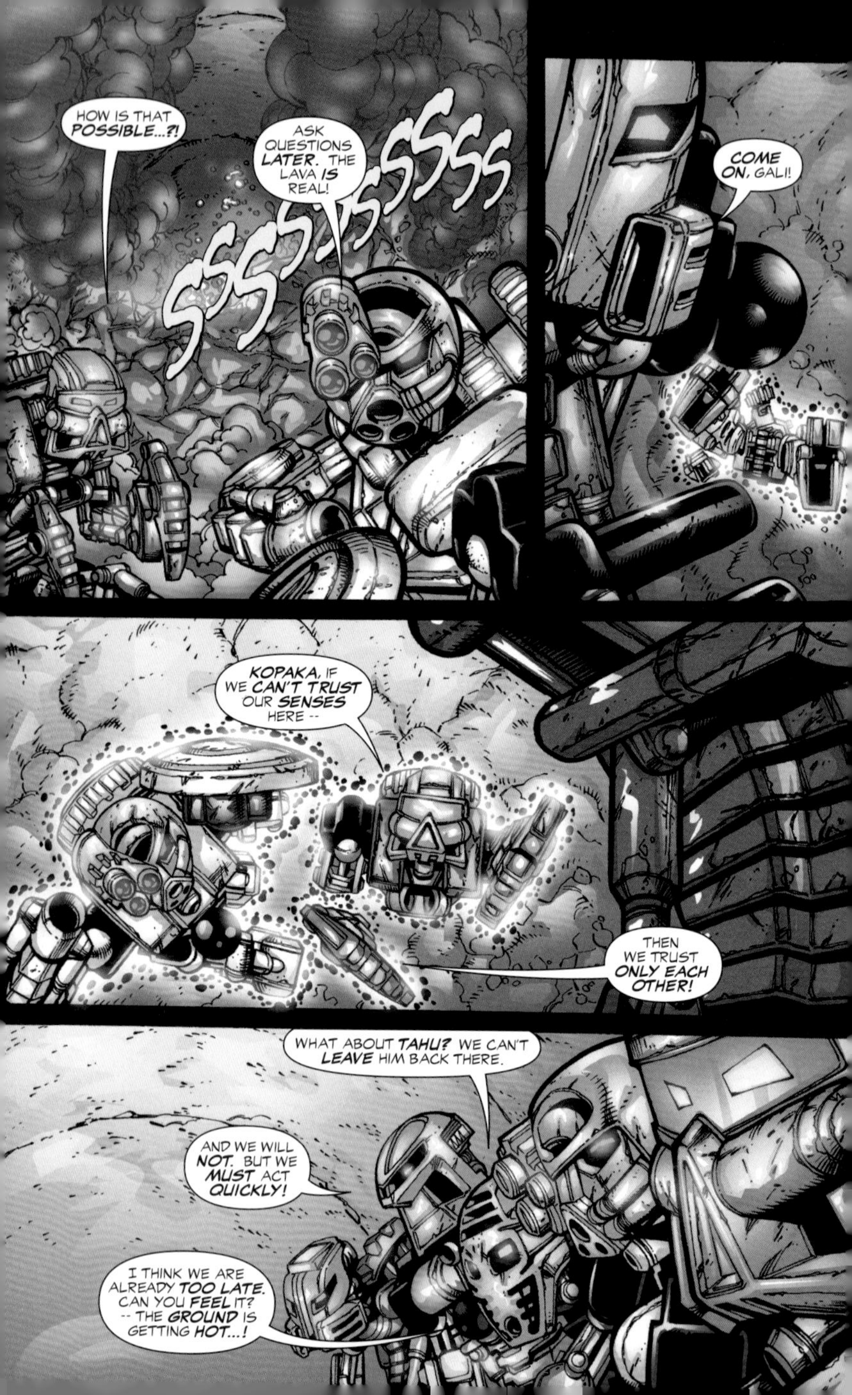
HOW IS THAT POSSIBLE...?!
ASK QUESTIONS LATER. THE LAVA IS REAL!
SSSSSSSSSS
COME ON, GALI!
KOPAKA, IF WE CAN'T TRUST OUR SENSES HERE --
THEN WE TRUST ONLY EACH OTHER!
WHAT ABOUT TAHU? WE CAN'T LEAVE HIM BACK THERE.
AND WE WILL NOT. BUT WE MUST ACT QUICKLY!
I THINK WE ARE ALREADY TOO LATE. CAN YOU FEEL IT? -- THE GROUND IS GETTING HOT...!

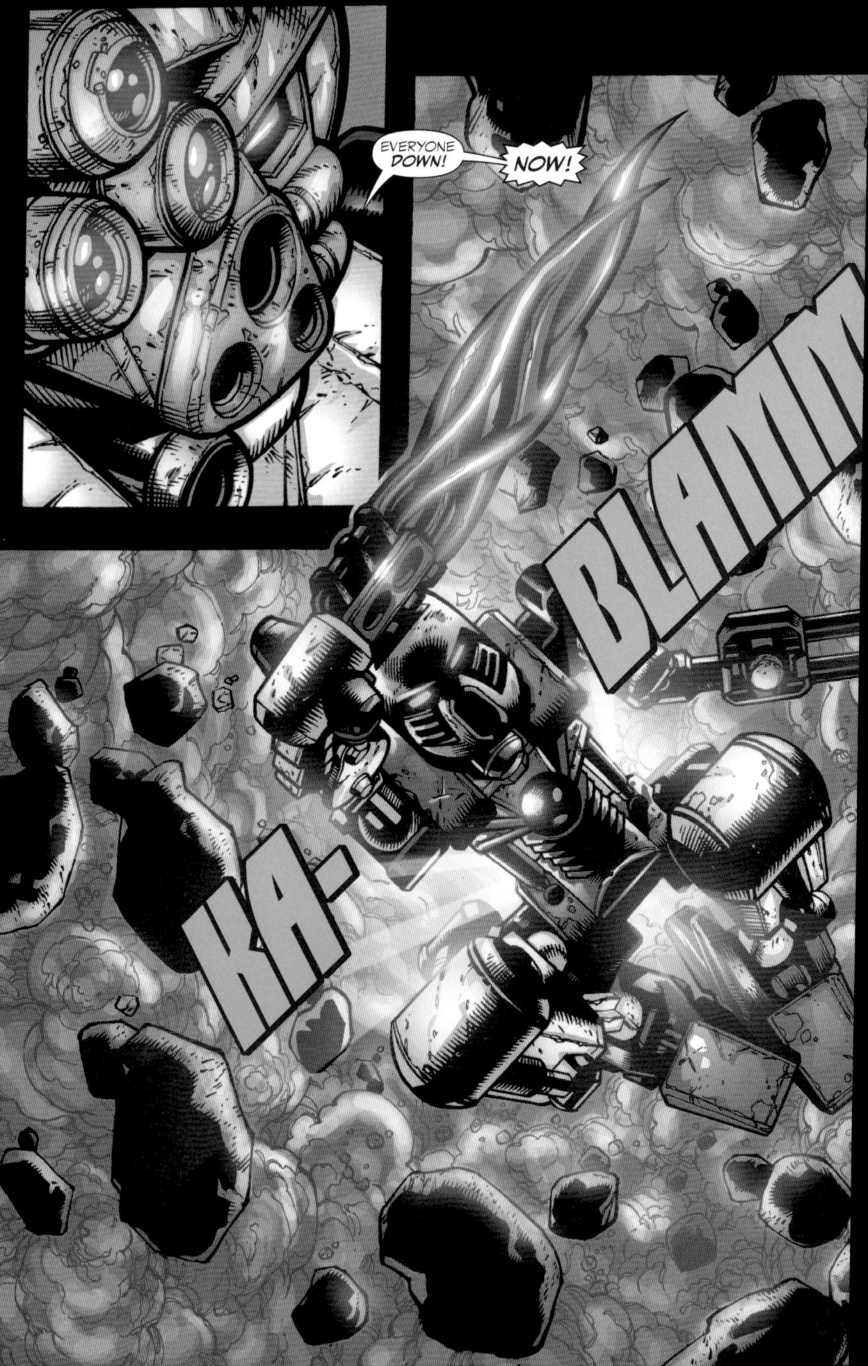
EVERYONE DOWN!
NOW!
KA-
BLAMM

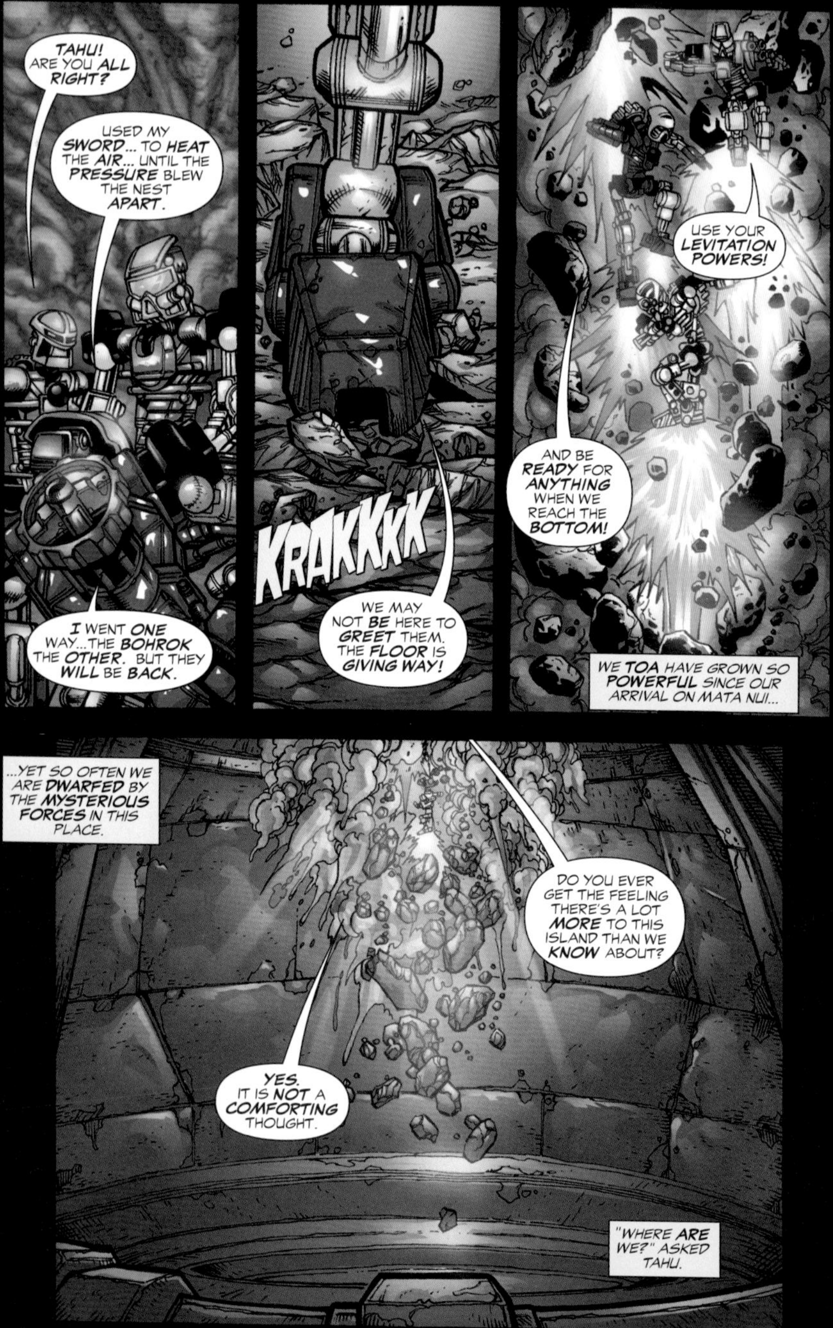
TAHU! ARE YOU ALL RIGHT?
USED MY SWORD... TO HEAT THE AIR... UNTIL THE PRESSURE BLEW THE NEST APART.
I WENT ONE WAY...THE BOHROK THE OTHER. BUT THEY WILL BE BACK.
KRAKKKK
WE MAY NOT BE HERE TO GREET THEM. THE FLOOR IS GIVING WAY!
USE YOUR LEVITATION POWERS!
AND BE READY FOR ANYTHING WHEN WE REACH THE BOTTOM!
WE TOA HAVE GROWN SO POWERFUL SINCE OUR ARRIVAL ON MATA NUI...
...YET SO OFTEN WE ARE DWARFED BY THE MYSTERIOUS FORCES IN THIS PLACE.
DO YOU EVER GET THE FEELING THERE'S A LOT MORE TO THIS ISLAND THAN WE KNOW ABOUT?
YES. IT IS NOT A COMFORTING THOUGHT.
"WHERE ARE WE?" ASKED TAHU.

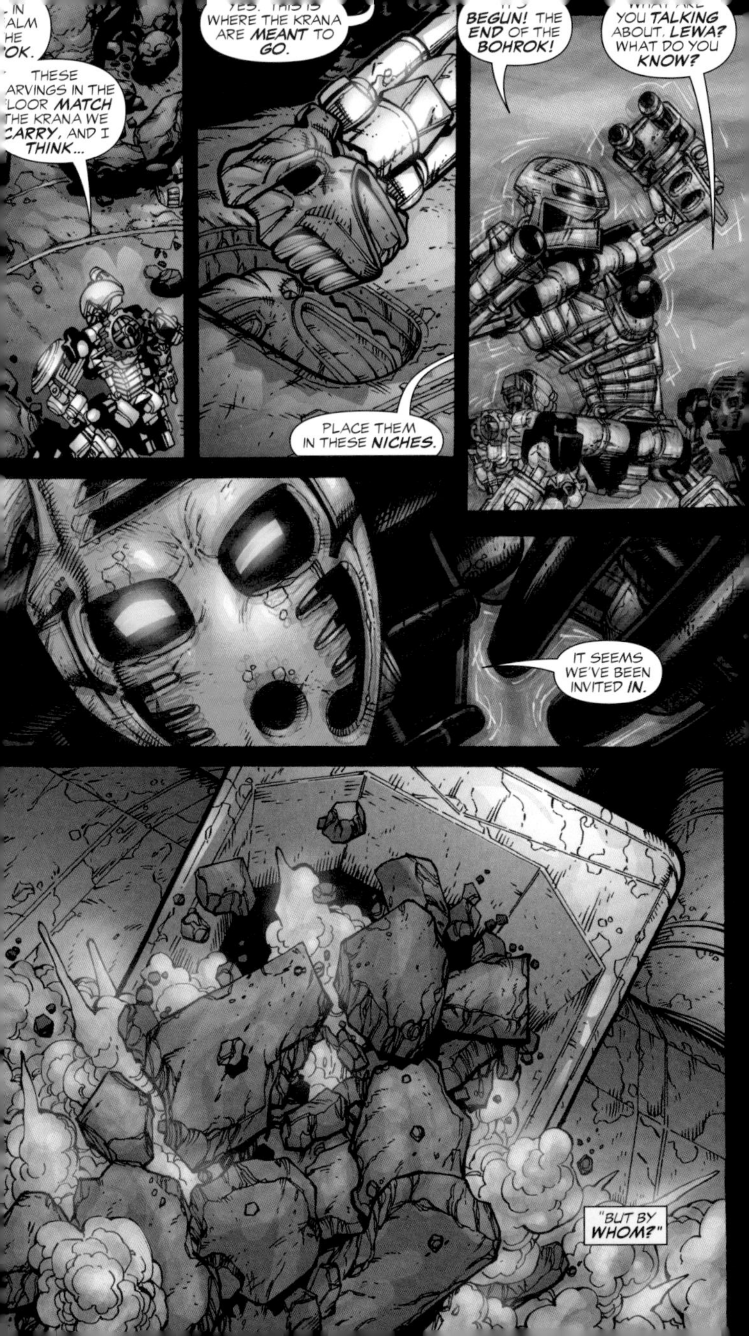
THESE ARVINGS IN THE LOOR MATCH THE KRANA WE CARRY, AND I THINK...
YES. THIS IS WHERE THE KRANA ARE MEANT TO GO.
PLACE THEM IN THESE NICHES.
BEGUN! THE END OF THE BOHROK!
YOU TALKING ABOUT, LEWA? WHAT DO YOU KNOW?
IT SEEMS WE'VE BEEN INVITED IN.
"BUT BY WHOM?"

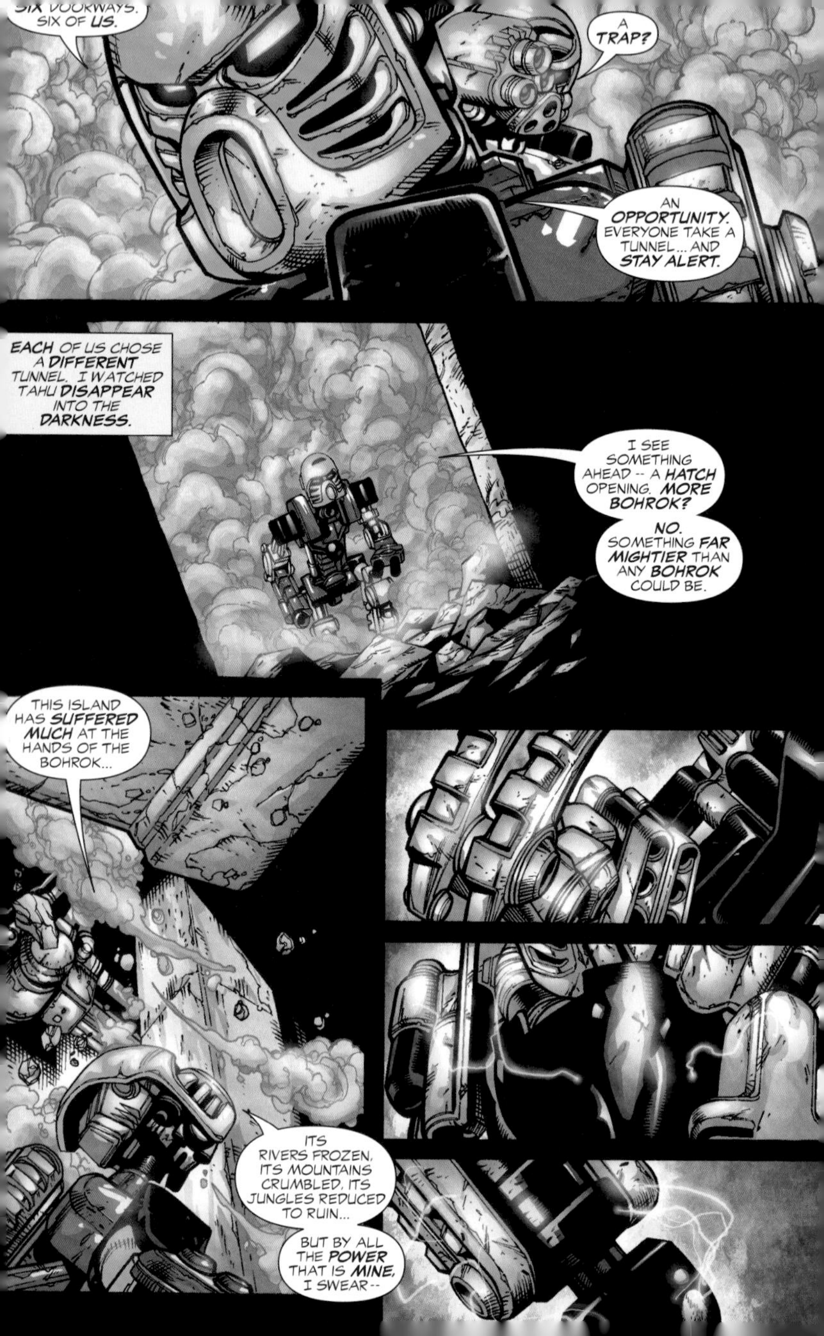
SIX DOORWAYS. SIX OF US.
A TRAP?
AN OPPORTUNITY. EVERYONE TAKE A TUNNEL... AND STAY ALERT.
EACH OF US CHOSE A DIFFERENT TUNNEL. I WATCHED TAHU DISAPPEAR INTO THE DARKNESS.
I SEE SOMETHING AHEAD -- A HATCH OPENING. MORE BOHROK?
NO. SOMETHING FAR MIGHTIER THAN ANY BOHROK COULD BE.
THIS ISLAND HAS SUFFERED MUCH AT THE HANDS OF THE BOHROK...
ITS RIVERS FROZEN, ITS MOUNTAINS CRUMBLED, ITS JUNGLES REDUCED TO RUIN...
BUT BY ALL THE POWER THAT IS MINE, I SWEAR --

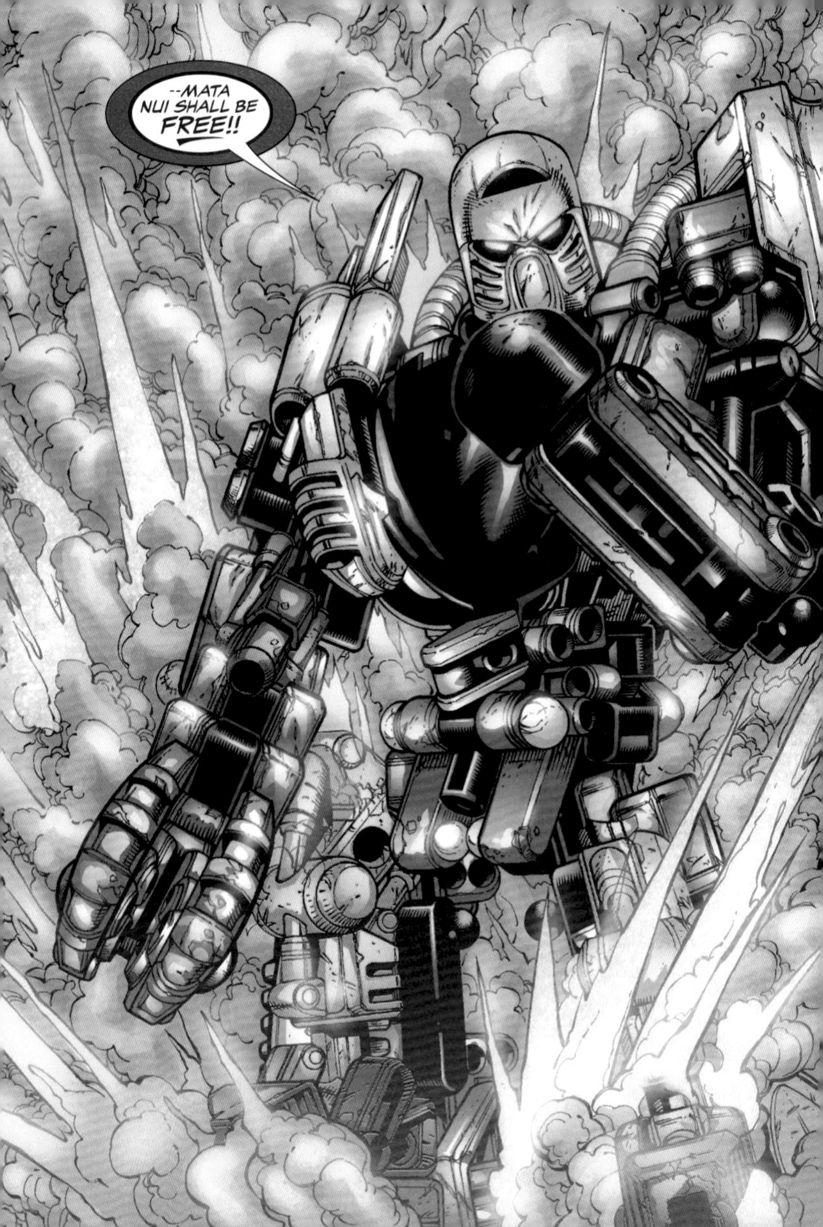
--MATA NUI SHALL BE FREE!!

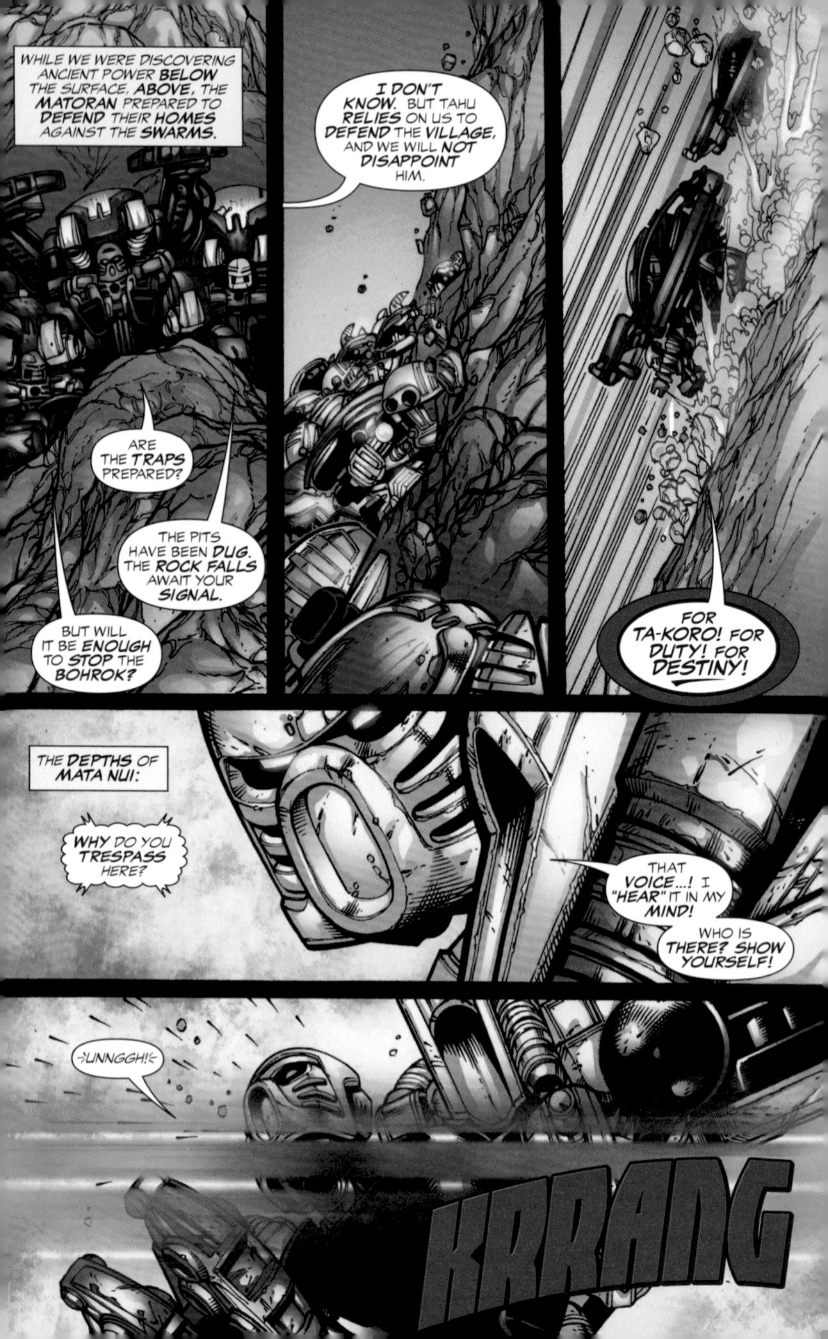
WHILE WE WERE DISCOVERING ANCIENT POWER BELOW THE SURFACE, ABOVE, THE MATORAN PREPARED TO DEFEND THEIR HOMES AGAINST THE SWARMS.
ARE THE TRAPS PREPARED?
THE PITS HAVE BEEN DUG. THE ROCK FALLS AWAIT YOUR SIGNAL.
BUT WILL IT BE ENOUGH TO STOP THE BOHROK?
I DON'T KNOW. BUT TAHU RELIES ON US TO DEFEND THE VILLAGE, AND WE WILL NOT DISAPPOINT HIM.
FOR TA-KORO! FOR DUTY! FOR DESTINY!
THE DEPTHS OF MATA NUI:
WHY DO YOU TRESPASS HERE?
THAT VOICE...! I "HEAR" IT IN MY MIND!
WHO IS THERE? SHOW YOURSELF!
UNNGGH!
KRRANG

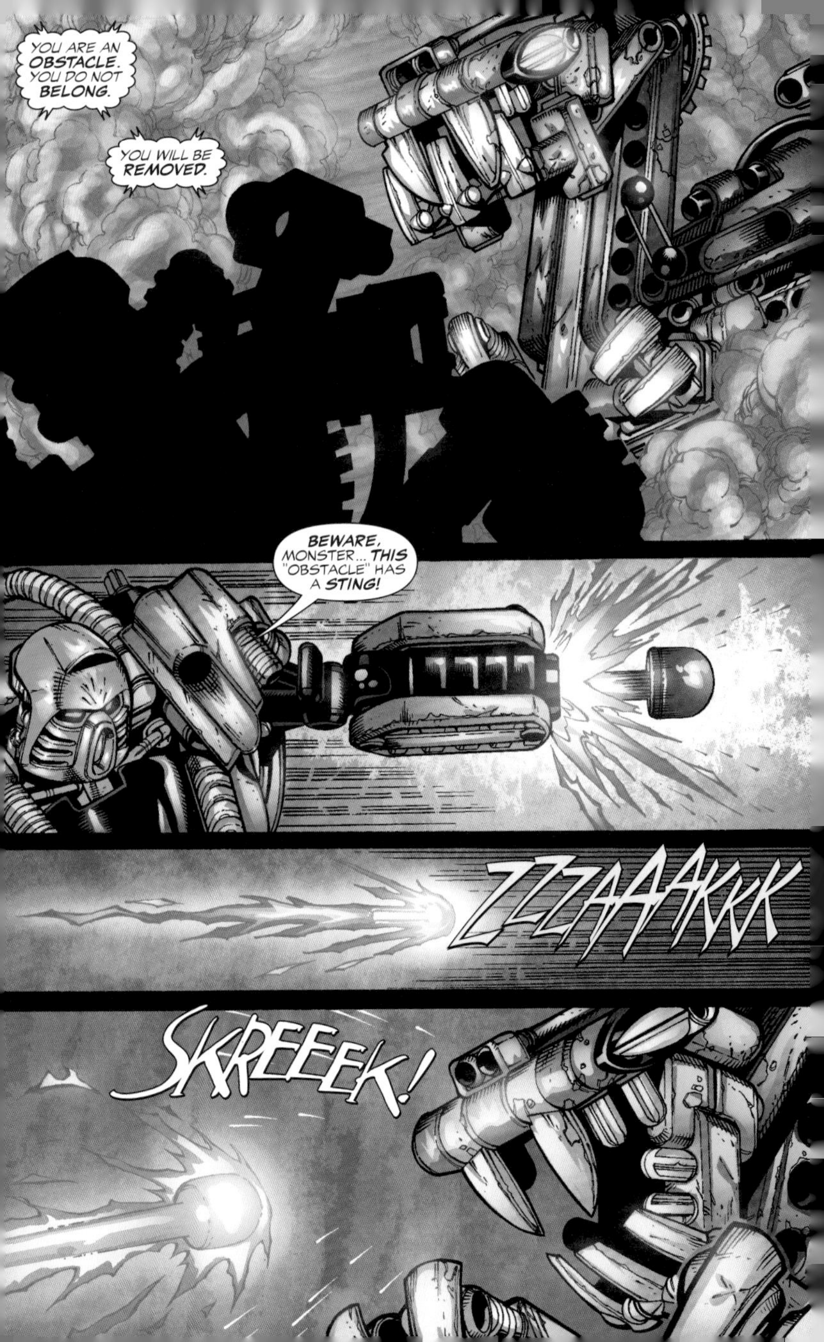
YOU ARE AN OBSTACLE. YOU DO NOT BELONG.
YOU WILL BE REMOVED.
BEWARE, MONSTER... THIS "OBSTACLE" HAS A STING!
ZZZAAAKKK
SKREEEK!

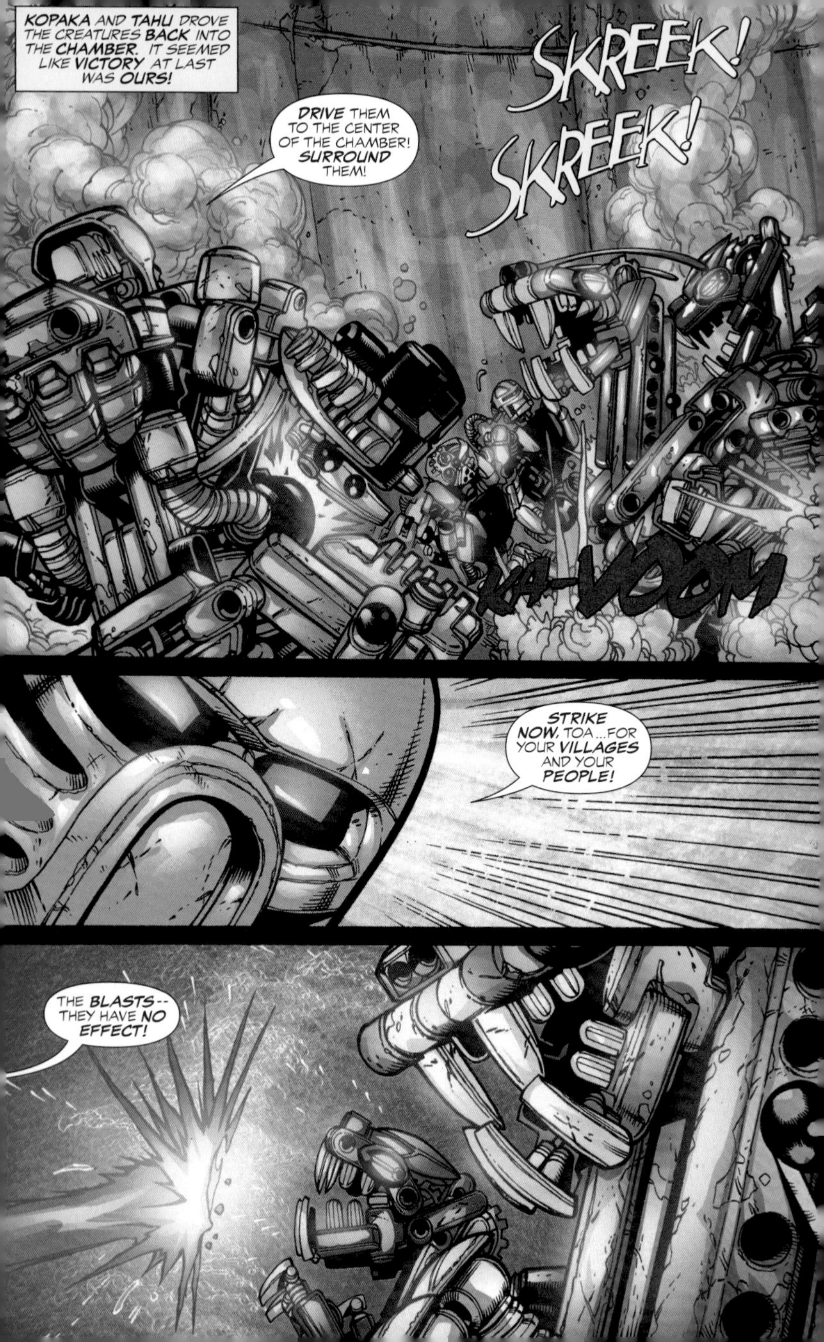
KOPAKA AND TAHU DROVE THE CREATURES BACK INTO THE CHAMBER. IT SEEMED LIKE VICTORY AT LAST WAS OURS!
SKREEK! SKREEK!
DRIVE THEM TO THE CENTER OF THE CHAMBER! SURROUND THEM!
KA-VOOM
STRIKE NOW, TOA...FOR YOUR VILLAGES AND YOUR PEOPLE!
THE BLASTS-- THEY HAVE NO EFFECT!

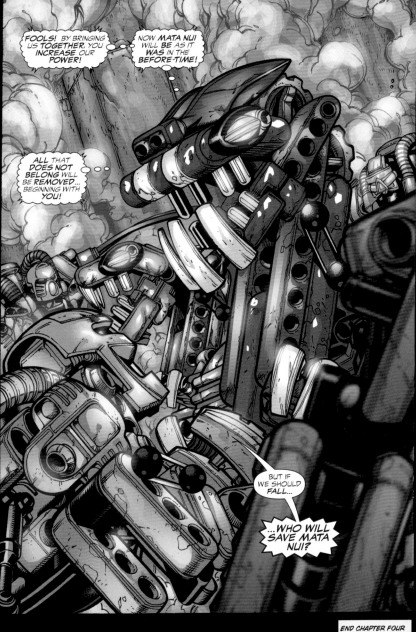

FOOLS! BY BRINGING US TOGETHER, YOU INCREASE OUR POWER!

NOW MATA NUI WILL BE AS IT WAS IN THE BEFORE-TIME!

ALL THAT DOES NOT BELONG WILL BE REMOVED... BEGINNING WITH YOU!

BUT IF WE SHOULD FALL...

...WHO WILL SAVE MATA NUI?

**END CHAPTER FOUR**

# THE BOHROK SAGA
# CHAPTER FOUR

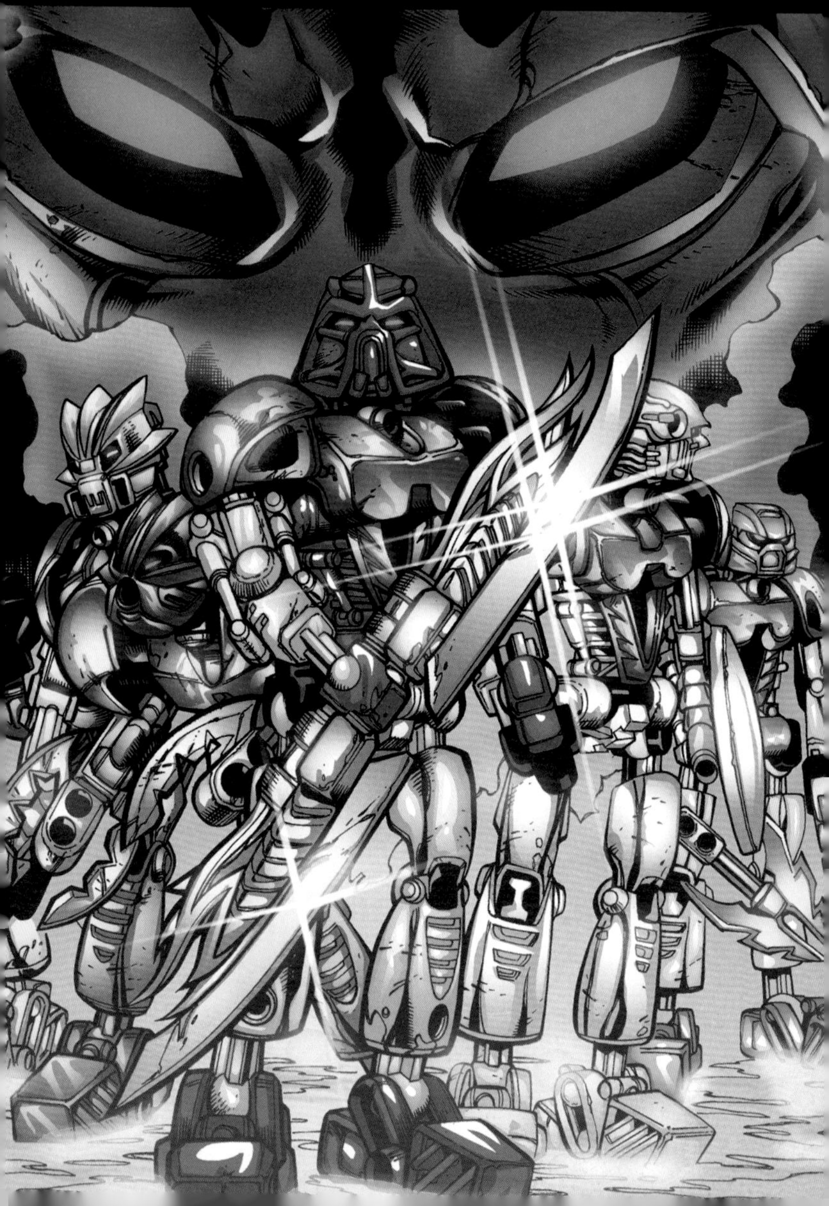

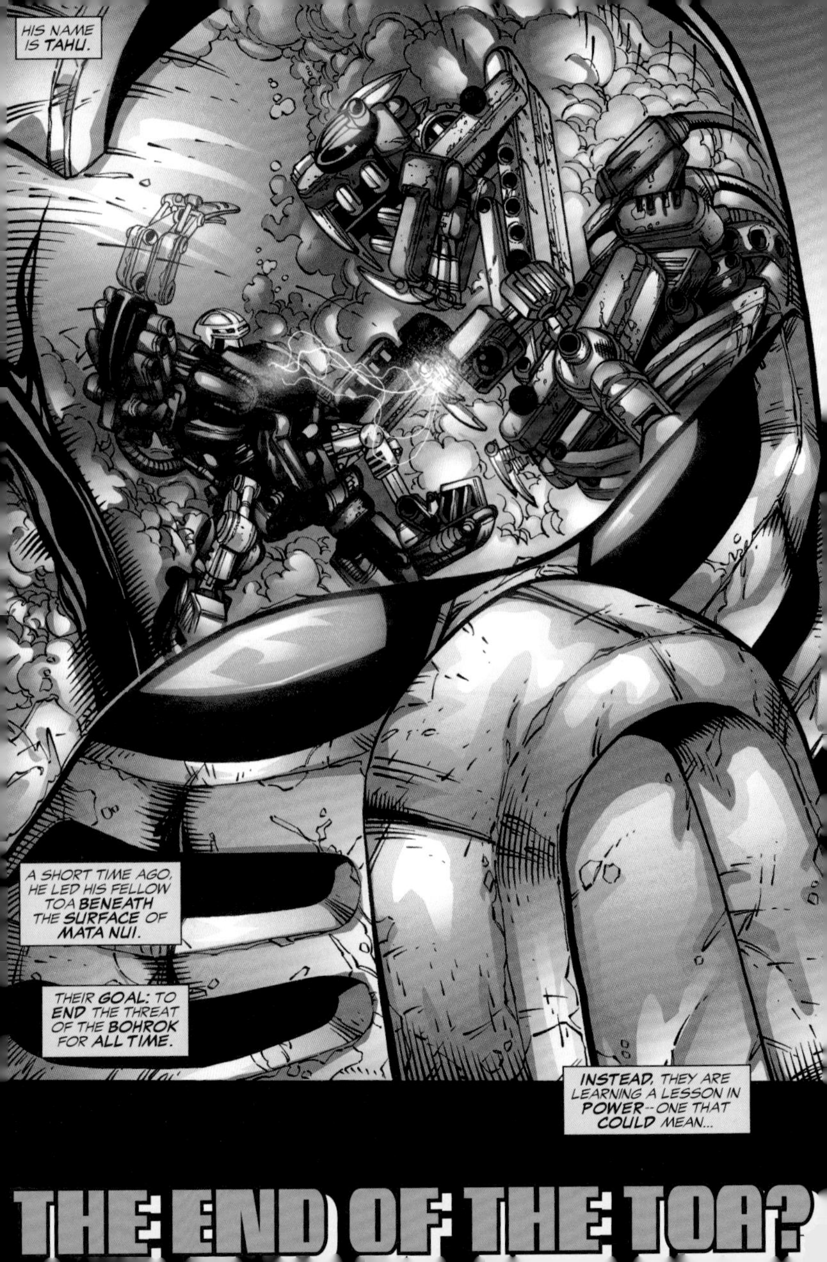
HIS NAME IS TAHU.
A SHORT TIME AGO, HE LED HIS FELLOW TOA BENEATH THE SURFACE OF MATA NUI.
THEIR GOAL: TO END THE THREAT OF THE BOHROK FOR ALL TIME.
INSTEAD, THEY ARE LEARNING A LESSON IN POWER--ONE THAT COULD MEAN...
THE END OF THE TOA?

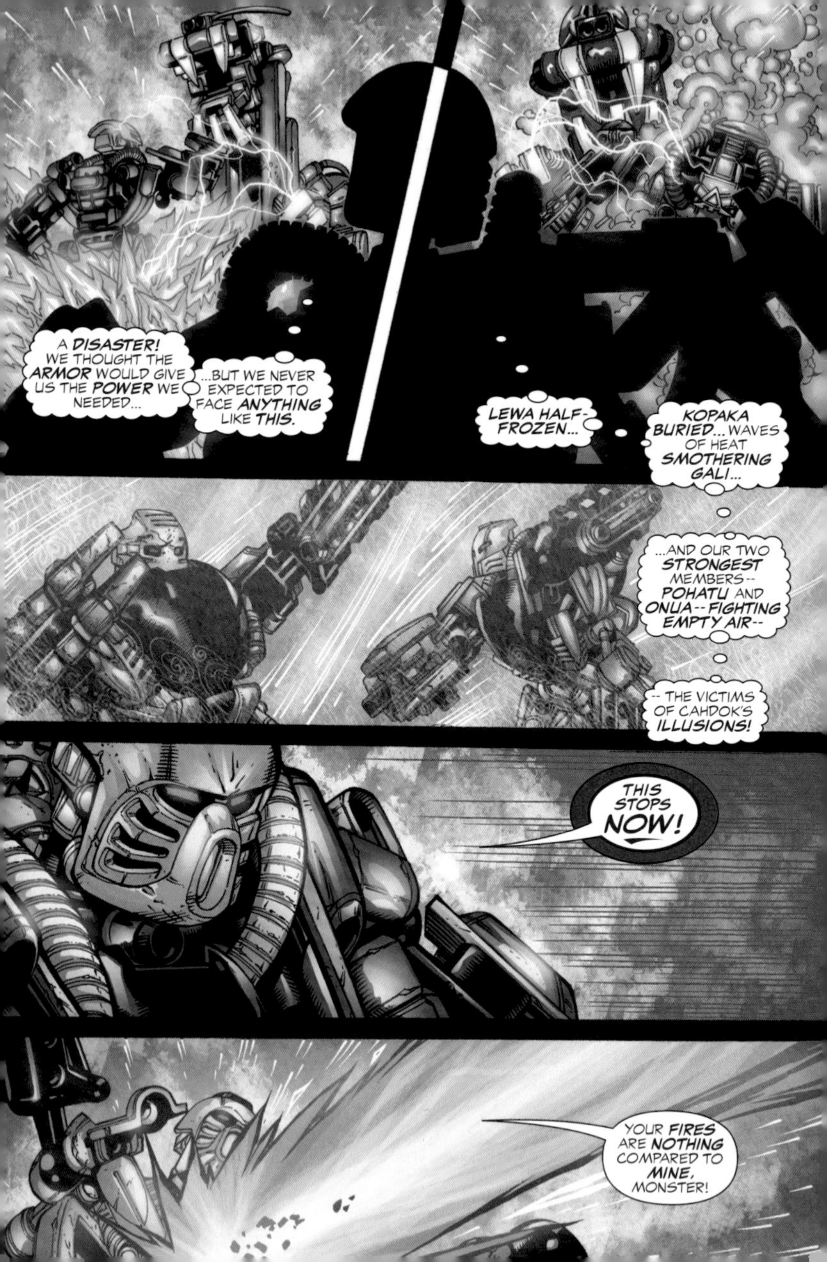
A DISASTER! WE THOUGHT THE ARMOR WOULD GIVE US THE POWER WE NEEDED...
...BUT WE NEVER EXPECTED TO FACE ANYTHING LIKE THIS.
LEWA HALF-FROZEN...
KOPAKA BURIED... WAVES OF HEAT SMOTHERING GALI...
...AND OUR TWO STRONGEST MEMBERS-- POHATU AND ONUA-- FIGHTING EMPTY AIR--
-- THE VICTIMS OF CAHDOK'S ILLUSIONS!
THIS STOPS NOW!
YOUR FIRES ARE NOTHING COMPARED TO MINE, MONSTER!

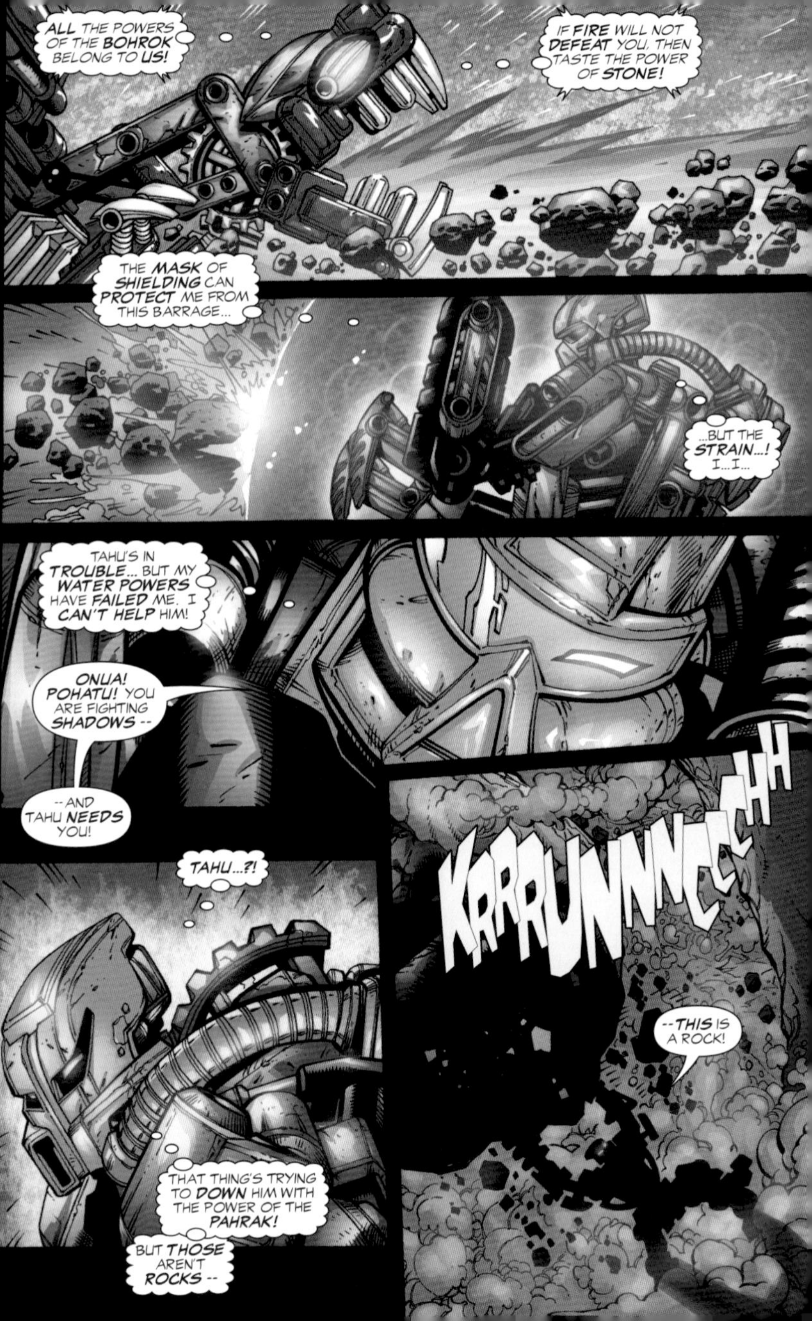
ALL THE POWERS OF THE BOHROK BELONG TO US!
IF FIRE WILL NOT DEFEAT YOU, THEN TASTE THE POWER OF STONE!
THE MASK OF SHIELDING CAN PROTECT ME FROM THIS BARRAGE...
...BUT THE STRAIN...! I...I...
TAHU'S IN TROUBLE... BUT MY WATER POWERS HAVE FAILED ME. I CAN'T HELP HIM!
ONUA! POHATU! YOU ARE FIGHTING SHADOWS --
-- AND TAHU NEEDS YOU!
TAHU...?!
THAT THING'S TRYING TO DOWN HIM WITH THE POWER OF THE PAHRAK!
BUT THOSE AREN'T ROCKS --
KRRRUNNNCCHH
-- THIS IS A ROCK!

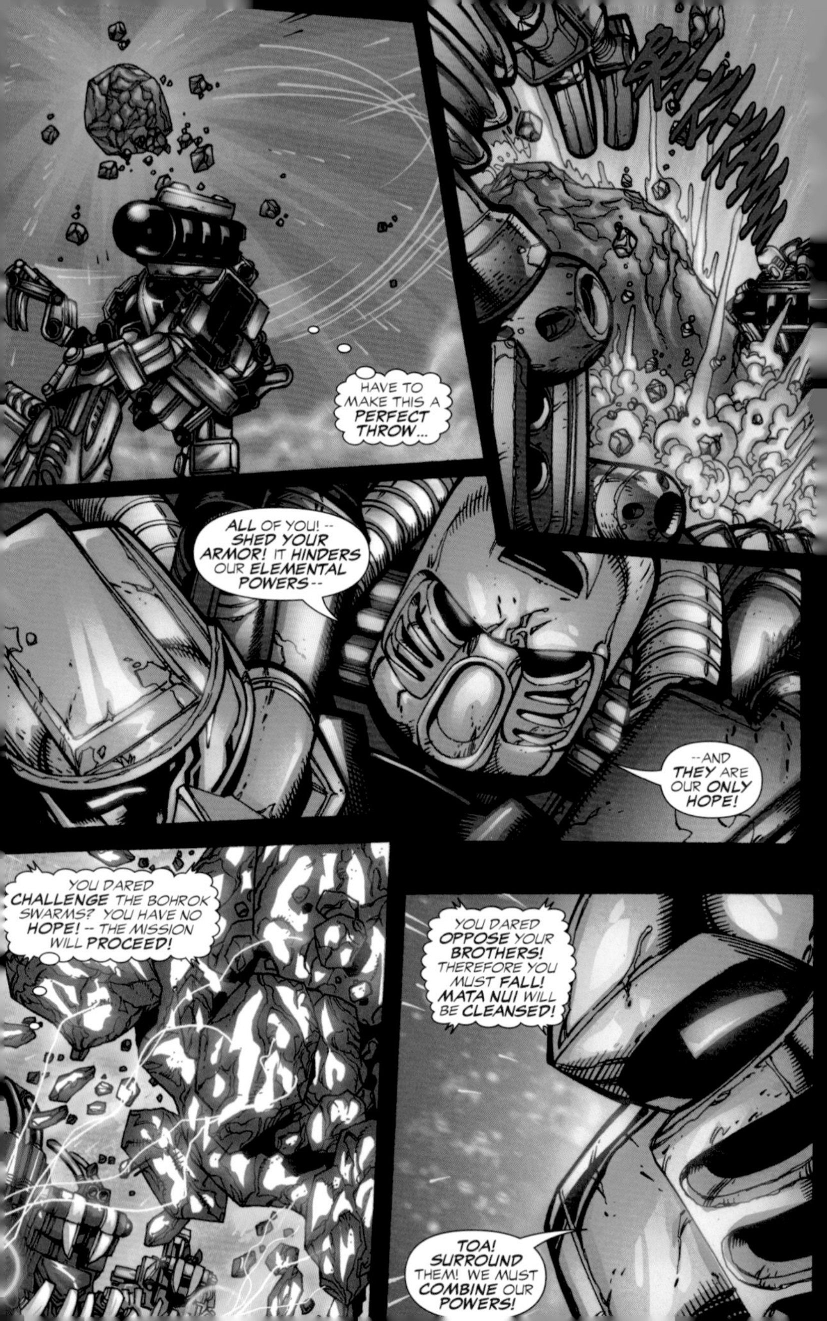
HAVE TO MAKE THIS A PERFECT THROW...
BRA-KA-KAMM
ALL OF YOU! -- SHED YOUR ARMOR! IT HINDERS OUR ELEMENTAL POWERS--
--AND THEY ARE OUR ONLY HOPE!
YOU DARED CHALLENGE THE BOHROK SWARMS? YOU HAVE NO HOPE! -- THE MISSION WILL PROCEED!
YOU DARED OPPOSE YOUR BROTHERS! THEREFORE YOU MUST FALL! MATA NUI WILL BE CLEANSED!
TOA! SURROUND THEM! WE MUST COMBINE OUR POWERS!

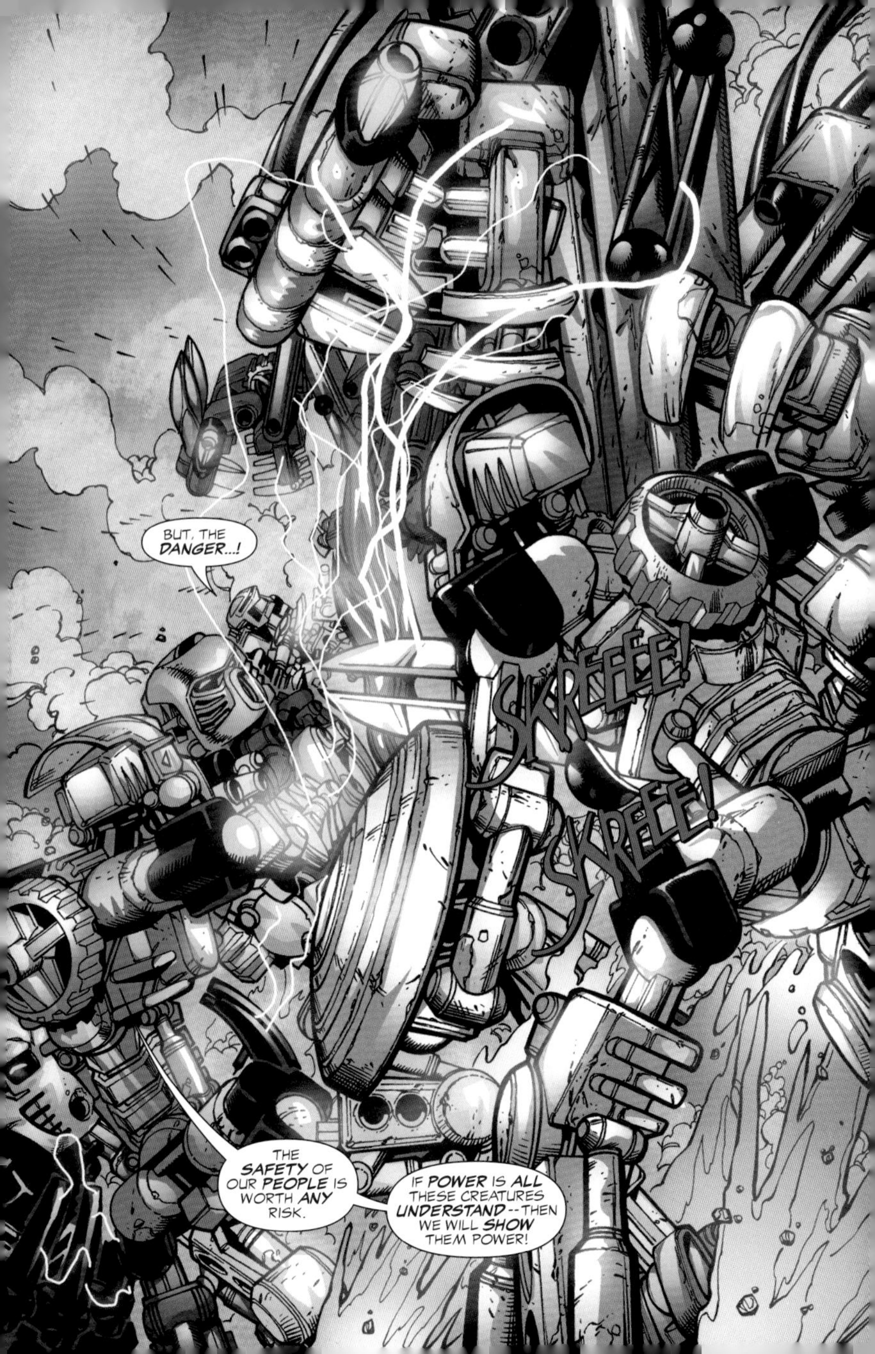
BUT, THE DANGER...!
SKREEEE!
SKREEE!
THE SAFETY OF OUR PEOPLE IS WORTH ANY RISK.
IF POWER IS ALL THESE CREATURES UNDERSTAND--THEN WE WILL SHOW THEM POWER!

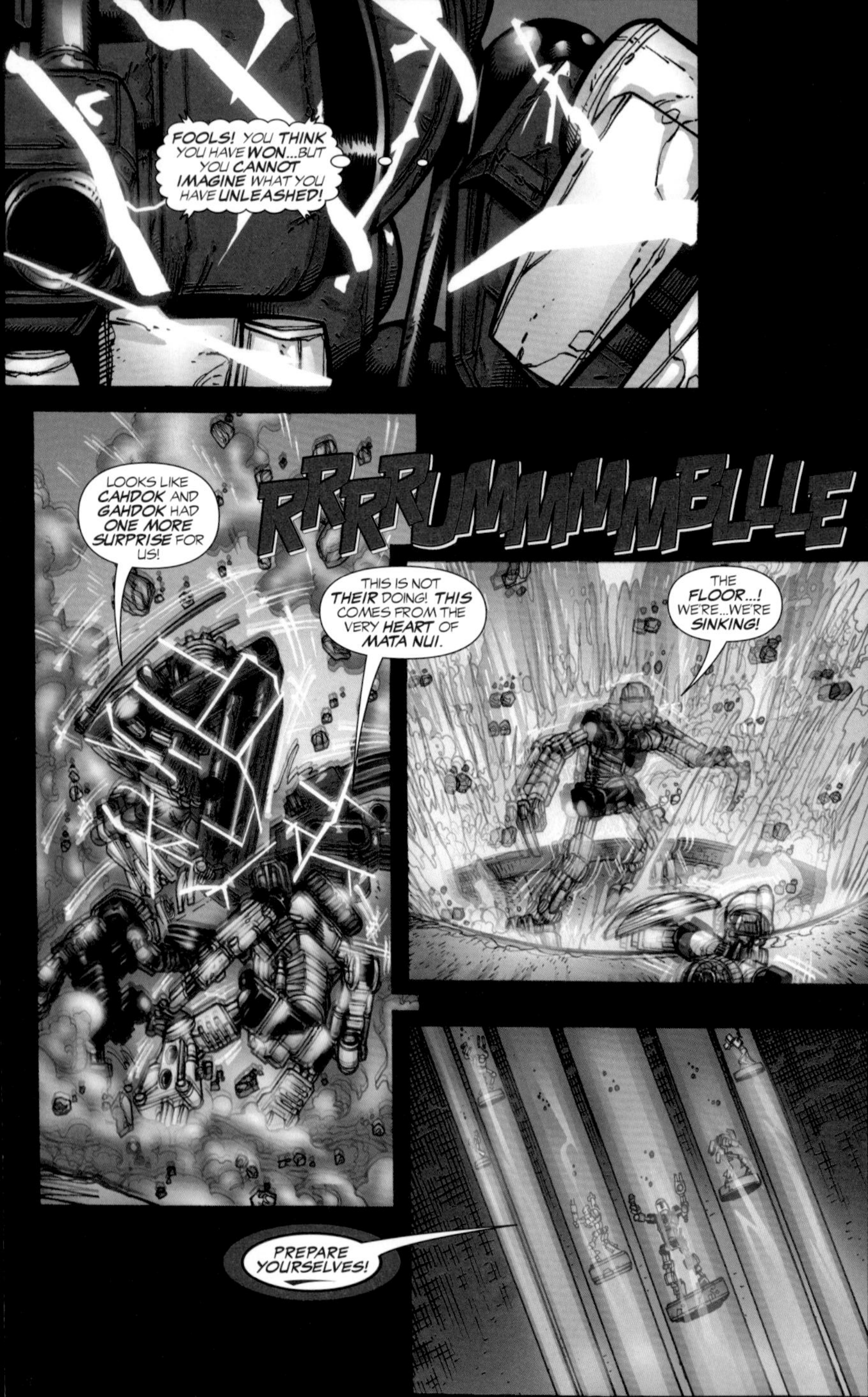
FOOLS! YOU THINK YOU HAVE WON...BUT YOU CANNOT IMAGINE WHAT YOU HAVE UNLEASHED!
RRRRUMMMMBLLE
LOOKS LIKE CAHDOK AND GAHDOK HAD ONE MORE SURPRISE FOR US!
THIS IS NOT THEIR DOING! THIS COMES FROM THE VERY HEART OF MATA NUI.
THE FLOOR...! WE'RE...WE'RE SINKING!
PREPARE YOURSELVES!

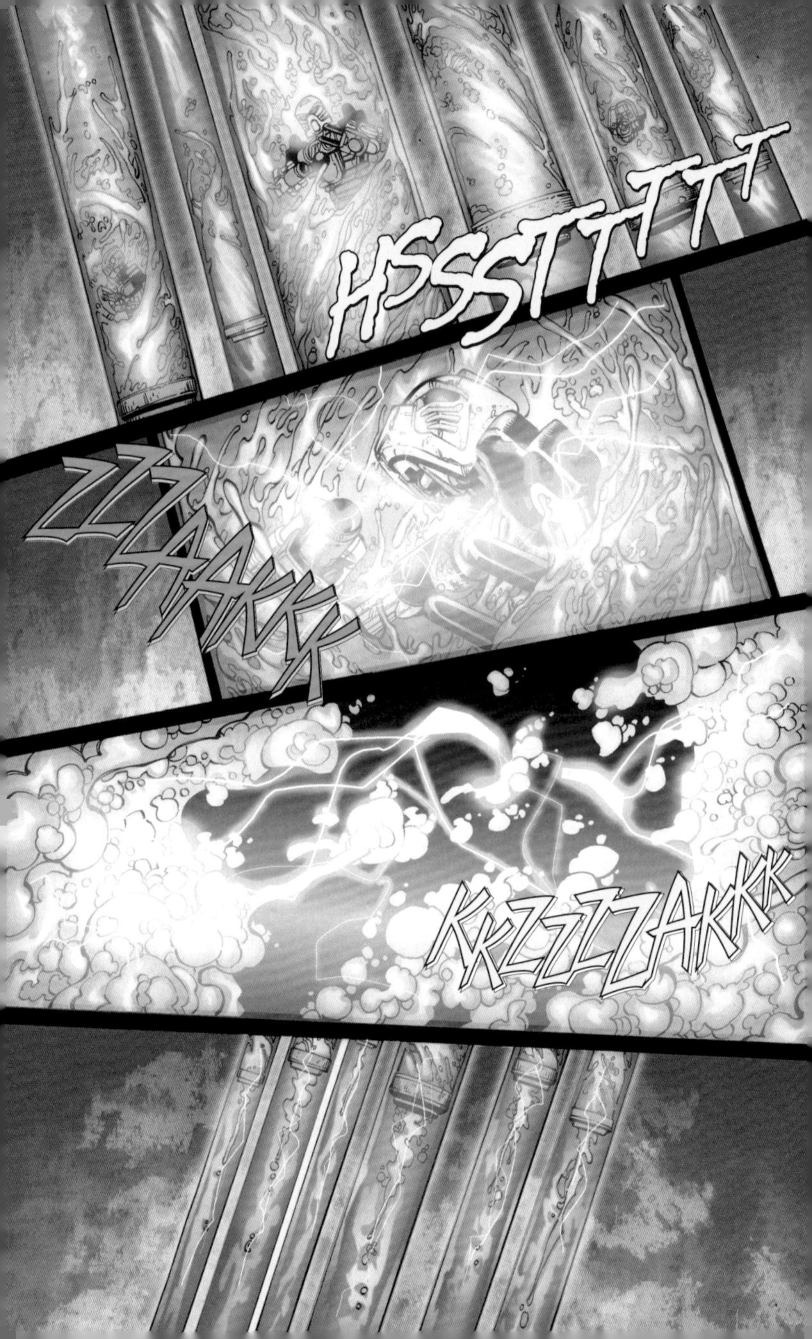
HSSSTTTTTT
ZZZAKKK
KKZZZZZAKKK

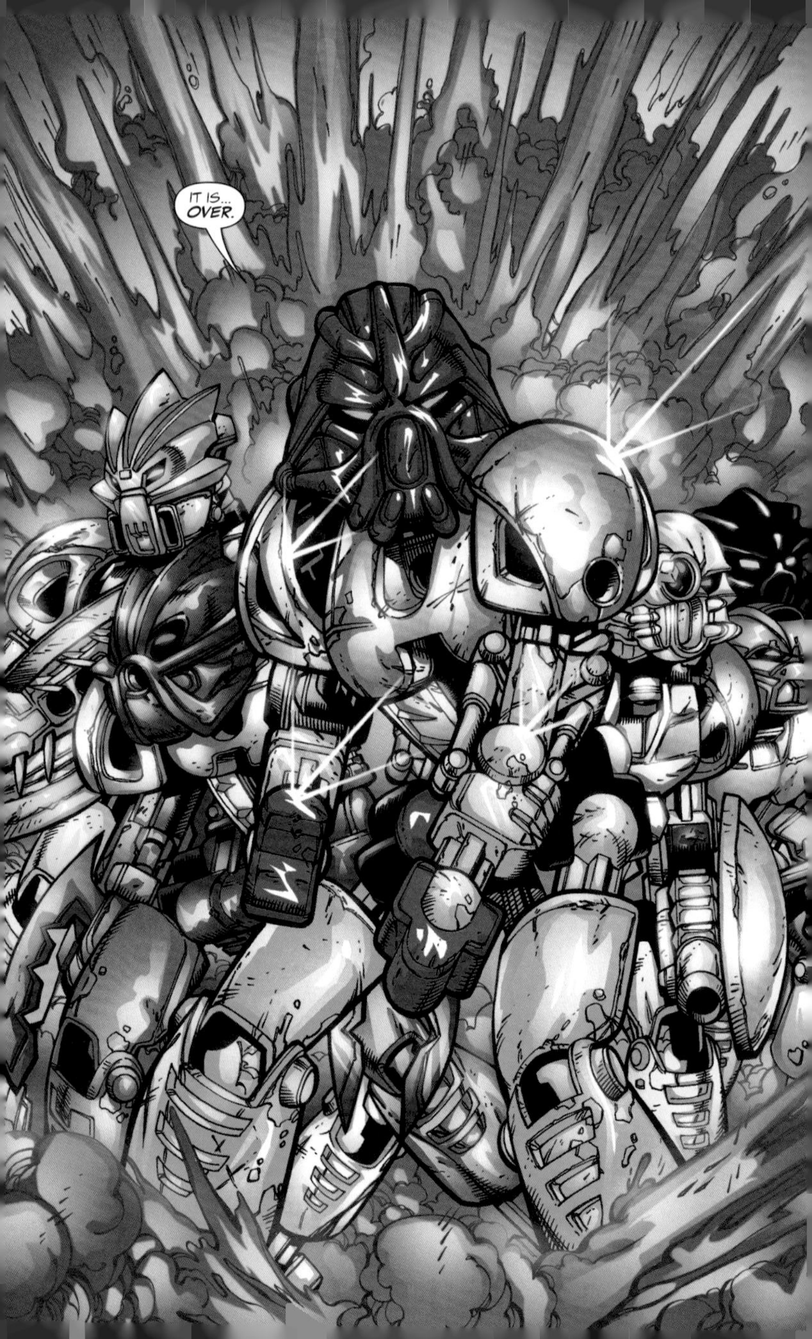
IT IS... OVER.

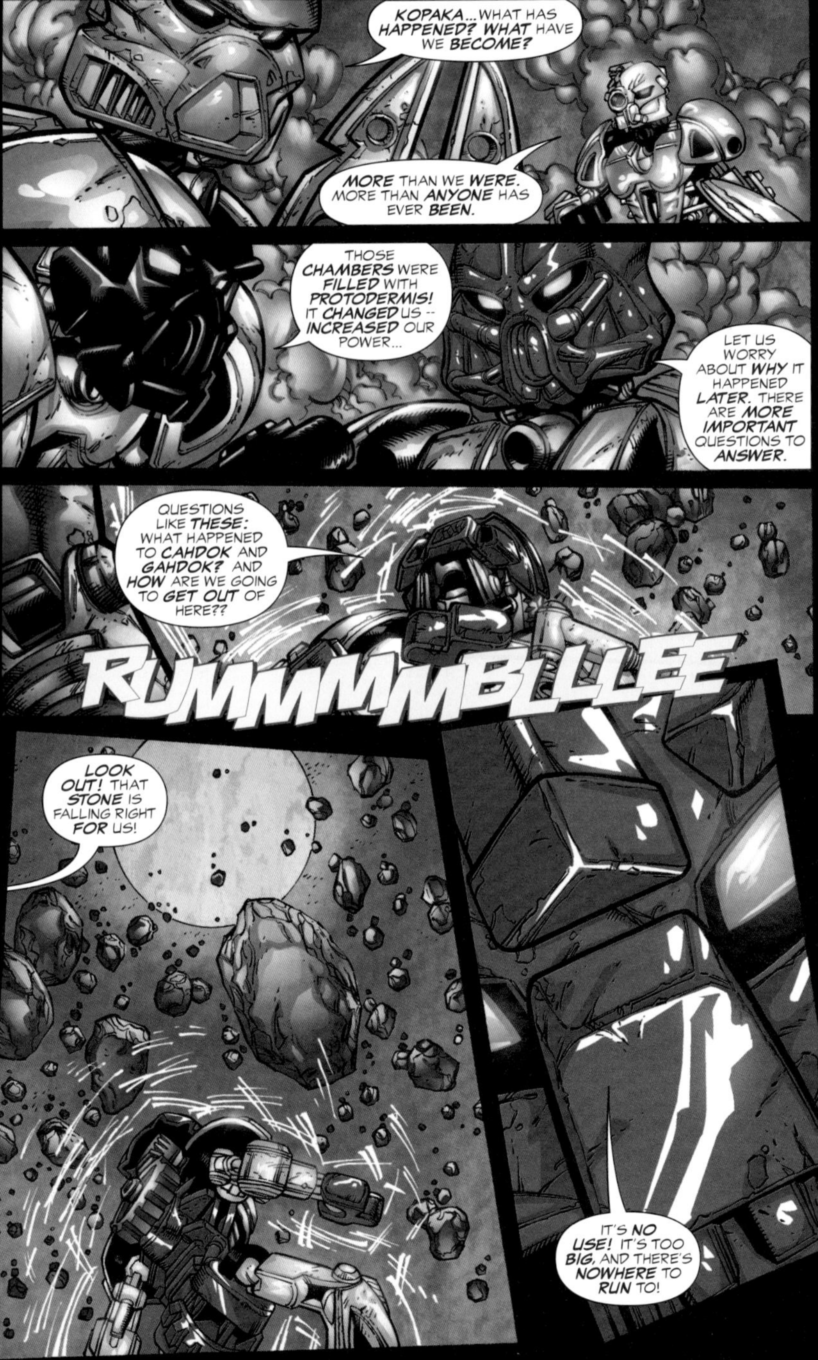
KOPAKA... WHAT HAS HAPPENED? WHAT HAVE WE BECOME?
MORE THAN WE WERE. MORE THAN ANYONE HAS EVER BEEN.
THOSE CHAMBERS WERE FILLED WITH PROTODERMIS! IT CHANGED US -- INCREASED OUR POWER...
LET US WORRY ABOUT WHY IT HAPPENED LATER. THERE ARE MORE IMPORTANT QUESTIONS TO ANSWER.
QUESTIONS LIKE THESE: WHAT HAPPENED TO CAHDOK AND GAHDOK? AND HOW ARE WE GOING TO GET OUT OF HERE??
RUMMMMBLLLEE
LOOK OUT! THAT STONE IS FALLING RIGHT FOR US!
IT'S NO USE! IT'S TOO BIG, AND THERE'S NOWHERE TO RUN TO!

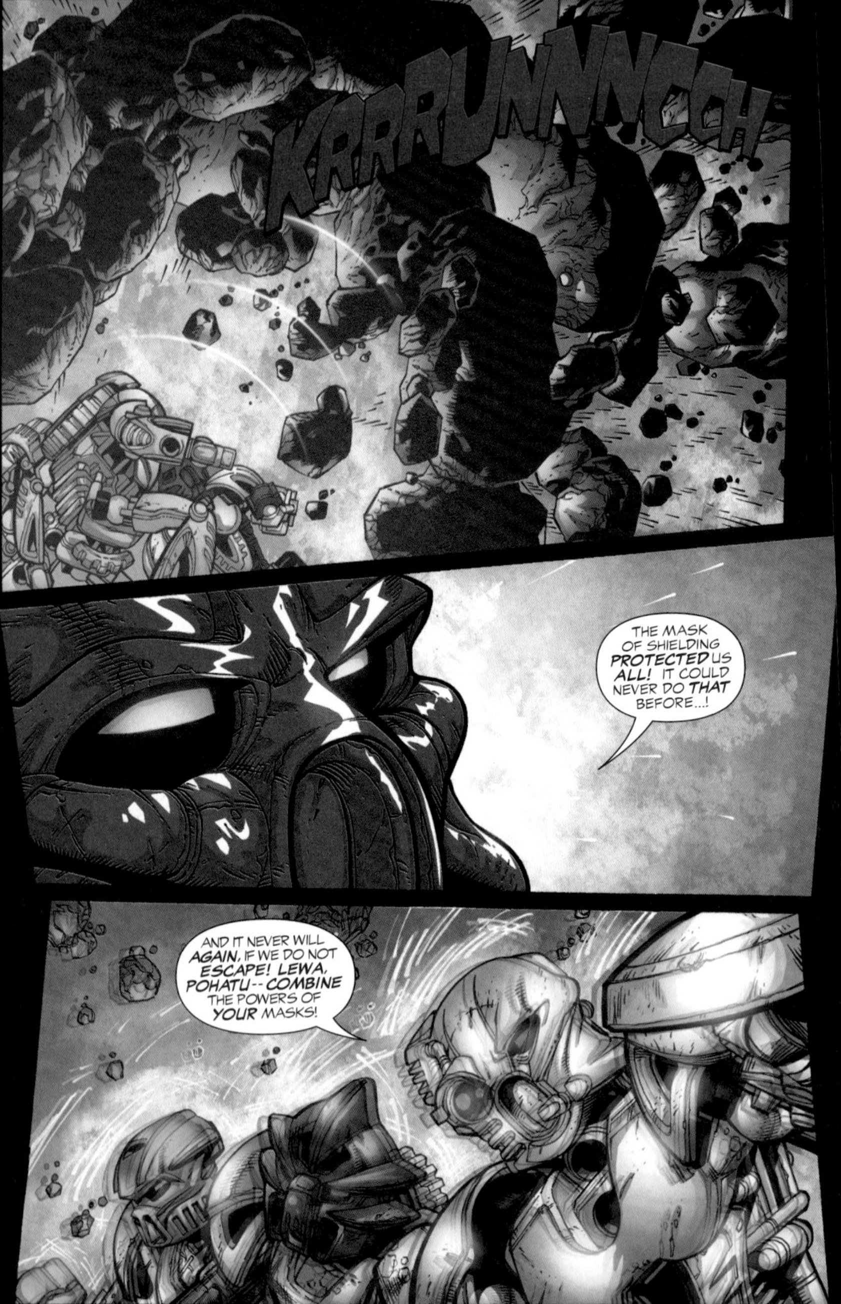
KRRRUNNNCH!
THE MASK OF SHIELDING PROTECTED US ALL! IT COULD NEVER DO THAT BEFORE...!
AND IT NEVER WILL AGAIN, IF WE DO NOT ESCAPE! LEWA, POHATU--COMBINE THE POWERS OF YOUR MASKS!

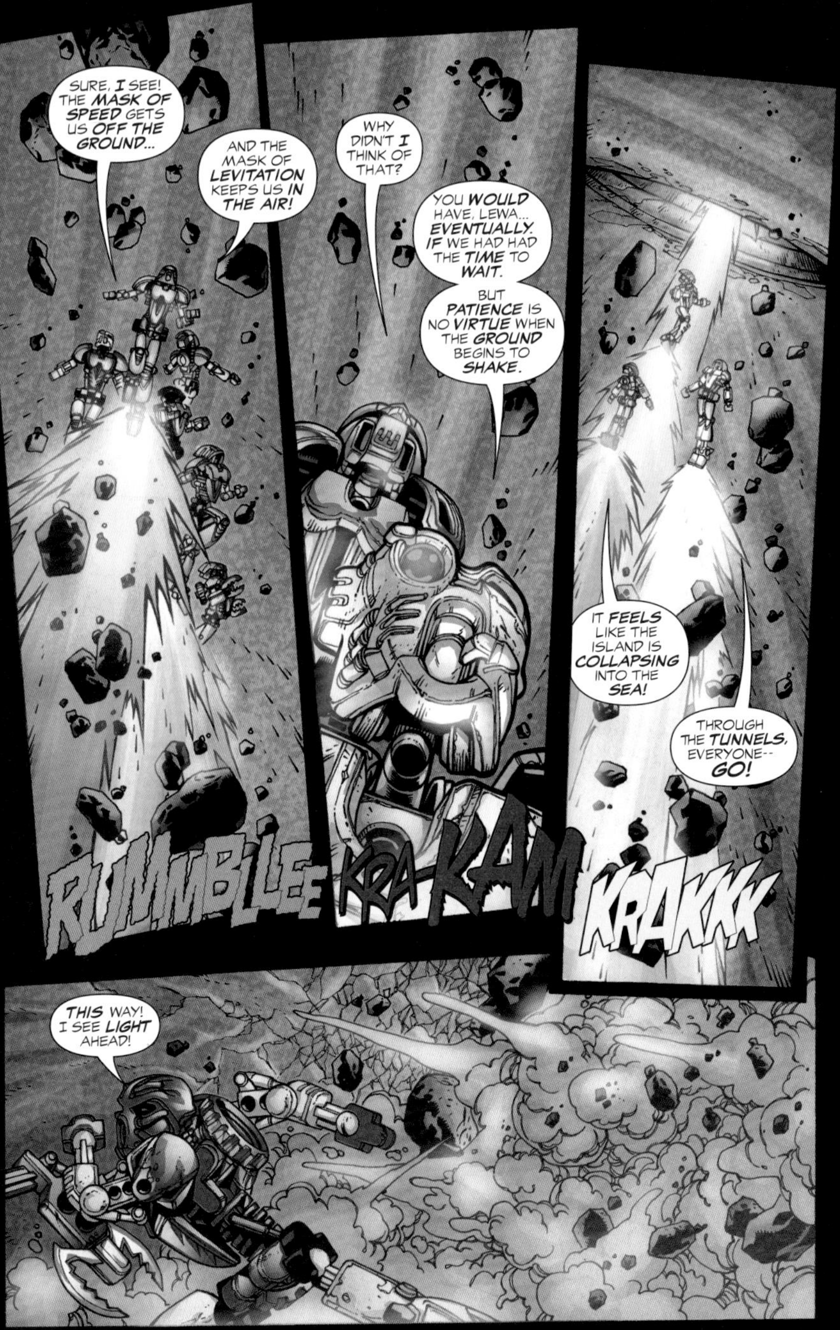
SURE, I SEE! THE MASK OF SPEED GETS US OFF THE GROUND...
AND THE MASK OF LEVITATION KEEPS US IN THE AIR!
WHY DIDN'T I THINK OF THAT?
YOU WOULD HAVE, LEWA... EVENTUALLY. IF WE HAD HAD THE TIME TO WAIT.
BUT PATIENCE IS NO VIRTUE WHEN THE GROUND BEGINS TO SHAKE.
IT FEELS LIKE THE ISLAND IS COLLAPSING INTO THE SEA!
THROUGH THE TUNNELS, EVERYONE-- GO!
RUMMBLEE
KRA-KAM
KRAKKK
THIS WAY! I SEE LIGHT AHEAD!

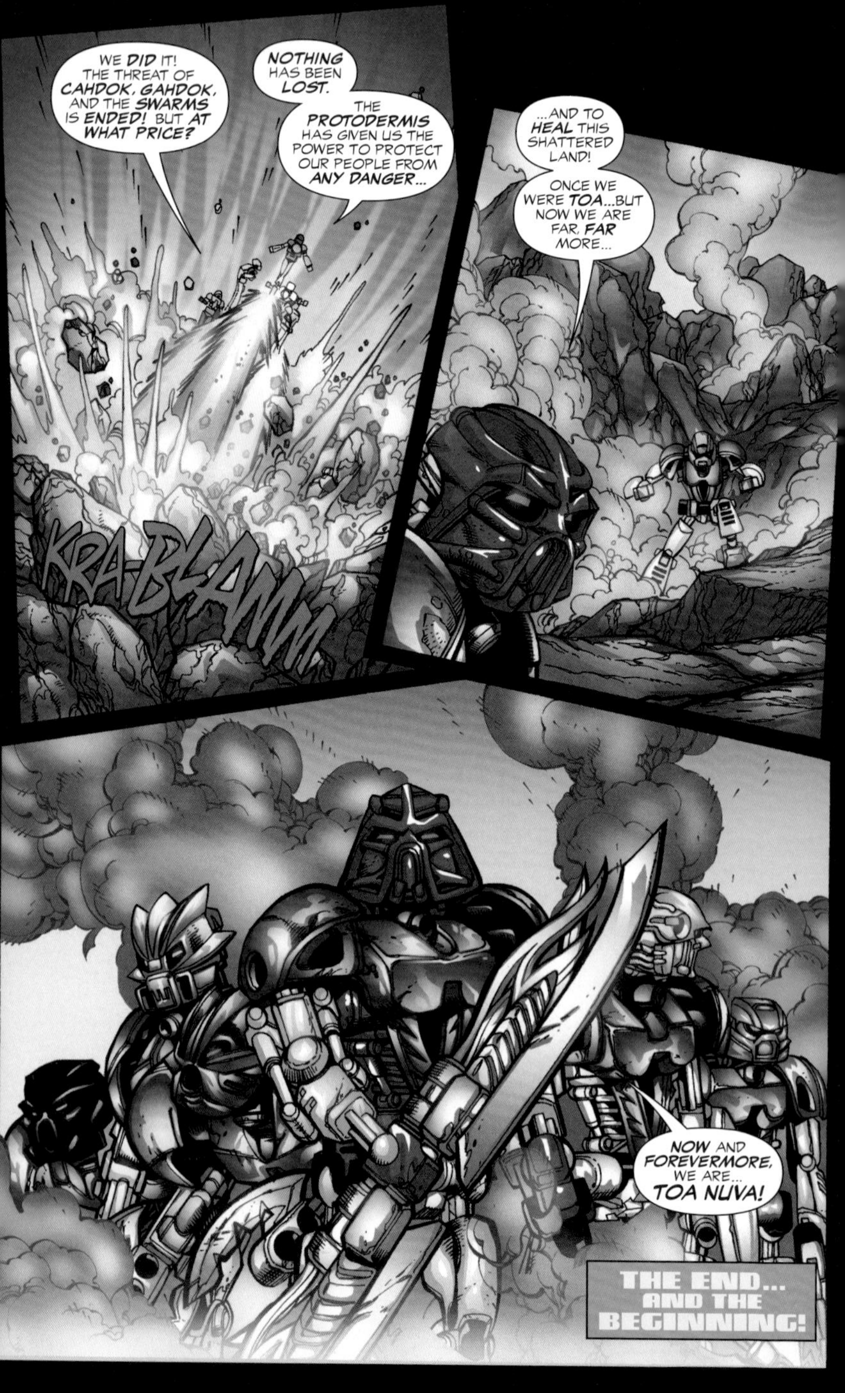
WE DID IT! THE THREAT OF CAHDOK, GAHDOK, AND THE SWARMS IS ENDED! BUT AT WHAT PRICE?
NOTHING HAS BEEN LOST.
THE PROTODERMIS HAS GIVEN US THE POWER TO PROTECT OUR PEOPLE FROM ANY DANGER...
KRA-BLAMM
...AND TO HEAL THIS SHATTERED LAND!
ONCE WE WERE TOA...BUT NOW WE ARE FAR, FAR MORE...
NOW AND FOREVERMORE, WE ARE... TOA NUVA!
THE END... AND THE BEGINNING!